MY KINDA

Mess

USA TODAY BESTSELLING AUTHOR

LACEY BLACK

My Kinda Mess
Summer Sisters Book 4

Copyright © 2017 Lacey Black
Cover Design by Y'all. That Graphic
Editing by Kara Hildebrand
Format by Integrity Formatting

Published in the United States of America.
All rights reserved.

ISBN-13: 978-1-951829-23-0

MY KINDA Mess

Lexi

It's a Summer sister tradition that on the first Saturday of each month, the six of us get together. We take turns picking the location or activity, anything from margaritas and a movie to wine and painting classes at the small gallery uptown. One thing, though, is as certain as the sun rising over the Chesapeake Bay every morning: there will be alcohol involved.

Always.

Pumpkins and turkeys and wooden signs about being thankful cover every wall and flat surface inside the salon I call home five days a week. Thanksgiving looms in just a few weeks, and I'm not even close to being in the holiday spirit. My life is a mess, of that I'm sure, and I just can't seem to get it together enough to care about the one holiday where you focus on all that you're thankful for.

Sad, isn't it?

Like many nights, I'm surrounded by laughter. Two of my sisters, Abby and Jaime, each sit at my side, our feet soaking in warm, fragrant water in pedicure chairs. Meghan and Payton both sit at one of the manicure desks, while AJ has her shoulders worked over at the massage table. Of course, it wouldn't be a sisters' night without booze. Tonight, we're each holding red solo cups with fruity rum and pineapple juice concoctions. They're yummy and provide just enough buzz to take my mind off the drama in my life.

But we don't need to go there yet.

Tonight, we've taken over Hair Haven. I'm one of four stylists at the busiest salon in town. Home is Jupiter Bay, a small, friendly place in Virginia along the Chesapeake Bay, where everyone knows you and your business. During the summer months, we become a tourist trap with easy access to beaches, waterfront condos, and hotels to make your stay more comfortable.

You heard me mention my sisters, and damn, there are a lot of us. Six, to be exact. The oldest is Payton. At thirty-three, my eldest sister has finally found her happiness. She lives with her boyfriend, Dean, and his six-year-old daughter, Brielle. Payton plays with flowers all day at the flower shop she owns, Blossoms and Blooms, while Dean is an accountant at one of the best accounting firms in town. They've started the adoption process, and I'm so excited for Payton to officially become Brielle's mom. Earlier in the year, she informed us all that she was diagnosed with PCOS, or polycystic ovarian syndrome, and her chances for conceiving a child naturally was slim to none. She's keeping her head up, though, and focusing on what she has, instead of what she doesn't.

Next comes Jaime. At thirty-one, she works at Addie's Place, a local nonprofit organization that helps kids who are less fortunate with after-school care. They do everything from homework to movies, to just playing outside. It's a great organization that many of us didn't even really know about until she delivered flowers there one afternoon and fell in love with the place. Jaime's engaged to Ryan, a construction contractor, and their wedding plans for this spring are in full swing.

Third in line is AJ, or Alison Jane as her birth certificate states. She teaches math at the junior high and is the cheer coach. At twenty-eight, AJ's been through her fair share of frogs and remains single. It's not that she hasn't tried to find her Prince Charming. I think she's looking in all the wrong places. You know, bars and beach parties. Like me, AJ likes the bad boys, and usually finds herself disappointed or with a broken heart.

Then there's Meghan. Oh sweet, brokenhearted Meghan. Earlier this year, Meg lost her fiancé in a car crash. It was devastating for her, as well as our entire family, who all loved Josh from the moment we met him. He was pure goodness and treated her like she walked on water. Watching her grieve the loss has been especially hard in light of what's happening on my home front. I actually had the wedding, have the house and husband, and don't want any of it anymore.

Meg will be okay; I know it. She has the love and support of her family who will make sure that she gets up every day and smiles as much as she can. That's our goal: to wipe away the tears and replace them with more smiles.

Finally, there's Abby. She's my twin, older by six minutes. We may look the same, but we're as different as night and day. Abby's quiet, shy, reserved, and I'm, well, not. She's dating her best friend, Levi. (It's about damn time.) These two have been pussyfooting around it for so long, we all thought they'd never get their heads out of their asses.

Abby is an editor for a major publishing house in New York and works from home. I used to be jealous of the friendship they've had since we were ten years old, but not anymore. Abby and Levi have been in love with each other before they knew what love was, and while their time with each other would take her away from me, I realized that their relationship was inevitable. Like the sun setting and the stars shining. They fought it; Lord help us all, they fought hard. But in the end, their love was too powerful.

Abby is my best friend. My other half. The six of us are all close, but nothing compares to the bond Abby and I share. It probably comes from sharing such tight living quarters for almost nine months.

In a way, I'm still jealous of her. Not in a vindictive or petty way, but more out of love. She found her soul mate, the person she's going to spend the rest of her life with. No, that doesn't mean Levi slid a ring on her finger–yet. But it's coming. Even though they've only been a couple for a few months, it's happening sooner rather than later. My jealousy stems from the fact that I thought I had found that. I believed I was marrying my best friend, the person I was going to grow old with, have babies with, and rock in chairs on the front porch with when we were old and gray.

I was wrong.

"When are we going dress shopping?" AJ asks Jaime.

"Right after the new year. There's no way I'm interested in battling the holiday shoppers right now," Jaime replies with a groan as Ella, our newest stylist, massages the soles of her feet. "That feels so wonderful. Will you come home with me and do this every night?"

"Kinky. I didn't realize Ryan was into that kinda thing," I quip with a smile. The alcohol definitely makes me feel no pain.

"Not *that* kinda thing. I don't share my toys, Lex." Jaime laughs.

"Neither does Abby," AJ says with a mischievous grin. I knew someone would bring it up. We've been teasing her about Levi's penis piercing since we found out about it last month. We make sure to embarrass her as much as humanly possible.

And for the record, no I'm not really interested in seeing it. Even though I might tell her I am, he's like my brother and that would just be gross. Throw in the fact that we found out about it from our Grandma, and you've got a story legends are made from.

"Here we go," Abby groans, her feet soaking in the tub and her back being massaged by the chair.

"Seriously, Abs. We just want details about it. It's not every day you find out someone has an Apa," Payton chimes in, her fingernails drying beneath the lamp.

"Agreed. I did some research on them after that night and wouldn't mind seeing one in the flesh. They look interesting online." Everyone stops and stares at Meghan. Even Barb, the salon owner, who's painting her nails a dark shade of red, stops, her mouth hanging open.

"I'm not having my boyfriend show you his penis, even for the sake of education, Meggy," Abby giggles, slurping another drink dry.

"Who needs a refill?" I holler, pulling my feet from the hot water. All of my sisters, as well as my three co-workers, each respond with some form of yes. Drying my feet off on the towel, I head towards our break room and mix another pitcher of Malibu and pineapple juice.

I've probably been drinking more than normal this last month, but it's to be expected when your life is tossed in the washer and turned on spin cycle. You know, when your heart, soul, dreams, and future is thrown into a blender and puréed.

It's hard to believe it was only a month ago that my world shattered. One minute I was married to my high school sweetheart, living in a cute little house on Porter Avenue, and the next I was packing my shit and leaving in the middle of the night without looking back.

That's how it happened.

My dad had just dropped me off from one of our monthly sisters' nights. This one was different because everyone was there. Not just us girls. I felt like a big fraud the entire night, smiling and laughing, when in reality, I was dying inside. I had discovered something just that morning. A very big something that I couldn't unsee, couldn't forget. After another night where Chris said he'd "try" to stop by at the gathering, I found myself completely alone. Not physically, because the asshole was sleeping in the bed we shared, but emotionally.

I had been betrayed. I had been gutted. I had been broken.

There was only one thing for me to do. I packed a big overnight bag (carefully, as to not wake the sleeping douche), left a copy of the paper I had stumbled upon with my wedding ring on the kitchen counter, and walked out the door.

Considering it was somewhere around one in the morning, I knew my destinations were limited (even though any one of my sisters would have taken me in, without a question asked). I ended up driving to Abby's place that night. I knew she's be staying with Levi, so my plan was to sneak into her apartment and deal with her the next day.

Unfortunately, they busted me in the parking lot. Well, I guess you could say I busted them. I'm pretty sure I pulled up at the tail end of road-head, which we had all been discussing earlier in the night. When I pulled up and got out of my car, Abby saw me from Levi's truck. She was adjusting a pretty rough looking ponytail, and when I questioned her on it, all I got was a horrible blush. Levi, on the other hand, looked as relaxed as possible, with this big dopey grin on his face.

That grin disappeared quickly when they saw my bag and realized what was going on.

Abby let me stay at her place without question, and I've been there for four weeks.

My dad and grandparents stop by often; you know, just to check up on me. See, my mom died when I was ten from ovarian cancer, leaving six young girls and a husband behind. Dad has done everything a father would do for his kids, but realized he needed help. That's where my grandparents came in. My mom's parents, Orval and Emma, moved in with us after she died to help take care of us. They're incredibly embarrassing and wildly inappropriate, to say the least, but I wouldn't want them any other way. Well, maybe less talk about blowjobs and sex toys from the elders, but whatever.

We're one big, dysfunctional family.

"Hey! Did you get lost in there? Where's the booze!" Jaime hollers from the main area of the salon, pulling me from the memory I was lost in.

A few moments later, I rejoin my sisters with a fresh pitcher of drinks. After topping off each of their cups, I make my way back to the chair where Ella is waiting. "Your turn," she says with a smile.

"Hey, Abs, where'd you hang your new swing?" Payton asks with an ornery grin as she heads over to the massage table.

"I wish you'd all get amnesia and forget about that," Abby says, her face three shades of red.

"Have you used it?" I ask my twin who picks out a deep shade of purple for her toes.

"No way!"

"Why did you get the sex swing? Lexi's more likely to use it," AJ says, as she gets ready to have a manicure.

The sex swing is just one of the many radical gifts we've received over the years from our grandparents. Orval and Emma don't know the meaning of boundaries, and think it's natural to talk about *the sex* with their grandkids. It doesn't matter how old we get, it's still just wrong to witness their constant groping, fondling, and sex talk. And now that some of my sisters are in relationships, there's a never-ending supply of new stories, unwanted advice, and crazy gifts showered upon us.

But for as inappropriate as they are, it's who they are. (Well, maybe less closet nooky would be nice. Do you know how many times I've opened the door and found them in a *compromising* position?) Looking at them, that's the way love is supposed to be. Even after sixty-plus years of marriage, they can't keep their hands off each other.

Theirs is nothing like my marriage.

"Lex, how's the apartment hunting?" Payton asks, causing everyone to look my way. Finally, someone addresses the elephant in the room. My sisters found out that I left my husband the day after, but haven't pushed me for details.

Abby glances my way. I can feel her stare, but refuse to look her way. If I do, I'm liable to cry, and I hate crying. Hate. It. It makes me feel weak and vulnerable, two things I despise as of late. Mostly because that's all I feel. Inept. Weak. Used.

"Actually," I start, clearing my throat. "I think I'm going to stay with Abby and take over her lease."

All eyes turn towards Abby. "And that means…" Meghan starts, letting it trail off so Abby can fill in the rest.

"I'm going to move across the hall to Levi's," my twin says with a shy smile.

"Finally," Jaime says, her green eyes full of excitement.

Abby blushes again, a darling shade of red.

"Has he contacted you?" AJ asks.

Adjusting myself in the seat, I confirm, "Yeah. Every day."

"Every day?" Meghan asks.

"He thinks I'm going to come crawling back, but I'm not," I add, shaking my head and taking another healthy drink of my booze. "Besides, I'm sure he got the point yesterday when the divorce papers were sent to him," I add with a smirk.

"So this is it, huh? There isn't a cooling off period or spending time apart to make the heart grow fonder?" Meghan asks, sadness in her green eyes.

"Hell no," I tell them. "I'm done. D. O. N. E. Done. Just stick a fork in me." And to punctuate my statement, I finish off the rest of my cup of alcohol.

I feel their eyes on me as I set the empty cup down in the holder beside my pedicure chair. "It's going to be okay, all right? I'm going to get through this because I have you guys. I don't need a man who won't make me a priority, and that's what I realized I wanted to be. Hell, that's what I deserve to be." I don't need to convince myself. I've already spent the last month doing that, building up the courage to be confident and content in my decision.

My sisters all nod their heads and give me a smile. Even though this is going to be hard, and Chris isn't going to go down without a fight (his words), I know this is for the best. Plus, I can't live with a liar, and that's what he is. A liar. A thief. A dream killer.

With tacky nails, wet feet, and teary eyes, my sisters surround me, wrapping me in their arms and their love.

I don't need him, I remind myself.

I don't need a man to make my dream come true.

I got this.

Linkin

Lately, it's rare that I find a moment's peace. Between working two jobs and catching a little bit of sleep, I barely have time to eat, let alone sit on the couch and catch up on some grease monkey show on television. But that's what I find myself doing this Sunday afternoon.

My apartment is a mess–like always–but that's just because of the pair of yahoo visitors I had over last night. Two days' worth of dishes are stacked in the sink, there's crumbled cereal on the floor in front of the couch, and my laundry pile is big enough that I wonder if I even have a pair of clean jeans to wear to work tonight. But there's a smile on my face.

There's always a smile on my face when Jack and Jeff are here.

Ignoring the mess, I choose to relax a few minutes before heading to Lucky's to work my shift. I'm a mechanic and restorer at Stapleton Auto, a small family owned auto business who restores classic and antique cars to their original state. The Stapletons have been in business two generations, from servicing cars and trucks of all makes and models, to specializing in the classics. One job restoring a souped-up a '69 Shelby Mustang, that won fucking car shows all over the state of Virginia, changed the business. Sure, we still get the occasional standard repair job, but for the most part, we just refer them to the shop down the street.

Most nights, after the shop closes, you can find me slinging drinks at Lucky's up town. I'm there four nights a week, including weekends. I get one Saturday night off a month and I use it to take my little brothers off my mom's hands. At eight, they're a handful, and without any help from the asshole who fathered them, I do everything I can to lend a hand.

And then some.

I grew up in another small town in Virginia called Westville, where I lived until about six months ago. Things happened between my mom and the asshole sperm donor of my little brothers that caused us to have to relocate. Staying in Westville wasn't much of an option; not when everywhere she looked, everyone was watching with their fucking judgmental eyes.

Life hasn't been easy for her and the boys, and I'm doing everything I can to make it simpler on them. That means working two jobs and living on little sleep so that I can be available when she needs some assistance.

A loud knock echoes from the hall. Glancing at the clock, I realize it's getting close for me to head to the bar. I almost make it to the bathroom when the banging rings out once more, followed quickly by a voice. And he sounds pissed.

The voice doesn't belong to Levi, the guy cattycorner to me. His voice is deeper and more masculine. This voice has a higher pitch to it, which instantly grates on my nerves. After the third round of pounding, I decide to find out what in the hell is going on.

The hallway is empty except for a guy standing in front of Abby's door. My neighbor is quiet, never causes a problem, and is sleeping with the dude across the hall. I've talked to Levi more in the last month than I did total the five before it. He's an all right guy, comes into Lucky's every once in a while. I helped him carry some groceries and shit up to his apartment one day. We chatted for a bit about music and cars before I headed back to my place.

It doesn't take a rocket scientist to realize the man standing before her door isn't Levi. This guy is much shorter than my six-four frame, with barely an ounce of muscle to him. His Dockers are pressed and his polo spotless. He screams trust fund douche from a mile away, and I instantly don't fucking like him.

And I haven't even seen him from the front side.

"Hey, man, if you're looking for Abby, she's probably across the hall," I holler from my doorway, eager to get the guy out of here.

"I'm not looking for Abby," he says, turning and facing me. His lighter colored hair is styled with more product than I've used in my lifetime, and his eyes are a mix of blue and green. But what really catches my attention is the disdain dripping from his lips when he says, "I'm looking for my wife."

"Wife?" I ask more to myself than the asshole in front of me.

"Alexis. Abby's sister," he says, walking towards me.

"You mean Firecracker?" I ask, instantly perking up a bit more as I recall the gorgeous spitfire I had a run-in with in the hallway a while back.

The jerk's eyebrow rises to his hairline. "You know my wife?" he asks, skeptically.

"Uhhh, just met her once in the hallway with Levi. She was eating his ass for something."

"My wife can be… difficult at times."

"You don't say," I quip, fighting the grin that threatens to take over when I think about the way those hypnotic green eyes turned on me that morning several weeks back. I had never been so damn turned on by a woman threatening to cut off my balls before in my life. Hell, I thought about her for weeks after I left her standing in the hall with Levi, a look that can only come from Satan himself reflecting in those gorgeous eyes.

I was hooked from that moment on.

"I'm Chris Jacobson," he says, extending his hand towards me.

My gut tells me he's more trouble than meets the eye, but I'm not about to cause a scene in the hallway of my building. This guy's obviously married to the woman I jerked off to more times than I can count, which probably puts me safely in the same douchebag category that I've got Chris safety tucked into. "Linkin Stone," I say as I shake his hand, squeezing a little tighter than necessary.

"So you live next door?" he asks after pulling his hand from mine and giving it a slight shake. Probably to get circulation back in his fingers. Fucker.

"Yep." Dumbass.

"You haven't seen Alexis lately, have you?"

And because I can't help myself (and I really don't like this guy), I ask, "You don't know where your wife is?"

He stammers and stutters a few moments before averting his eyes. "Well, we've had some trouble lately. She was staying with her sister for a short period of time, but I've come to collect."

"Collect her?" What is this, the 1950s?

"Yes. It's time she comes home. Where she belongs," he says very matter-of-factly, like it's a no-brainer.

"The only place I belong is away from you," I hear behind me in a voice that screams sex. It's raw and full of passion. Of course, there's enough venom laced in those words to kill a cobra, but that just adds fuel to the burning lust I already have for her. What can I say? Her attitude and take-no-shit demeanor turns me on.

Bad.

"Alexis," Chris says, stepping around me and walking towards his wife. Yeah, that fucking hurts to think about. Her eyes are hard with laser-sharp beams shooting straight at the man in front of her.

"Firecracker," I whisper, not meaning to say it aloud. But when her eyes clash with my own, I swear the entire earth moves. Those deep green eyes soften a little and her breath catches. She scans my face, then takes in the way my black shirt molds to my arms and chest, before returning her gaze to my face. My dick goes from zero to sixty in less than a second.

My view of her is cut off when the douche steps in and kills the fantasy. "Listen, Alexis, I know you're upset, but we can work this out. It's time to come home," he says directly, but I can hear the desperation in his words.

"Ain't fuckin' happenin', Chris. There is no home. There is no us! There is nothing left because of you, and what *you* did!" she exclaims, stepping around him and heading towards the apartment next door.

"Sweetheart, I know you're upset, but if you'd -" he starts, but is cut off when his wife spins around and gets in his face.

"If I'd what? Just listen to reason? Screw that and screw you, Chris. You got the papers Friday. This marriage is over. Over. Done. Finished. I want you to leave," she says with force before turning her attention to opening her door.

"Alexis, don't be difficult," Chris says behind her, and I swear I can actually feel the loathing roll off her body. Of course, it's not directed at me, but I can feel it the same. With my arms crossed over my chest, I relax against the wall and watch the show.

"Difficult? *Difficult?!*" she hollers. "Read my lips, Chris. I want a divorce. I want you out of this building and out of my life. There's nothing difficult about that. It's a simple signature on the indicated line. You sign, I sign, and we both get what we want."

"That isn't what I want. At all."

"Yeah, well, now you know how it feels." I have no clue what she's talking about, but the asshole must. He lowers his head. "Go."

"This isn't over," he whispers.

"It's over," she confirms with conviction. "Go."

"I'm not leaving until we talk this through. We can make this work," he starts, and that's when I move. I'm walking up to them before I have a chance to consider my actions.

"I think the lady asked you to leave," I state, arms still crossed at my chest.

He opens his mouth as if he's ready to argue, but must think better of it. My face is hard as I give him my best "try me" face. I've perfected the look over the years; it comes with bartending at some pretty rowdy joints back in Westville.

"I'll be in touch," he says, turning and heading towards the elevator. Fortunately, it's still on our floor since Lexi's arrival just a few minutes ago.

"You can contact me through my attorney," she replies, her own arms crossed at her chest. Only her actions push her perfect tits up and spilling out over the top of her shirt. It's a marvelous view.

Silently, we watch and wait for him to leave, my eyes shifting to the elevator.

When the door is closed, I turn my attention back to her. "So, that was the husband, huh?"

"Ex."

Stepping forward, I invade her personal space. Her eyes are alive with fire, but not in the way they were a moment ago with the douche. No, her eyes dance with a heady mixture of excitement and lust as she glares back at me. "Watching you tear him apart and eat him alive was so fucking hot," I confess, touching the side of her cheek with my finger.

Her gasp echoes in the hall, invading my soul and filling my mind with dirty images. Ones of her and me, naked, and making little noises just like that. "I hear cold showers work wonders to help cool you down," she suggests with a smirk.

"Are you joining me in said shower?"

"Not in this lifetime, bucko."

"Shame. I'm sure you'd really know how to turn up the heat in the shower, Firecracker." Again, I touch her face. I can't seem to stop touching her. She should probably run in the other direction, fast. Hell, I should run the other way as quickly as possible. The last thing I need is a woman clouding up my brain, distracting my focus from helping my mom.

But I'm just a man.

A man with urges and needs, and those are directed at this little spitfire of a woman who makes me want to turn all caveman on her and throw her over my shoulder. I bet I could extract another of those sexy little gasps if I were to swat her ass.

Plus, throw in the fact that she's technically married. That point alone is enough to make me want to look away. But I can't. I'm drawn to her, like a moth to a flame. This desire I felt, even after only a brief meeting several weeks ago, clearly isn't going away anytime soon. Not when she stands there with fire dancing in her eyes and a sadistically little smile on her lips. Oh, this woman is trouble, and I'm going to get burned.

"Well, whether that's true or not, I guess you'll never know," she quips. My brain is picturing exactly what she'd look like naked in the shower. Of course, having my eyes glued to her ass when she turns to walk away helps those images. A lot.

"Maybe," I reply with a smile.

"No maybe," she fires back, returning her attention to me. Or at least I think she turns it back to me. I can't tell. My eyes are still focused on the same spot her ass was just occupying. When I glance up at her eyes, I swear I'm scalded from the heat.

"Stop looking at my ass," she chastises.

"It's a nice ass," I defend, refusing to look away from those hypnotizing green orbs.

"You're impossible."

"You like me."

"No, no, I don't. You're… annoying and impossible and just like rattling my chain."

Stepping closer yet until I can smell the scent of her lotion and see her throat bob as she swallows hard (a result of my nearness), I say, "You. Like. Me. You just don't know what to do about it."

Rolling her eyes, she fires back, "Don't be so sure of yourself. You're not that likeable."

Lexi reaches back and finishes unlocking the door. Before she steps inside, she pauses, making my heart skip a beat and my boner stand up and say hello. "Thank you for helping me get rid of him," she says softly, without turning and looking my way.

"Anytime he gives you trouble, come get me."

Before she can slip inside and disappear on me, I reach forward and touch her arms. My gut tightens as my fingers dance along smooth, soft skin. I've never had a reaction like this to a woman. Never. So why her? Why this little hellion in heels? She's already given me sleepless nights and wet dreams and I don't even know her. I should stay as far away from her as possible, but if I know one thing about myself, it's that I love a challenge.

And Lexi is that challenge.

I need to know if she'd be as dynamic in my bed as I imagine. I need to know if her skin tastes as sweet as a peach. I need to know if the rest of her body is as perfect as the parts I can see. I need to know the answers like I need my next breath. She's ingrained on my mind, and there's only one way to work her out of it.

The problem is, I just don't see myself willingly letting go once I've had a taste.

Maybe I'll end up being just like the douche who just left. Can't let go, even though she's clearly done. Though, I'm one hundred and ten percent sure there's more to the story than. I'm nothing like that bastard, except that my eyes are set on her. I don't know what their story is, but I'll find out, and then I'm going to convince her to give in to this chemistry I know she feels. She'll fight it, obviously. She'll fight me. But in the end, she'll cave. I know it.

Oh, it's going to be damn fun convincing her.

3

Lexi

I can still feel his eyes on me, even after the door closes.

Those dark chocolate orbs I feel clear down to my soul.

It's amazing how one pair could render me speechless, helpless, and ready to throw my panties out the window, all at the same time. And the worst part is: he knows it. I can tell by the way he gives me that cocky smile (something that also wets my panties).

Setting my stuff down on the counter, I head into the bedroom to change my clothes. Most of my stuff is still in boxes in Abby's old office, but there are a few pairs of comfy leggings in her dresser. As I peel off the sweater and slacks I wore to lunch with my grandparents, I can't help but think about the man on the other side of the wall. I can still feel him; it's as if his eyes are penetrating the wall and watching me. You'd think I'd be creeped out, but I'm not.

Not even a little bit.

I'm so far on the opposite side of creeped out it's not funny. The way his dark hair looks a little shaggy on top begs for my fingers. The hairdresser in me could get lost for hours, tugging and playing with those locks. Throw in that yummy scruffy beard, rich chocolate eyes, broad shoulders, muscular frame, and those tattoos that make me want to trace them (with my tongue), and you've got one dangerous and heady combination of man.

That's why I need to stay away from him.

He's everything I want, and nothing that I need. Oh, he'd probably show me a good time, just like they always do, but then he'd walk away, leaving me heartbroken and yearning for more. I read enough romance novels to know that the bad boy is always ready and willing to engage in a little extracurricular sexual activity, but will up and leave without so much as a warning. The hero doesn't fall in love with the heroine like in those books.

Not in real life.

With a new sense of resolve in my grip, I set out to start to unpack my stuff. It's very fortunate that I don't have to actually search for an apartment and furnish it. I'd say the timing was about perfect when I finally got the balls to step away from my marriage. Abby and Levi are practically living together anyway, and after me staying with her for one week, he made it official. She was torn, at first, between wanting to move across the hall with her man and staying behind with me. She was worried that they hadn't dated long enough to warrant moving in. Of course, once he reminded her that they've loved each other for years, it made her decision to go a little easier.

Abby only took a few pieces of furniture with her: her desk and cabinets from her office, as well as her kitchen table, which is bigger and nicer than the one Levi had. Lucky for me, I went ahead and took his old, smaller one, which made the apartment perfectly furnished. I love the mismatched pieces, mostly because they're nothing like the perfect things I had in my old house with Chris.

My husband always wanted the best of the best. We may have started our marriage with hand-me-down furniture, but as soon as the money started rolling in, we started replacing them with new, sleek pieces. Before long, everything I had didn't feel like my own. It felt like I was living someone else's life, trapped in someone else's dream.

My dream?

Well, that's simple.

I want a baby. I've dreamed about becoming a mother for so long, I feel like it's all I've ever wanted. I had the house, the husband who doted on me, and the job I loved. Even if that was all a façade. The doting husband started off flawless, but things quickly changed. Once he graduated college, Chris became focused on his career. He wanted it all, the best that money could buy.

The problem was when he was out chasing his dream, he left me and mine behind.

He rarely attended anything like family functions or random lunches with friends. He chose to work, always reaching for the next rung on the ladder. I was lonely.

When I told him I wanted a baby, he was hesitant. He wanted to wait until he secured the promotion at work, until we built a new home, until the time was right. Well, the time was never right. I didn't need all of that to be a mother. In fact, the more I wanted it, the less he seemed interested. We went from having sex almost nightly to never. Once I broached the subject of having a baby, something changed in my husband. I went from being his first priority to being kicked off the list. Every dream, every goal he had was pushed to the front of the line, leaving me alone and sad.

But not anymore.

I'm determined to make the most out of my newfound freedom. I have a job I love, a family I adore, and a place to call my own, thanks to taking over Abby's lease. I don't need a man to make my dreams come true.

With a new sense of pride and determination, a new plan starts to take shape.

One that will secure me just what I need to make my dream come true.

"Did you hear that Clayton Cooper caught Lisa with his brother?" Christine whispers conspiratorially as I add color to the strip of hair I'm holding between my fingers.

"Seriously? Didn't he ask her to move in?" I ask, wrapping the hair in foil.

"Yes! I heard she told him she had to think about it. Then he caught her that night at his brother's house, doing the horizontal hustle on the couch," Christine exclaims.

"When did this happen? I swear I just saw them not that long ago."

"A month ago, I guess."

"Wow, poor Clayton. He was always a nice guy in school."

"He was," Christine says, averting her eyes to her lap. Even though she's wearing a cape, I can still tell she's wringing her hands together. That was always one of the tells she had back in school when she got nervous or upset.

"You guys were close in school, right?" I ask, finishing up the highlights in her chestnut hair.

"Yeah." Her response is a whisper, the way she bites her lip nervously, even though not directed at me, is her tell.

"You liked him," I state, starting to connect the pieces.

Her blue eyes cloud with tears as she stares at me in the mirror. "We were always friends, but then he started dating Lisa right out of school. They've been together since right after graduation, and he didn't really have time for me anymore."

"Christine, I'm so sorry. I didn't realize you had a thing for him."

"Don't worry about it."

Turning her chair so that she's facing me, I add, "You know, Abby and Levi were always friends, but they finally realized they loved each other. Give him time to get over the cheating hussy, and ask him for coffee."

Together, we walk over to the dryer. "What? I can't ask him out!" she exclaims dramatically.

"Why not?"

"Because he's... well, there's just... I don't know."

"You can, and you will. Not right away, obviously, because they just broke up, but maybe in a few weeks or months."

"Yeah, maybe." She has that look in her eyes that tell me she's just humoring me and that she has no intentions of asking Clayton out for coffee. Christine is sweet, good looking, and funny. Any man would be lucky to have her. Especially Clayton.

An idea starts to take shape and I can't help but smile.

"What's with the smile?" she asks, suspiciously.

"What smile?" I ask, grinning like a loon.

"That smile. I know that smile. You're planning something."

"Time to dry your hair, Christine," I say in a singsong voice. Before she has time to open her mouth and argue, I turn on the dryer, drowning her out.

Again, I smile mischievously before turning and heading back to my station. With my phone in my hand, I fire off a quick text message. He responds almost instantly, bringing a Cheshire cat smile to my red lips.

Oh, Christine is going to be so mad at me.

After thirty minutes, I retrieve my friend from the dryer and set out to wash her hair. I've always loved playing with hair; you know, digging your fingers into someone's scalp and using your nails to scratch and massage the shampoo into their head. Once she's conditioned and ready for her cut, I lead her back to my station.

Right on time at eleven, the door opens. I try to fight my smile, really I do, but I fail miserably. "Hey, Clayton!" I holler at my friend as he enters the salon.

"Hey, Lex," he replies, walking towards the front counter.

"Ella will be with you shortly," I tell him, ignoring the tension radiating off my other friend sitting in my chair.

"Thanks for squeezing me in. I'm way overdue," he says, running his hand through his sandy blond hair. Then his eyes lock on Christine. "Hey," he adds with a slight smile.

"Hi," she squeaks, fidgeting in her seat.

Bending down so that I'm close to her ear, I say, "You're gonna have to sit still or I'll whack off a big chunk of your hair."

She glares at me in the mirror. "You did this." It's an accusation, and it's right on target.

"Did what? How was I supposed to know he was coming in for a cut?"

"He said you squeezed him in."

"Oh," I reply, glancing up at the ceiling. "Fine, I did, but do you know what? You'd never have the balls to talk to him if I didn't orchestrate this little get-together. You can thank me in your wedding toast."

Christine closes her eyes and shakes her head, but it's the smile and laugh that slips from her lips that lets me know she's secretly thankful. Sure, she's going to pretend to be offended, but I know better.

Ella finishes her cut and waves Clayton over.

Did I mention Ella's station and mine are right next to each other?

I take my time cutting her hair, reveling in the feel of her wet tresses between my fingers. I know, I'm weird. After Ella washes Clayton's hair, she seats him beside Christine, who seems even more fidgety than before.

"So, whatcha been up to, Clayton?" I ask as Ella places the cape over his body.

"Working, mostly."

"Yeah? Still out at the farm?"

He gives me a look that lets me know he's onto my game. Yes, I know damn well that Clayton still lives and works at his parents' farm. He resides in the small house at the back of the property where the farmhands used to live back when his great-grandparents bought the land and started working it seventy years ago. "Yes," he says, drawing out the word.

"I thought so," I reply with a wave.

"Christine, weren't you telling me that you wanted to learn to ride a horse?" I ask, offering her a sweet smile.

She glares back at me. "I know how to ride a horse."

"Oh, that's right. You were saying something about wishing there was a place to ride in the area," I concede. "Hey, Clayton, don't you have horses out at the farm? Maybe Christine could come over sometime and ride with you. You know, since she's been looking, and everything."

Both of them stare at me in the mirror. A small smile tickles the corner of Clayton's mouth, while Christine looks like she can't decide if she's mortified or wants to throw up.

"Sure, anytime you want to come out and ride, Chris, just give me a call," he says, turning his attention to her and giving her a smile.

I feel so good right now. Just call me Lexi Summer, matchmaker extraordinaire.

While blow-drying her hair, I catch several long glances her way from Clayton in the mirror. Christine doesn't realize it though, because she's too busy staring a hole in the cape.

I finish styling her hair at the same time Ella removes Clayton's cape from his neck, and we make our way to the front counter about the same time. Clayton pulls out his wallet and hands Ella a twenty, and Christine pulls out her checkbook to cover today's visit.

"Oh, shoot," I say aloud, scanning my appointment book. "I completely forgot that I have a noon appointment coming in. Christine, I don't think I'll have enough time to get lunch today."

"Lunch?" she asks, confusion written all over her pretty face.

"Yeah, sorry, babes. I can't reschedule this appointment so late in the game." Glancing over at Clayton who's watching with humor dancing in his eyes. "Hey, Clayton, you're probably hungry, right? Would you mind accompanying Christine to lunch?"

Clayton smiles widely at me, while Christine gasps beside him. "No, that's okay. You don't have to," she says, turning her panicked look towards him.

"No, actually, I'm starving. I'd love to go," he says, offering her a smile. "If you don't mind, that is."

She blinks several times before opening her mouth. "I don't mind."

"Good, then it's a date," he adds before placing his hand on her back and leading her towards the door. She glances over her shoulder with a murderous, yet thankful, gleam in her eyes.

When they're both out the door and walking down the sidewalk towards the café, I bust up laughing. "My work here is done."

"That was evil genius, right there," Ella replies with a wide grin.

"Excellent work," Cecelia adds from her workstation. She's cutting the hair of Mrs. McGill, the now-retired schoolteacher that had taught all of us in school at one point.

"Alexis Summer, you haven't changed one bit," Mrs. McGill says with a broad smile. I blanch at the way she uses my full name. Chris has always favored calling me Alexis, even though I preferred Lexi.

I sweep up the hair around my area, and stick my combs inside the sanitizing solution. My stomach growls loudly, reminding me that I should grab a quick bite to eat before my one o'clock appointment. I'm so focused on cleaning up my area that I don't hear the jingle of the bell as the door opens behind me.

"Can I help you?" Ella asks, smiling at whoever is behind me.

"I was hoping to get a cut." The deep voice is familiar and makes the hairs on the back of my neck stand up.

"No appointment?"

"No, ma'am."

"Well, let me take a look at the book," Ella offers.

My brain is telling me not to turn around, but the need to see him is too great. Slowly, I move until I'm facing him. He's wearing a dark t-shirt that's slightly dirty and molded to his arms and chest. My tongue practically dangles from my mouth, and I don't even care. His powerful legs are wrapped in light colored, well-worn denim, and his feet covered with work boots. And those tattoos. My word, the ink on his arms is downright panty-melting. He looks good enough to eat, even though he's a bit greasy, and that thought just turns my insides to jelly.

"Lex, you have time before your one o'clock," Ella says.

"I'm going to lunch," I tell her, turning back to grab my purse. "Have someone else grab it."

"I promise it won't take long. Just a quick cut. Ten minutes, tops." His voice is close, not that my body wasn't hyperaware of his proximity. I seem to get all tingly anytime he's near.

When I turn back around, I'm staring at those deep, dark eyes that seem to invade my thoughts continuously. He's looking at me with a bit of humor, and a whole lot of excitement laced within them. "Did you know I worked here?" I ask, reaching for the cape and pointing to the chair.

"I did not," he says as he walks around me. "You're not going to wash it?"

"Do you want me to wash it?"

"Best fucking part of a haircut, Firecracker," he replies with that devilish smirk.

Without replying, I walk over to the wash stations. The room is fairly quiet, which tells me that everyone is well aware of the effect this man has on me. They're watching me with their beady little hawk eyes, waiting for their moment to swoop in and use any ounce of my discomfort against me.

I feel his eyes on me as he leans back in the chair and places his neck in the lip of the sink. I make sure the water is warm before I start to wet the dark strands. My fingers already itch with excitement. The first slide of my fingers through his hair is almost orgasmic. No, I'm not in a habit of getting all worked up when I touch a guy's hair. Even when I'd wash and cut Chris's. But there's something about Linkin's hair that gets me all sorts of squirmy and excited.

With a quarter-sized drop of shampoo, I start to lather up his head. My nails dig and scratch at his scalp, causing him to groan. My eyes fly to his face. His eyes flutter around before closing, a relaxed grin playing on his lips. I'll be honest: I scrub around on his head a little longer than necessary. I can't help it. His hair is just so fucking fabulous.

I add conditioner and work it in good and hard. Good and hard. Yeah, can you tell it's been a while since I've gotten any? My face blushes, something that's completely foreign to me. My twin has a fierce blush like you wouldn't believe, but me? I don't flush when I get embarrassed. Hell, I rarely get embarrassed.

When I glance back down, his chocolate eyes are locked on me and I feel the impact clear down to my toes. My gut tightens and my panties are useless. I can't believe how much he affects me with something as simple as a look.

"All done," I whisper, shutting off the water. And because I'm weak, I slide my hands over his head, pushing back the water as I go.

"Are you sure? You can wash it again if you'd like," he quips with a half-smile.

"Get in the chair."

"I like it when you talk rough to me."

Rolling my eyes, I can't ignore the way my heart flutters and my stomach lurches at his statement. My fingers graze the back of his neck when I snap the cape, and I can feel his eyes glued to me in the mirror. But I don't look. Instead, I grab my comb from the solution and get to work.

"Just a trim?"

"Mmhmm."

I keep my eyes on his head while I cut off the ends of his hair. We don't talk, but it's not uncomfortable. He watches me work, though. I can feel it.

After trimming up around his ears and his neck with my trimmers, I take a look at the results. My hands go to his hair (completely on their own). The tips are already drying, his hair soft and fragrant from the product I used.

Quickly, I remove my hands from his hair and grab the snap. "All done," I say, lowering the chair and walking towards the counter.

"How much?" he asks, digging some bills from his wallet.

"Fifteen."

"Here," he says, handing me a twenty.

"Let me get you change." Grabbing my moneybag from the drawer, I slip the twenty in and look for a five.

"Keep it. Just a small thank you for squeezing me in at lunch."

"Well, thank you," I reply, sticking the five back in the bag and closing the drawer.

"Come eat with me. It's the least I can do for making you miss most of your lunch," he says, drawing my attention back to him. He's standing on the other side of the counter, his arms casually crossed over his chest.

"I don't have time," I reply, standing up across from him. Even with a counter between us, I can't help but feel so small in his looming presence.

Linkin glances at his watch. "You've got thirty minutes before your next appointment."

Just as I'm about to make some excuse for not going, my stomach growls, loudly. He doesn't say anything, just raises his eyebrow at me as if in challenge.

"Fine. You're buying," I say, turning around and grabbing my purse from where I set it by my workstation. "I'll be back in thirty," I holler at my coworkers, who are all smiling and watching me. Assholes.

Outside, the sun is shining brightly in the November sky. The air is clear and crisp, a trace of salt coming from the Bay. Linkin's hand is large and warm against my lower back and he guides me towards the café.

"Wait. We can't go there," I say, stopping in my tracks. Christine and Clayton are down there, and if they see me come in, they'll know I totally lied to get them to go to lunch together. Of course, I'm pretty sure they both know anyway, but I don't feel like letting them call me out right now.

"We can head down to the burger joint back that way," he says, pointing behind us.

"I love Fast Burger," I state, more to myself than anyone else. Chris was never a fan of the greasy fast food burger joint, which makes my visits there that much more joyous.

"Me too. There's something about a big, juicy double burger with fries."

"Agreed."

Together, we make our way down the block and into the small burger place. There's a line at the counter and only a few tables open. The good thing about the place is that they're usually quick, hence the name, so it shouldn't be a problem to order, eat, and get back before my next appointment.

"Why don't you grab a table and I'll order," he offers, pointing to one of the open spaces.

"Okay."

"What would you like?"

Well, isn't that the loaded question? I find myself wanting more than I probably should when my sexy neighbor is around. He's arrogant and cocky, but I'm drawn to him just the way I was to all of the bad boys in high school.

"A double with everything and fries. Cheese on the side. Oh, and a cherry cock." Realization sets in, causing my cheeks to flame for the second time in a short period of time. "I mean Coke!"

Oh. My. God.

Leaning down, Linkin looks me square in the eye. "Anytime you want it, sweetheart."

My cheeks burn under the fluorescent lighting, but I can't seem to look away. I feel his gaze burning through my eyes, down my face, and into my soul.

Without waiting for a reply, he heads up to get in line to place our order. I, on the other hand, consider slipping out the door and running as far away as I can get. Guam, perhaps? But then reality slaps me upside the face. The man knows where I work and lives next door to me. Chances of another encounter are pretty damn good, you know?

Sighing, I take a seat at one of the remaining tables. To occupy my time until our food is ready, I check my phone. Two texts from Chris that I ignore and an email from my attorney. All things that can wait until later tonight, after I've had a glass of wine and am better prepared to deal with his brand of drama.

Linkin sets a tray of food down on the table and pulls out the chair across from me. He looks so large in the average sized chair, which makes me wonder how tall he is.

"Six four."

"What?" I ask as he sets a wrapped burger in front of me.

"You asked how tall I was. Six four."

I said that out loud?

"Yes," he answers with a smile.

"Stop that," I command, though he didn't really do anything wrong. It's the way he's smirking at me, like he can read my thoughts or something. I don't like it.

"How long have you been doing hair?" he asks before shoveling half of his first burger into his mouth. Chris had impeccable manners. Not only would he not eat here, but he wouldn't shove his food into his mouth like it's the first food he's eaten in days.

"Since I was twenty. I went to cosmetology school after high school and started with Barb as soon as I graduated. What about you?" I ask while taking a much smaller bite of my burger.

"What about me?"

"I don't know what you do."

"I'm a mechanic at Stapleton by day and I tend bar at Lucky's a few nights a week."

"I thought you looked familiar."

"I've seen you there a few times. With your sisters. How many of them?"

"Six total. Payton, Jaime, AJ, Meghan, and Abby's my twin."

"I'll never remember that."

"I don't expect you to. It's not like you're going to be hanging out with them," I state, kinda feeling like a bitch for being so blunt and cold to him.

He doesn't seem fazed, though. Linkin just smiles at me from across the table before sticking a handful of fries into his mouth and slowly chewing. How he can chew with a smile on his face is beyond me.

After our food is gone, I glance at my watch. It's five to one. "I need to get back."

"Me too. My lunch is over in five," he says while collecting the trash and dumping it in the garbage can.

"You don't have to walk me back," I tell him as we step outside and head towards the salon.

"My bike is there," he says, pointing to the bike parked across the street from Hair Haven.

"Oh." We quietly walk towards my work. "You have a bike?"

Oh. Em. Gee! Could he get any hotter? A freaking bike? I think my panties just melted.

He chuckles next to me and replies, "Yeah."

My eyes slip back to the bike and I can't help but wonder if he'd ever give me a ride. I haven't ridden since I used to sneak out of the house in high school, and even then, my dad would have had a heart attack if he knew about the motorcycle rides.

"Anytime."

"What?" I ask, stopping in front of the salon door.

"Anytime you want a ride. Just say the word." Those chocolate eyes roam over my face and slide down my front, making my entire body spark with sudden desire and need.

"Am I speaking out loud or can you read my thoughts?" I ask quietly, watching the way he watches me.

Bending down until his mouth is beside my ear, he replies, "You're not that hard to figure out, Firecracker. Underneath that tough, feisty exterior is a woman who wears her heart on her sleeve and shows her emotions on her face. But you have to look to see it. You have to look beneath that glare and that badass persona you hide behind." He runs his nose against my jaw causing my entire body to shudder. "I see it, though. I see you."

And before I can formulate a smart ass response, he's gone, walking away from me and crossing the street. When he reaches his bike, he slides on and fires up the motor. It rumbles deep and loud, causing a chill of excitement to race through my blood. His boot flips the kickstand and he maneuvers the beast of a bike onto the road. When he's directly across from me, he glances at me from behind a pair of dark glasses. I know because I can feel his eyes on me.

I wave before he turns his attention back to the road, giving it gas and taking off like a bat out of hell. My heart beats wildly in my chest as I watch until I can't see him anymore. I can smell the gas and the burning rubber from where I stand. I can see the smoke lift from the mark he left on the street. I can feel the bad boy worming his way into my life.

But not my heart.

Never my heart.

Linkin

I park my bike behind the shop with a smile on my face. Honestly, I had no clue Lexi worked at the hair place uptown, but I'm damn glad she does. I'm pretty sure I'll never go to another barber or beautician as long as I live. Not now that I know what it feels like to have Lexi's hands in my hair.

Holy shit, that was fucking hot.

I was already sportin' a chubby just by being near her, but when she started massaging my head? And when she groaned? And then her eyes rolled back in her head with pleasure? Mother of God, I swear I almost blew my load in my pants. I've never been so turned on during a haircut in my life. And that includes the time I was sixteen and the young new girl washed my hair and dragged her tits across my face.

Lexi just does it for me.

Even though I can tell she's trouble, I can't stay away. I want more time with her. The sound of her voice, the way she smells, the softness of her skin, I want to discover everything I haven't even had the chance to wonder about yet. And I'm doing a shit-ton of wondering. Ever since running into her douche ex and then her in the hallway last Sunday, I've been wanting to know more about the fiery little brunette with the sexiest green eyes. No, I don't want to know.

I *need* to know.

"Damn, look at you, pretty boy. Someone got a snazzy new haircut," Jacob, the garage prick, says behind me. I'm gathering up my tools, gearing up to rebuild the Chevy big block 454 motor that's going into the Nova on the lift. It's a sweet-ass car that I wouldn't mind owning, if I were actually able to buy it.

Jacob runs his mouth for a bit more, but I tune him out. He's a year younger than me, a whopping twenty-five years of age, but you'd think he's got decades on me. I've been working in a garage since I was old enough to hold wrenches, but this ass thinks he's better than me because he's been here longer. Even Ernie, the shop owner, knows the kid's full of shit, and that's why he's still doing basic jobs like oil changes and tire alignments. He doesn't get his hands on the big blocks and the tight front ends that the bad boys want.

Not like me.

"Did you see Ella while you were there?"

"What?" I ask, turning around and facing him.

"Ella. She's hot. Just turned twenty-one. I think she wants me," Jacob smirks while making lewd gestures with his hands.

"I wasn't introduced to them, man. I was just there for a cut."

"Who'd ya get?"

For some reason, I don't want to tell him. If I knew any of the other two stylists that were there, I'd happily give him another name. There's something about this guy that just rubs me the wrong way. Unfortunately, the only name I have (besides Ella) is the one I fantasize about. "Lexi."

"Alexis? Damn, that bitch is fine too. I wish I grew hair faster; I'd get it cut every week. Show both of them a good time with ol' Jacob."

"Don't call her that." My ears burn red as I try to keep my temper in check.

"What?"

"Lexi. Don't call her a bitch."

"Sorry, man. What? You doin' her? I heard she left the stiff she was married to. She's probably looking to bang every cock in town. Bitches on a tight leash always go buck wild when the shackles are gone, man. Heard she was a wild one in school."

Just the thought of Lexi with other men makes my blood pressure elevate. It's embarrassing the impact she has on me. Hell, even just the thought or mention of her gets me all worked up.

"Whatever you say, man," I say before turning and grabbing my impact driver.

"No, seriously. When we were in school, she dated all the bad boys. Not like her sister. She was quiet and read a lot. Great ass, though. Not my type, but I'd still tap it."

"You might not want to let her boyfriend hear you say that," I quip, positioning myself at the open hood of the Nova.

"Levi? Yeah, I heard they were together. He's a lucky son of a bitch. That ass, man. Mmmmmm," he draws out, my fist itching to connect with his jaw. "I'd like to bite it. But seriously, you tapping Lexi? She's probably dynamite in bed, dude. You hit it, you gotta tell me, 'kay? Maybe I'll go up there and get a cut too. I bet she'd love to blow my mind right about now," he adds, adjusting his crotch and flexing his hips.

I'm spinning around and pinning him to the side of the Nova before he even knows what's happening. My forearm has his shirt and neck pinned and my legs have his caged in. "What the hell, dude!"

"Listen to me, you little prick. Quit talking about Lexi and her sister like they're a piece of fucking meat. Show a little respect." I lean my weight into his body to show him that I'm not messing around.

"Sorry, dude. Didn't mean no disrespect. I didn't realize you were hittin' it, 'kay?" he says. "Jeez, you don't have to be so touchy."

"I'm not hittin' it. Your ass would be knocked the fuck out on the ground if I were. I just don't want to hear you running your trap about them, okay?"

"Yeah," he says quietly, adjusting his shirt and taking a retreating step away from me. "Yeah, got it."

Turning my attention back to the car, I get to work. Jacob pisses me the hell off pretty much all the damn time, especially when he's running his mouth about women. But when he mentioned Lexi and her sister, I saw red. See? This is why I should stay the hell away from her. She gets in my head and messes with me. All I want to do is reach out and grab her, holding her close.

Preferably naked.

My phone rings just as I'm clocking out to head home.

Mom.

"Hey, Mom," I say in way of greeting as I walk towards my bike. It's starting to cool off already, the sun starting to drop behind the trees. Even for November, the weather is somewhat mild, which is why I'll ride my Harley as long as possible.

"Hey, Link. Done with work?" she asks, a screech from one of the boys echoing in the background.

"Just heading out to my bike."

"I hate that thing. It's dangerous," she tells me for the ten thousandth time. No more dangerous than the drinking, drugs, and gambling that got us into the fucked up situation we're in now. Of course, I'd never say that to my mom.

"So what's up?" I ask, steering the conversation towards safer ground.

"Uhh, I was called in to work. Someone called off, and you know, I could really use the money." Mom's working at the café part time, but has been able to grab extra shifts every now and then. She's the first one on the list to go full time when a position opens up. In the meantime, she's cleaning houses while the boys are at school, just to pull in as much extra cash as possible.

"I can run home and grab the car. I'll be there in fifteen," I tell her, throwing my leg over the bike.

"You're off tonight, right?"

"Yeah," I confirm. "See you in a few."

She signs off and I clip my phone onto my belt. Without waiting for the Harley to warm up, I throw it in first and take off towards my place.

So much for a nice, relaxing night off. I'm about to be terrorized by two eight-year-old mini-mes with a chocolate milk and chicken nugget addiction.

Fifteen minutes later, I'm pulling my old Blazer into Mom's driveway and stopping with my ass end sticking into the street so I don't hit the bikes lying at the end of the drive.

"Knuckleheads," I grumble as I head towards the front door. Before I raise my hand to knock, the door flies open.

"Link!" Jeff hollers before tearing through the door and jumping into my chest.

"He's here," Jack yells, sneaking around the side of the house and throwing himself on my back.

"Tweedledee and Tweedledum!" I exclaim, grabbing a hold and twisting them until one is in each arm. "Ready to go?"

"Yep!" the both exclaim in unison.

"Go pick up your bikes from the drive or Mom will run them over when she leaves," I tell them, setting them down on the old porch. As I slip into the small, rundown house, I make note to grab some boards and fix the bad ones on the porch as soon as I can.

"Hey," I holler as I step inside.

There's minimal furniture, all well-worn and mismatched pieces. The living room has a small television, old floral couch that might have survived the seventies, and an ugly green recliner that smells like sweat and cheese when the temperatures get too hot. The only thing on the wall is an old portrait of the three of us boys, taken seven years ago when the boys were barely a year old.

"Hey," Mom replies, stepping out in a pair of clean jeans, white tennis shoes, and a standard white polo shirt with the café logo on the front. "Where'd they go?" she asks, looking around the small living room.

"Outside to pick up their bikes. They left them at the end of the drive again."

"One of these nights, I'm going to run one over."

"Probably," I confirm. "They're not as well behaved and mild mannered as I was at their age," I quip, holding back my smile.

Mom rolls her eyes. "Oh, please. You would have been jumping your bike off the front steps and riding with no hands in the street."

That makes me laugh, mostly because I had done both on numerous occasions.

"Their bags are packed and book bags ready. Do you want me to come over in the morning and get them for school?" she asks, collecting her purse and apron.

"Nope. I can take them before I head to the shop."

Her matching brown eyes are tired, showing just enough of the exhaustion I'm sure she feels. Long hours and raising twin boys alone, unfortunately, makes Mom look older than her forty-four years. I'm sure she survives on less sleep than I do, and even less food. She'd lost too much weight while we were in Westville, dealing with the aftermath of the boys' father leaving. Now that we've all started new, she's put a few pounds back on and eats a decent meal on nights she works at the café. The boys will always have enough to eat and will never know the lengths Mom goes, to keep them warm and healthy. I, on the other hand, have been old enough to see it for years.

And it fucking kills me.

"Well, their book bags are by the door with their overnight bags. They did their homework when they got home from school, so you don't have to worry about that."

"Okay," I tell her, gathering up their bags and heading out the front door.

The boys are already in my car, Jeff pretending to drive, while Jack hangs out the passenger window, *Dukes of Hazzard* style. They talk to each other on the Ninja Turtle walkie-talkies I got them for Christmas last year. Well, Santa gave them. It's one of the handful of gifts that I threw under the tree on Christmas morning so that the boys wouldn't feel the disappointment of not having much to open on the one holiday that's supposed to bring unlimited joy and happiness to a child's life.

Shaking my head, I turn around and give Mom a big hug. "Make sure you eat a big meal on break and catch up on some sleep," I tell her in my best son-knows-best voice.

"I will," she replies with a smile and tears in her eyes. Reaching forward, she runs her hand along my jaw. "I don't know what I'd do without you."

I choke on the ball of emotion that lodged itself in the middle of my throat. She's said this before – hell, tons of times – and every time it gets the same result. "You'd be just fine without me. You're the strongest woman I know," I tell her kissing her forehead.

"Don't let them watch *The Hangover* again. Last time I had to explain what a hooker was," she chastises with a raised eyebrow.

"Fine," I reply with a hearty laugh. "Buckle up, knuckleheads. We've got a full night of shenanigans and debauchery to partake in," I say just loud enough so Mom can hear.

"Yay!" they both holler in unison, diving into the back seat and sitting in their booster seats. They hate them, but I won't let them ride in the old truck without them.

"Let's go!" Jeff yells, pointing down the road.

"To de-batteryyyyyyyy," Jack adds, big, dirty smiles swept across both of their faces.

Lexi

My last appointment left shortly after seven, typical for a Thursday night. I always work late on this particular day of the week, which helps me slim back my schedule on Saturdays to only half days.

The cute little silver flats are stylish, but not so great when you're on your feet eleven hours a day. Sure, I was able to steal a few moments to rest my feet between clients, and lest we forget my quick lunch with Linkin, where I was able to sit down for twenty whole, uninterrupted minutes.

Linkin. I'm not sure what to think of him. He has that bad boy persona down pat, but every once in a while, I catch glimpses of a sweeter side with manners and charisma. I don't hate him, that's for sure. In fact, I find myself drawn to him, which is just crazy talk because I don't even know him.

I don't know his last name. I don't know where he's from. And I definitely don't even know how he takes his coffee. Though, if I had to guess, I'd say black. Definitely tall, dark, and rich. (And now I'm thinking about him drinking coffee. In my kitchen. Naked.)

The elevator drudges up to the third floor, my shoes already off and in my left hand. I don't even care at this point that the floors are probably super gross. I'm that exhausted. And hungry. My stomach is loudly reminding me that I haven't eaten since my lunch date with Linkin.

No. Not a date.

Just lunch.

When the door opens, a plastic sword is thrust in my face. "Halt, my fair maiden! Hand over the pizza or die by my sword!"

I'm so startled in place that the elevator doors almost close- with me still inside.

Loud giggles erupt as I slowly step off the elevator. Two little boys stare up at me with matching mischievous grins and twinkling brown eyes. Both train their plastic battle weapons at my body, their own bodies covered in some sort of tin foil armor.

"Where's the pizza?" one asks real low and menacing like. Of course, the giggle that follows kills the threatening appearance he's shooting for.

"Pizza?" I ask, looking between the two boys who are obviously twins.

"Hand it over," the other growls.

"I didn't bring any pizza." It's hard to hide the smile threatening to spread across my face as I gaze down at these two boys ready to do battle for a pizza.

"What?! No pizza?! Off with her head!" the one on the left shouts just before fake swords are thrust at my face.

I start to laugh as the two boys attack, causing me to drop my shoes in the process. Reaching out, I use the only weapon I have at my disposal: my hands. Grabbing the closest one to me, I start to tickle his waist, while he thrashes and squeals against my assault.

"You'll never take my brother," the other yells, swinging his sword around and nearly taking my head off for real. Thank God those things are fake.

I grab the other boy and start to tickle. He kicks his feet outward, swinging around and yelling like a banshee. He ends up dropping his plastic sword as I really dig my fingers into his side. The first brother I tickled picks up both dropped toys and raises them above his head. Just as he lets out a war cry that's a spot-on depiction from the movie *Braveheart*, he thrusts one sword into my side.

Dramatically, in what could be my best Oscar award winning performance to date, I let go of the captured boy and swagger around in the hall, disoriented and dazed. My arms drop and my legs buckle beneath the weight of my body. I slowly fall to my knees, then completely onto the ground, gasping for my last breath.

As I die, the boys stand over me, triumphantly, with their swords held over their heads. "We got her!" one twin says to his brother, who's bending down and feeling for my pulse in my elbow.

"Hey, knuckleheads? Why did you kill my neighbor?"

I'd know that voice anywhere. Cracking my eyes open, I see Linkin standing in his doorway, a broad smile on his lips and his arms casually crossed over his expansive chest, the tattoos on his arms on full display.

"She didn't bring the pizza," the one checking my pulse answers, crossing his arms over his little chest to mimic the stance of the man before him.

There's a strong resemblance, from the dark hair to the brown eyes. If these are his sons, he's older than I thought. That or he started earlier than most. I can just picture a young Linkin, sweet-talking and charming the panties off all the girls in high school.

"She's not the pizza delivery person, Jack."

"Well, how were we supposed to know?" he says looking down at me. That's when I realize I'm still sprawled out on the floor, body posed perfectly for the chalk outline.

"Yeah, you told us to watch for the pizza."

"I meant from inside my apartment. You're not supposed to open the door without me, right?" Linkin asks with a firm voice. Both boys look down, nodding their heads. Linkin points inside his place, and the twins take off, a whole mess of noise in their wake.

"Sorry 'bout that," Linkin says, towering over me. "They were supposed to listen for the pizza delivery guy while I took a quick shower," he adds, extending his hand down to me.

"It's okay. I haven't taken a sword to the gut in a while. It was nice to brush up on my dying skills," I reply, shaking the nastiness off my pants. Glancing around I find my flats and purse that I dropped on the floor right before the tickling commenced.

As I turn around to face him, my personal belongings clutched in my hands, I finally get a good look at the man before me. His hair is still wet from his shower and his beard is trimmed neatly. His jeans are well worn and faded, and hang dangerously low on his hips. His blue shirt is tight and wet around his neck–probably from not being fully dried before throwing on the garment–and his feet are bare.

He's positively edible.

And I want him.

No, no I don't.

But I do. I really do.

"Yeah, they're going through a gladiator phase. Ever since we watched that movie, they've been obsessed with fighting to the death."

"Sounds like fun," I say with a smile.

"I go through so much aluminum foil," he responds with a matching grin.

I'm about to excuse myself to my apartment when the elevator opens. The delivery kid from the local pizzeria steps out, two large boxes in hand. "Uh, I'm looking for Stone?"

"That's me," Linkin says, digging his wallet out of his pocket.

"Twenty-seven fifty."

Linkin hands him a handful of bills and takes the boxes. "Thanks," he tells the kid just before he slips into the elevator and disappears.

"I should get going. I'd hate for your boys to behead you. It would make an awful mess on the carpet," I say, stepping towards my place.

"Wait." Unable to resist the pull I feel, I slowly turn to face him. "They're not mine."

"What?"

"Jack and Jeff. They're my brothers."

"Oh." That's all I've got; I have no idea what to say. Instead of speaking, I grab my keys and take another step towards my door.

"Lexi?" Again, I turn. My breath catches in my throat at how truly gorgeous this man really is.

"Yeah?" My voice doesn't even sound like my own. It's breathy, husky, and just plain embarrassing.

"Want some pizza?"

"Oh, no, I shouldn't."

"You should," he insists, taking a step towards me. "Well, if you don't mind watching *The Gladiator* while two eight-year-olds jump on the couch and pretend to duel it out to the death." The left corner of his lip curls upward and my heart skips a beat.

I just start to open my mouth, ready to politely decline, when he interrupts. "Please. I've got plenty, and this way you don't have to cook anything. Plus, you'd be doing me a favor, actually, because your dying skills are far superior to my own and it would make their evening to be able to slice and dice you, piece by piece."

My eyebrow shoots into my hairline. "That might be the worst dinner invitation I've ever received," I quip.

"I aim to please, Lexi. Come on," he says, nodding towards his open doorway.

As if my legs had minds of their own, I follow behind him as he steps through the opening, holding the door until I pass, and securing it tightly behind me. Stepping into his place, I notice that the layout is identical to mine. The furniture is older, worn, and mismatched and the floor littered with toys and Nerf bullets.

"Knuckleheads, the pizza's here," Linkin says, setting the pizza boxes down on the counter. Two heads fly by me at Mach 10 and dive in to the two pizzas as if they haven't seen food in days.

"Hungry?" I say aloud to no one in particular.

"Mom said she fed them before I picked them up. They're like human garbage disposals. They eat nonstop," Linkin says as he places plates in front of them to place their food on, instead of in their hands. My stomach growls again as Linkin hands me a plate of my own. "Eat up before the twins take all the food."

Stealing two slices of pepperoni, I slowly make my way into the living room. The boys are eating at the coffee table, swords lying on the carpet beside them, and their eyes are glued to the screen. As soon as I take a seat on the couch, one of them notices my presence and moves to join me on the couch.

"What are you doing?" Linkin asks when he comes into the living room, sitting on the chair. He's so big that the chair is child sized in comparison to his large frame.

"Sittin' by the pretty lady," the boy says with a shrug.

"That's Jack. You gotta watch him. He's the charmer," Linkin says with humor and fondness laced in his eyes.

"Do you like *The Gladiator*?" the boy I now know as Jack asks.

"It's okay," I answer before taking a bite of pizza.

"It's the best," he says, shaking his head and leaning towards me. "If you get scared, you can hold my hand." He's so serious that I can't help but smile.

"I'll keep that in mind." My smile is genuine and my body is relaxing for the first time in I don't even know how long.

"Keep your hands to yourself," Linkin reminds his little brother.

"Whatever, man. If I kiss her first, she's mine. You snooze, you lose." Jack's eyes are burning into his older brother's, but I can see the laughter in Linkin's. He's trying not to smile as he stares down his little eight-year-old brother.

"Noted," Linkin replies, shoving a piece of pizza into his mouth. As he slowly chews, that smirk that I'm becoming quite fond of, is still plastered on his face. He throws me a wink before turning his attention towards the television.

After, when there's nothing left of the pizzas but crumbs and the movie is nearing the dramatic ending, both boys are showing no signs of slowing down. They're acting out the movie, scene by scene, as they gear up for the big finale. Someone's going to die; I just can't decide which one of them will fall under the other's big plastic sword.

That's when they make their move.

Both boys attack their older brother sitting in the chair. Jeff, in the blue shirt, jumps on the back of the chair to cover his arms, while Jack works to secure Linkin's legs. The noise reaches deafening levels as the boys screech and wail with each thrust of their swords and grab with their hands. I'm laughing as Linkin pretends to be overtaken by the hellions, but it's clear that he's just playing along for their sake.

"Pretty lady, help us! We can beat him and take over the castle. Then we'll order pizza every night!" Jack yells.

"And ice cream!" Jeff adds.

Unable to keep myself on the couch, I move to the chair where the boys are attacking their older brother. Seeing a window of opportunity where they have Link's arms and legs occupied, I dive into his ribs, digging in and giving him a full force tickle. His eyes widen as he squirms beneath us. The boys laugh as they watch him wiggle, my fingers refusing to lighten up their assault.

Suddenly, he moves. With two boys attached to him, he gets up and sets them down on the ground. Then he starts to tickle. They scream in protest, begging for mercy, for him to stop. When he concedes to let them breathe, I feel the air in the room shift. Then, just as quickly as he stood, I'm sprawled out on the carpet, Linkin's body pressed firmly over mine. My eyes must widen bigger than the plate we just ate dinner off of, and it isn't until his small smile turns into a big wolfish one, that I realize what's about to happen.

"No, no, no," I beg just before his hands wrap around my ribs and he starts to tickle. "Oh my God!" I squeal, wiggling and gasping for air. The boys both jump up and down, cheering and encouraging their big brother.

When I'm two seconds away from peeing my pants (yeah, wouldn't that be awesome), Linkin lets up on his wicked assault. It's then, panting and gasping for breath, that I realize he's practically laying on top of me, one of his hands pinning both of mine above my head, and my legs wrapped around his waist.

How in the hell did that happen? Bad legs!

"You asked for it," he quips, most likely referring to the tickling. Yet, my mind is focused on the erection he's pressing into the V of my legs, and all I can think now is that *yes, I'm asking for it.*

Begging, actually.

"Did not," I retort, lifting my chin.

"You did. It's in your eyes." I'm suddenly wondering if we're actually talking about the same thing.

"I should go. The boys probably need to get ready for bed," I tell him, neither of us moving. Not that I could move anyway. I'm still pinned beneath two hundred pounds of solid muscle.

"They do," he replies, seemingly reluctant to move.

"If you kiss her first, you get to keep her," Jeff says, bending down and getting right in our faces.

"Dang it!" Jack pouts, making both Linkin and I laugh.

Linkin's face moves closer, his breath fanning across my forehead. "What are you doing?" I whisper, conflicted between wanting him to kiss me and knowing that he shouldn't.

"He said I get to keep you if I kiss you first. I can't let my little eight-year-old brother win, now can I?" he whispers. My body sparks to life and burns with a fierce need that seems to be associated with only him.

"Is that a good idea?" I ask aloud. I'm not really sure if I'm asking him or myself.

"It's the best idea in the history of all ideas, Lexi. But when I kiss you, there won't be an audience. There won't be anything holding me back from taking what I want."

"What do you want?"

"You." That one word sends shivers up and down my spine. His conviction is written plainly in the depths of his dark chocolate eyes.

He blinks before offering me a small smile. Then places a tender kiss in the middle of my forehead.

"There! Now she's yours!" Jeff declares to his brother with a pat on the back.

And I'm afraid he might not be that far off base. There's something pulling me, some invisible force that's drawing me towards the man I'm still wrapped around like a cat climbing a tree.

It's something that I'll continue to think about as I head back to my lonely apartment, crawl into my cold bed, and dream about the way those brown orbs looked down at me, seemingly undressing me with his eyes and ravishing me alive. Oh, there'll be no sleeping tonight. Not with dreams of a certain neighbor who makes me feel more alive than I've ever felt before.

6

Linkin

Thanksgiving came and went in a flurry of food and work. Mom was called in to work extra shifts in light of the influx of people back in Jupiter Bay for the holiday. She was more than willing to grab the extra shifts, which translates into extra cash in her pocket. There's no way I could begrudge her that, considering she's still working her ass off to dig her family out of the hole *he* created.

He would be my asshole former stepfather.

I picked up extra shifts, too, in the evenings. The night before Thanksgiving is what is known as Black Wednesday, where all of the locals hit the bars and tie one on, making sure they're hungover and miserable when they stuff their bellies with food on Thanksgiving.

Mom worked Thanksgiving at the Café. The knuckleheads and I spend time watching football before heading up there at lunch for their traditional Turkey Day feast. Then, when she got off at four, I had a small roast with potatoes in the oven already cooking for dinner. The last thing I wanted was for her to have to come home and cook a big meal after serving them all day.

Friday night was packed at Lucky's. We had the local band that Levi plays in, and the bar was wall-to-wall with partiers. It was a damn good tip night for me, which I tucked away in the coffee can in my kitchen cabinet with the rest of my extra cash. I'm close to hitting my next goal, and can't wait to see another payment done and fucking gone.

Tonight, however, was a different story at the bar. The Beaver hosted their annual Thanksgiving bash. Where we were busting at the seams last night, we were practically dead tonight. Hell, even the few regulars only stopped by for one, before heading over to The Beaver.

Bossman ended up letting me go at eight, which sucks balls, but there was no point in me hanging around and competing for what very little tips were being offered by the two men left at the bar.

That brings me to now.

I've heard doors opening and closing for the last thirty minutes, and I'm wondering if there's a party somewhere on my floor. Hell, maybe I should crash it. Might be a good night to go out and make the acquaintance of the female variety. It's been a while since I've spent the night with a woman, and I'm definitely feeling the need to scratch that particular itch.

But my mind only pictures one woman.

My body responds anytime she's near, and over the last few weeks, my need for her has only increased. That night she ate pizza with us and I ended up nestled snuggly between her thighs? Had to jack off twice that night just to get any sleep. And that was *with* my brothers sleeping in their room across the hall, so that's telling right there just how deep she's wormed her way into my mind… and my pants.

I've only run into her a few times since that night, and our pleasant greetings in passing in the hallway wasn't anywhere close enough to quench my thirst for her. If anything, it's only fueled the fire.

Loud music suddenly pulses through the wall, a hard and fast beat with deep bass and screaming vocals. Rock music. My kinda music. My eyes zero in on the white wall that divides her place from mine. I can practically feel the beat vibrating the floor, shaking the mismatched plates in the cabinets.

What in the hell is she doing? Lexi doesn't strike me as the classic rock kinda girl, but hell, I find myself questioning everything I've come to expect and assume about the fiery brunette. She's completely turning my world upside down, keeping me on my toes in the best way possible. She's unexpected, that's for sure, but for some reason, I don't seem to find the strength to give a single fuck.

I'm picturing her now, relaxing after a long day at the salon in a bubble bath with some Jack Daniels. Her hair is up and all wild-like as Def Leppard rocks her into a deep state of peacefulness. Fuck, that's my kinda woman, right there.

Unable to stay away any longer, I slide my boots onto my feet, forgoing lacing them up, grab my keys, and head out of my apartment. The music isn't horribly loud, but I'm surprised she has it up as loud as she does. It makes me wonder who lives below and above her that wouldn't be bothered too much by the blast of her stereo.

My knuckles rap hard on her door and a new wave of excitement rushes through my body. It starts at my fingers and ends at my cock, making me crazy-hard in about two point four seconds. That's probably a new record since I stepped out of my adolescence.

After a few very long, sexually charged seconds, the door flies open and a little old woman stands there, a bright smile on her worn face. She's on the short side, like Lexi, and is looking at me like she's about to eat me alive. Now, let me clarify that I was perfectly content, and well, *hoping* to have this look greet me, but that was when I assumed Lexi would be opening the door. But now? I'm not diggin' it so much.

"Come in, come in! I'm so glad you're here! We're ready to celebrate!" she exclaims, pulling on my arm until I'm inside the apartment.

It's somewhat dark inside, with only the overcast from the kitchen light illuminating the living room. I stop dead in my tracks when I see four girls, with drinks in their hands, all staring back at me with a mixture of eagerness and embarrassment written all over their faces. But what draws my attention is the woman sitting in the middle of the room, blindfolded.

It's Lexi.

Or Abby.

No, definitely Lexi. I've never gotten a boner just by being in the room with Abby before.

"It's time to get this thing started!" the little old woman hollers behind me, walking by and swatting me on the ass. "Oh, that's nice," she adds with an ornery grin and a wink.

What in the hell is going on here?

"We're ready. Go!"

"Go?" I ask, confused, and rubbing the back of my neck with my hand.

"Strip! It's why you're here, right? My granddaughter, Alexis, is celebrating her divorce, and what a better way to rejoice than with a stripper! Oh, that agency was right. You are a delicious, big ol' slab of meat. So, take it off! Take it off!" the woman chants, the girls standing off to the side giggling and chugging whatever is in their glasses (probably alcohol).

"Grandma, this is completely not necessary," Lexi says from the chair.

"Zip it! It's completely necessary to welcome you back into the dating world with some naked man meat. This is a cellllllllebrationnnnnnn, Alexis."

"Stop calling me that. I'm not even divorced yet."

"Semantics." Walking up to her granddaughter, the old woman whispers loudly, "Hey, maybe you'll get to sleep with the stripper. He's super hunky with a great ass," she adds with another wink sent my way.

"Please don't do this," Lexi begs from her chair.

"Too late. I've already paid the beefcake. Just sit there and enjoy. I know I'm ready," Grandma says, pulling a folding chair nearby so she gets an up-close and personal view.

My heart is hammering in my chest as I take in the room. The other occupants are staring at me expectantly, while Grandma grabs her phone, presumably to take pictures or video.

Strip in a room full of woman?

For Lexi?

Fuck yes!

Suddenly, the music changes to Warrant. "Cherry Pie" blares through the speakers, and I realize I'm at a fork in the road. I can get the hell out of this apartment, away from the crazy old woman who's apparently into buying her grandkids strippers, and hide away from Lexi and her whacked family for the rest of my time in this building.

Or, I can stay.

And strip.

A broad smile stretches across my face as I take in the anxiously nervous woman sitting before me. I wonder why she hasn't removed her blindfold, and upon closer inspection, I realize her hands are also tied to the back of the chair.

Perfect.

I let the beat of the music wash over me as I make my way to the gorgeous woman who's front and center in the room. Ignoring the gazing eyes of those around me, I bend down and run my nose up the side of her neck, inhaling her scent as I go. She shivers, a little gasp slips from those lush lips.

She pulls against the restraints where her hands are bound and she turns into me. Her nose is against my own neck now as she inhales deeply. I wonder if she knows my scent as well as I know hers?

Not wanting to end the game before it really begins, I stand up and straddle her lap. Then I start to move. Grabbing the back of her chair for leverage and grinding and dipping to the heavy beat of the music, I slowly lower myself until my cock is all but rubbing the tops of her thighs. There's hooting and hollering echoing in the room behind me, but I don't pay them any attention.

Instead, I reach behind my neck and pull my tee over my head in one quick motion. Using the shirt as my new prop, I wrap it around her neck and pull her face into my chest. The feel of her breath against my body sends these amazing bolts of lust straight to my hard dick.

I take my finger and run it from the center of her forehead, down her nose. When my finger reaches her lips, I can't help but spend a little extra time touching them. Like a true dog, I imagine what it would be like to feel them wrapped around my cock as she sucked me off. The picture causes me to groan, and fortunately, it's drowned out by Warrant.

My fingers continue their downward trek as I graze her neck, her shoulder blades, and into her cleavage. She gasps beneath my touch, her chest heaving with each breath she tries to take.

Needing to feel her hands on my body, I reach behind her and untie the belt that's securing her to the chair. I continue to grind against her body and watch as she shakes her hands out before reaching for the blindfold.

Well, we can't have that, now can we?

I grab her hands and slowly pull them down to her lap. I know as soon as she removes the cover over her eyes that the gig is up. She'll probably throw me out of her apartment so fast, the door won't even have a chance to hit me in the ass on my way out. Keeping her hands in my own, I stretch them out to the side, as if she were forming the letter T.

Then I grind. Flexing my hips, I move forward until she can feel my erection against her chest. Again, she gasps as I dip my body back down to her lap and slide slowly along her thighs.

Letting go of her hands, I spin around, set my ass in her lap, and grind against her in beat to the song. When her fingers connect with my chest, I almost come in my pants. My eyes are closed as I move, reveling in her touch as she explores my pecs and down to my abs with her long fingers.

This might honestly be one of the greatest moments of my life.

And I haven't even fucked her.

Her hands are splayed against my abs as I dip and move, ignoring the burn in my legs from straddling her for so long. I rub against her body, feeling euphoric with each touch of her hands, my head falling back in the pure bliss of the moment. I don't even give a shit that people are watching me. All I know is that I'm touching Lexi and she's touching me.

And it's fucking amazing.

Turning back around, I slowly run my thumbs from her wrists to her shoulders, feeling her pulse thundering beneath my touch. I take her hand in my own, palm out, and slide it down my chest, bumping and grinding to the song. Hooking her fingers in my jeans, I slowly unbutton the snap and lower the zipper.

With her hands in my own, I slide her fingers into the elastic of my boxer briefs, watching as her throat bobs and her breath hitches. Movement catches the corner of my eye, and before I can register who has entered the room, I hear my name.

"Linkin?" I hear, barely, over the music.

Looking up, my gaze connects with the shocked one of Abby. With my name being said, three things happen very quickly. One, the music stops and we're surrounded by a deafening silence. Two, Lexi rips off the blindfold that's covering her eyes. And three, my dick ignores everything else and realizes that the fingers from one of her hands are still in my pants and very close to grazing the head of my cock. It's crazy hard (no pun intended) not to focus solely on that third thing.

"Oh my God," Lexi says, glancing down and noticing exactly where her hand remains. She rips it from my pants as if it were on fire (her hands or my pants, I'm not sure which) and covers that luscious little O her mouth is forming.

"Why is my neighbor taking off his clothes?" Abby gasps, her eyes bouncing from face to face and landing on the woman I now know as Grandma.

"Your neighbor is a stripper?" Grandma asks, smiling broadly with a drink from her folding chair. "How convenient!"

"You're a stripper?" Abby asks. I can feel all eyes burning into me, including the woman I just gave a lap dance to.

"Nope," I confirm, crossing my arms over my bare chest, a smile spreading across my face.

"You're not a stripper?" Grandma asks, confused. "Then who are you?"

"Linkin," Lexi answers at the same time Abby says, "The neighbor."

"And you're not a stripper?" Grandma asks, seeking confirmation, as she ogles my chest.

"No, ma'am."

"Shame. You'd make a damn good one," she chides, raising her cup before taking a long pull from her drink.

"Thank you?" I say, my reply coming out a question.

"No, thank you," she says with a playful grin. "You made my night."

"Why are you stripping off your clothes in my apartment?" Lexi asks, her emerald green eyes following my chest down to my abs.

"This is better than late night television," a girl on the other side of the room says to the women around her. Clearly, they're sisters. The resemblance is uncanny.

"Linkin!" Lexi hollers, drawing my attention back to her flushed face and sexy little mouth.

"Yeah?"

"You? Stripping? My apartment?"

"Making all of your fantasies come true, Firecracker," I reply, a wide smirk on my face.

"Hell yeah!" Grandma yells from her perch on the chair, her glass, once again, raised high in the air in toast.

This family might be a little crazy.

But I'm diggin' it.

A lot.

7

Lexi

I can't stop looking at his chest.

Stop looking at his chest!

But there were so many tattooed ripples and muscles that flexed and danced under my touch. I can't even believe that my hot neighbor was just performing a striptease for me, in front of my family, nonetheless. And worse, I didn't get to see it.

Though, I sure as hell felt it!

Linkin towers over me, gazing down with that little smirk I pretend to hate and pure wickedness reflecting in his eyes. This man is trouble. He's a potent cocktail of sexiness mixed with bad boy, garnished with a smirk that makes my body hum with excitement.

My mind replays the way his body felt beneath my fingertips. Without being able to see him, my other senses seemed heightened. I could smell his soap, mixed with aftershave and sweat. I could feel the warmth of his skin and every ripple and hard plain of his chest and abdomen. I could hear the steady beat of his heart and the way his breath sped up as he danced to the music.

But most of all, I could sense his desire. It flowed from him in waves and rolled through my own body. Everything started to tingle from where his finger touched my forehead, all the way down to my pink-painted toenails. Honestly, the entire experience was sexy has hell, and I didn't even get to see it.

Dammit.

"Seriously, Linkin. Why are you in my living room, not wearing a shirt?" I ask. I'm sure my sisters are loving the hell out of this.

"Because I was invited."

"By my eighty-one-year-old grandmother."

"You liked it."

"I didn't," I deny, but I'm pretty sure the breathiness in my words makes them fail to hit their mark. A single eyebrow shoots into his hairline just as a knock sounds on the door.

"I'll get it!" Grandma exclaims, jumping up and heading to the entrance. Linkin and I are still staring each other down when a commotion at the front door draws my attention.

"Look who's here! The stripper," Grandma coos, clapping her hands and practically jumping for joy.

"I think it's safe to say the party's over," I say, getting up and standing beside my neighbor. He's still shirtless, and my eyes automatically zero in on the broadness of his chest and the dark smattering of hair that was tickling my fingertips just a few minutes ago.

"What's your name?" Grandma asks the young man standing beside her.

"Xander."

"Xander," Grandma repeats, drawing out the name and clearly checking him out. He's definitely decent looking, but he doesn't have the height or muscle mass that Linkin has. I'd know. I recently had my hands all over him. "I'm going to need to see the goods, Xander. Take off your shirt."

The young man glances at us all, unsure of what to do.

"You might as well do it. She won't let you leave until she ogles your chest," Payton tells the young man.

He hesitates, but only for a moment, before stripping off his tight shirt.

"Not bad," Grandma says sitting back down in the folding chair. "I'm going to need to see you dance, Xander. AJ, start the music, please? Lexi, take a seat in the chair again."

"What? No," I state at the exact same time Linkin says, "Hell no." His stance is firm, his arms crossed over his chest, his eyes blazing something that resembles anger.

"Oh, don't be a stick in the mud, you two. I paid for a stripper and I'm going to get a stripper."

"But we already saw Linkin dance," Meghan says.

"Yes, we did," AJ mumbles, trying to hide her smile, as Abby shoves her elbow into her side. "What?"

"That was just a nice bonus. Yes, very nice, indeed," Grandma says and that's the moment I realize her frail little hand is sliding up and down Linkin's six-pack.

Suddenly, there's another knock at the door. I start to make my way in that direction, but am cut off by the oldest woman in the room.

"Oh, look! Another stripper!" Grandma hollers, holding the door open for a cop.

"Uh, Grandma, I don't think that's a stripper," Meghan says.

"I'm here to check out reports of loud music and a disturbance," the officer says, scanning the room, his eyes landing on the two half-naked men in the center.

"Yes, yes you are, Officer. Do me a favor and lose the shirt, will ya? We're already primed and ready to go, thanks to Linkin,"

Grandma tells the cop who's looking at her as if she grew a second head.

"Excuse me?"

"Your shirt. Your pants. Lose them. Or, as we used to say back at the club, take 'em off, hot stuff!"

"The club?" I ask, turning and looking at Abby, who's just as confused as I am.

"Did she tell him to drop his drawers?" Payton asks Meghan, who's looking at AJ like she might throw up.

"Yes, yes, the club. That's another story for another day, ladies," she says with a dismissive wave of her hand. Then she turns back to the officer who doesn't know whether to be amused, upset, or run for his life.

"Hot stuff?" the officer asks, his hands positioned firmly on his hips. As if it were happening in slow motion, Grandma reaches behind him and grabs a handful of ass, making him jump.

"No!" we all holler at the same time, but it's too late.

"Very nice. I'd like to see it in the g-string," Grandma says before finishing off her drink. "Now, let's be a good boy and show me the goods."

***

"Soooo, that was your grandma?" Linkin asks as I walk him to my door after he helped me clean up my apartment. Oh, I tried to get him to leave, but the stubborn mule was persistent.

"Don't remind me. I can't believe she felt up the cop."

"She's great," he says with a hearty laugh. "I'm still trying to figure out how she got out of being arrested."

"She's always had this uncanny ability to sweet talk her way out of anything, but even I'm surprised we weren't calling Grandpa to come get her out of jail," I say as we reach the door.

"What was the club?" he says, bending down to grab the full bag of garbage sitting along the way by the door.

"No clue. And honestly, I probably don't want to know either."

Linkin stares down at me for several seconds, making my heartbeat kick up a few notches. I'm suddenly aware that we're alone. In my apartment. At night. I've seen his gloriously naked chest, and suddenly, the thought of seeing said chest again is all I want to do.

Maybe touch it again.

And lick it.

Yeah, I definitely wouldn't mind licking it.

"Where'd ya go there, Firecracker?"

"What?" I stammer.

"You just got this far-off look in your eyes and your breathing got all heavy," he says, bending down until his mouth grazes against my ear. "It turned me on."

"Breathing turns you on," I whisper.

His chuckle fills my entire body with excitement. "You might be right there."

"You don't have to take that out," I say, nodding towards the garbage bag in his hand.

"I'm already going out. No sense in you putting on shoes to run down the hall and throw out a bag of trash."

"Well, uh, thanks for stopping by." *OMG, stupid. Why'd you say that!?* The look on his face is a cross between amusement and exhilaration. "Well, you know. Sorry about the disturbance."

Bringing his face close to mine (so, so freaking close), I allow myself the briefest moment of weakness and drink him in. His scent, the lines on his face, the way his lips curl upward just the slightest, and the way his dark eyes devour me from head to toe, everything about him makes me want to stand up and beg.

"I'm not. Tonight might have been one of the best nights of my life. But you wanna know what would make it better?"

Suddenly, too parched to speak, I just shake my head.

"If I could steal a kiss from the prettiest girl in town."

"You know Mrs. Williams down on the first floor? She used to be Miss West Virginia back in 1942," I reply, trying so hard to suppress my smile.

"Hmmm, I'm sure Mrs. Williams was hot in her time, but I was thinking of someone a little younger. Someone with brown hair and gorgeous green eyes. Someone who's feisty, stubborn, lives really close to me, and has a smart mouth. Damn, smart asses really turn me on."

"Should I be insulted that you called me stubborn?"

"Would you prefer persistent?"

"I'd prefer you not to think of me at all."

"See, Firecracker, I don't believe you. Your eyes and the way your throat bobs give you away. I think you like it when I think of you, knowing that you're consuming my thoughts and monopolizing all of my dreams. Because fuck, Firecracker, I think about you constantly. All. The. Damn. Time."

"You do?" I whisper, completely enthralled in the conviction of his words.

"Fuck yes, I do." Straightening up, he looks down at me from his full height. "I'll see you soon, Lexi. And then I'm going to get that kiss."

My heart skitters and stammers in my chest, making it entirely hard to think straight. Just the thought of kissing those full lips makes my heart race and my panties wet. Should I be thinking about kissing my neighbor, especially since I'm no closer to being divorced than the last time I saw him? Hell no. Do I want him to kiss me and make me forget about all of the BS that's weighing me down in my life? Hell. Yes.

Where do I sign up for that?

Before I can throw caution to the wind and my legs in the air, Linkin pulls my door open. Just as he does, a fist raps on his chest, making a weird thumping noise.

"Alexis?"

The sound of my name, coming from the person speaking it, makes my blood run cold and dread fill my body.

"Chris, what are you doing here?"

"Coming to see you," he says, glancing between me and Linkin.

"Why?"

"I wanted to discuss these papers with you," he says, pulling a wrinkled envelope from inside his jacket.

"At nearly midnight? There's nothing to discuss. Just sign them," I tell him, feeling the tension rolling off Linkin.

"No. I won't sign them. I don't want a divorce."

"I'm sorry, Chris, but I do."

"We can work this out, Alexis. I know it. Just let me in. I don't even care if you've been… entertaining a friend." The look Chris gives Linkin makes my stomach turn. It's full of disdain and hatred. But Linkin doesn't seem to care one bit. In fact, he sets the bag down on the floor, crosses his arms over his chest, and smirks at him. But it's not the smirk he usually throws at me. This one speaks of annoyance and indifference.

"No, Chris. You need to leave," I state with conviction.

"Why? Because you're seeing someone? You just left and you're already screwing another man? While we're married? Were you screwing him behind my back the whole time? Is that it?"

"Blow balls, Chris," I seethe through gritted teeth.

"You sound like your grandma," he fumes, narrowing his eyes at me. He never liked it when I cursed or used crude language. Fuck that.

"Don't turn this around on me. *You* are the reason we're separated. *You're* the reason you're holding divorce papers. But do you know what? You probably did me a favor," I say, softening just a little. "We were on different paths. I can see that now. We wanted different things."

"How is wanting you so bad?" he whines. "I just want you."

"Well, I no longer want you. I'm not trying to hurt you, Chris, but you need to leave."

"This isn't over," he retorts, glancing at the giant standing next to me once more.

"It's very much over." I hope he can hear the finality in my voice.

"But I love you," he whimpers, his eyes turning glassy.

I can only stare at him. I used to be able to say those words in return, but over the last year, it became harder and harder. Whether he changed, I changed, or a little of both, I finally realized that I fell out of love with my husband. It wasn't anything he did, per se, but something that gradually happened over time. We were too different. As much as I tried to make it work, I just couldn't do it anymore.

And finding that document under our bed was the final nail in the coffin.

A new wave of anger washes over me as I take in his haggard appearance. His clothes looks wrinkled and I'm pretty sure there's a stain on the end of his tie. His hair has seen better days and his nails look a little on the long side, like he's missed one of his monthly manicure appointments he insisted he keep. Frankly, he looks like hell. But that's not my fault or for me to worry about.

Not anymore.

"Go home, Chris."

"You're my home," he whispers.

"Not anymore." I hold the door, my grip turning white against the wood.

Chris glances at Linkin once more, a snide look crossing his tired eyes. Linkin doesn't seem fazed in the least, leaning casually against the doorjamb as if the entire exchange has bored him. Or maybe just that Chris has bored him.

That makes two of us.

Chris steps forward, his intentions clear. He leans forward as if to kiss my cheek, when a growl erupts from the man standing beside me. My soon-to-be ex-husband must reconsider his intended display of affection and quickly stands up straight, taking a retreating step. Honestly, the thought of feeling his lips on my skin makes me shiver.

And not in the way I shiver when I think of Linkin's lips on my body.

"Good night, Alexis. We'll talk soon," he says, glancing once more to Linkin before returning his eyes to me. They're pleading and full of sorrow, but I trample down a reaction. My reaction would be knee-jerk anyway and just cause him more pain.

That alone says something. Even though he's hurt me more than I ever imagined anyone could, I don't want to cause him any more pain. Our marriage might be over and it might be the result of something completely unforgiveable that he did, but that doesn't mean I want him to suffer.

I just want him to go away.

His shoulders are hunched as he makes his way to the elevator. Resolve fills my body as I watch him go, confirming that he just wasn't the one for me. Not if he can so easily do what he did, killing the only dream I've ever had in the process.

And killing me too.

But I refuse to let him keep me down.

In fact, I don't need him, or any man.

"Does he come by often?" Linkin says, pulling me from my thoughts.

"No. In fact, both times you've been here."

"Good," he smirks, those chocolate eyes lighting up with excitement. "I like being here, him seeing me with you."

"I'm not with you."

"Not yet."

"Whatever," I say, rolling my eyes and grabbing the garbage bag.

"You want me to kiss you," he says in a singsong voice, a wide smile crossing his too handsome face, as he takes the bag from my hands.

"Do not," I grumble, relinquishing the garbage and crossing my arms over my chest.

"Do too. But I'm not gonna, Firecracker. As much as you want me to, I'm not giving in to your taunts and reverse psychology," he says, walking over to the shoot down the hall and disposing of the bag.

"You are so full of yourself," I say with a smile.

"Maybe," he says, walking back over to stand in front of me. Bending forward so that I can smell his too familiar scent, he adds, "But you still want me to kiss you."

"I don't need your permission. If I wanted you to kiss me, I'd just do it myself."

"Doubtful," he smirks, that smugness written all over his face. It makes my blood boil, but not in anger. No, I realize my heated body is for an entirely different reason. One that I shouldn't entertain, but do anyway.

Suddenly, my lips are on his and my arms are wrapped around his neck. Linkin stumbles a bit as the force of my body plastering to his catches him off guard, but he recovers quickly. His arms wrap around my waist, his hands dropping to grab my ass. His lips are warm and soft as they fuse to my own, eagerly taking the lead and deepening the kiss.

My entire body flares to life with a need I'm unfamiliar with. Sure, I found Chris attractive and wanted to spend as much time with him naked as possible, but what I'm feeling with Linkin is so much livelier than ever before. It's dirty and raw and makes me grind like a cat in heat as my legs lock around his waist.

I'm pretty sure my cat is in heat right now.

His tongue slides against mine, hot and wet, just like my core. I throb in a way I didn't know was possible, and the thought of taking this to the next level with this man is probably the best idea. Ever. His lips command more as he moves, my back now pressed against the wall. That's actually perfect, because now I can shamelessly grind my cat against his extremely hard, extremely big erection.

Yay, me!

But suddenly, he slows his kiss, those talented lips nipping and sucking at my swollen ones. "I knew it," he pants.

"What?"

"That you wanted me to kiss you." Even though I can't see it, I can feel the smug smirk.

I give his chest a slight shove, putting a little space between us. Well, as much space as I can, considering I'm still wrapped around his waist like a jungle cat. "Technically, I kissed you," I respond, my mind still firing on only half its cylinders.

"Best first kiss ever."

"Yeah, well, don't be so sure about that," I answer as I lower my legs until he has no choice but to set me down. "That was a one-time deal."

"I'll let you have your moment, Lexi, but I can guaran-fucking-tee you that it wasn't an isolated incident. There will be more kisses, Firecracker. I know it."

"Whatever," I retort, lamely, knowing damn well that he's correct. There's no way that after tasting those lips I'll ever be able to stay away from him.

Which is why I must bid him farewell and head inside. Between the alcohol and the ex showing up, my mind is all whacky. I'm sure it has nothing to do with the earth-shattering, panty-soaking kisses he just administered. Nope. No way.

Except I'd be wrong.

Because those kisses were everything.

And that scares the hell out of me.

8

Linkin

The bar is pretty busy for a Saturday night without a band. The regulars are all here, as well as some fresh young faces that scream Christmas break. As the first Saturday of December, things have started to pick up as college kids come back home the closer we get to the holiday.

Mom's hours picked up too, which I'm grateful for. She needs the distraction, but most of all she needs to feel like she's contributing. The income from my second job at Lucky's, as well as part of it from my full-time gig at Stapleton's, goes to fix the damage her douchebag ex-husband has caused. No, I'd never say anything about him to the boys, but I've been tempted a time or two. Especially when they complain about missing him.

But the boys are too young to know what he did. They don't need me to spill the gory details of his addictions, tainting the few memories they have of him. That's why I keep my thoughts to myself. As hard as it is, especially in light of it jacking up my life too, I don't say a word in front of Jeff and Jack.

Enough damage has been done.

Speaking of damage, have I mentioned the destruction my sexpot little neighbor did on my brain? My little vixen swooped in with her tantalizing eyes and her must-have-her-now body and turned my world upside down when I wasn't looking. Just from one kiss, I'm left reliving every moment I was in her presence last weekend; I left with a boner that wouldn't quit and a dirty mind that wouldn't let me rest.

No, I haven't seen her since she left me standing in the hallway after the kiss to end all kisses. I had to go home and jack off just to get a moment's reprieve from the memory, and even then, she invaded my dreams like she was on the frontline in an active war zone. I remember the way her skilled mouth molded to mine, and then I picture how it would feel if that sexy little mouth of hers went down on me. Over and over again, I imagine what it would be like if I wouldn't have stopped that kiss.

And now I'm sporting a chubby behind the bar with a dozen dudes sitting on the stools.

Fucking awesome.

The knuckleheads wanted me to invite her over both nights they stayed with me. It was difficult not to go next door and drag her over to my place, kicking and screaming. And if I know my little firecracker at all, I know she loves to challenge me. The boys, on the other hand, adore her, and they only spent a few hours in her presence. Does that say something about her voodoo magical powers? I've heard all about the supernatural powers of the pussy before, but I never felt the effects until recently.

And I haven't even dipped my cup in the Kool-Aid.

That's what I'm talking about. She's completely entranced me with her witch powers and I didn't see it coming. My brothers would rather spend time with her (because she dies better than I do by their swords – their words, not mine) than me, and it's starting to piss me off a little. We used to be fine, just the three of us dudes, but suddenly, it's all "Lexi this" and "Lexi that." They ask about her all the time, pretending she's part of the games they play, and say goodnight to her through the wall.

We're all basically fucked.

I grab the glasses on the bar and top them off with more water. Levi and the other two guys to my left I've seen here before, but I wouldn't call them regulars. In fact, if you take into consideration the way they all watch the girls in back like hawks, I'd say the two I don't know are the other halves to some of Lexi's sisters.

Speaking of Lexi, I don't see her.

As soon as the girls came in, my heart kicked up a few beats in anticipation of getting to see her. Unfortunately, she's not here, but all five of her sisters are. When they first arrived and saw me behind the counter, there was a mix of embarrassment and shyness written all over their faces. It's like when you run into a one-night stand after a few weeks, and you don't know what to say. Yeah, they saw me half naked. Yeah, they witnessed me bumping and grinding on their sister. Yeah, their grandma might have felt me up.

Not wanting them to feel uncomfortable, I throw them a wave and smile and keep my customers happy behind the bar. Since they arrived two hours ago, they're playing pool in the back, drinking draft beer, and carrying on like lunatics, while the three sharks at the bar (who only arrived about twenty minutes ago) make sure every dick in the joint knows to stay the hell away from them.

I like these guys, and I don't even really know them.

Then the door blows open and the star of my late night fantasies walks in. Like a vision straight out of a magazine, she's wearing a tight black sweater and boner-inducing red skinny jeans with these little black heels that turn every head in the joint. One of the guys in front of me turns my way, grinning like a loon, making me realize that my growl was actually done out loud.

I try to return my focus to the guys at the opposite end of the bar, but it's fruitless. My eyes–completely on their own, mind you–zero back in on long brown hair and sparkling green eyes.

She's smiling brightly, a folder of papers in her hand, while she talks animatedly to her sisters.

Maybe it's her divorce papers? I mean, a guy can only hope, right?

Lexi sets the folder down on their table and grabs a cue stick. My cock jumps in my pants as I watch how masterfully she slides her chalked up thumb and pointer finger along the slick, hard wood. Her twin racks the balls as Lexi leans over the table and takes aim at the triangle. As soon as her sister is out of the way, she fires a shot straight into the cluster, sending them shooting down the table, sinking two solids into the holes.

Damn, my little firecracker can play.

Completely ignoring my customers, I watch her line up her next shot, bend over the table, and tap the cue ball. It moves fluidly towards the four and taps it softly, the angle perfectly knocking the ball into the side pocket. She moves around to the other side of the table and lines up her next shot. It's a hard angle that will have to be kissed just right to get around a striped ball almost in the way. I hold my breath as she takes aim and fires the cue ball into the six, which barely misses the obstructing striped ball, before sinking into the corner pocket.

She celebrates her sinking the difficult shot with a little shimmy and a shake that does nothing to help relieve the tightness in my pants. Sensing my eyes on her, she glances up at me, a wide smile on her gorgeous face, and winks at me. Fucking winks.

I think I'm in love.

The glass I didn't realize I'm holding shatters when it hits the old tile floor, pulling my attention away from the woman who seems to monopolize so much of it lately. Grabbing the broom, I sweep up the broken pieces and dump them into the trash before grabbing a new glass. I have work to do, and I'm not getting any of it done with her here.

Typical.

"I'm afraid you have it bad," the man at the end of the bar says. He's wearing a pressed button-down shirt, glasses, and a friendly smile.

"You think?" I ask, glancing up and offering him a grin of my own. I finish pouring the draft beer into the mug and slide it across the counter towards an older man who's here almost nightly.

"Definitely. I only speak from experience," he says, glancing over his shoulder towards one of the sisters.

"Which one?" I ask, tossing the towel over my shoulder.

"Payton, the oldest," he says, pointing to the taller and slightly thicker woman across the room. Her smile is wide and her face radiates happiness as she teases and jokes with her younger sisters. "Dean," he adds, extending his hand across the bar.

"Linkin," I answer, giving him a firm shake.

"The stripper?" the other guy I don't know asks, a wide smile sweeping across his face.

"The one and only," I reply with a laugh.

"Ryan," he says, offering his hand. "The one in the blue is mine," he adds, nodding towards the woman standing beside Lexi.

"How in the hell did you end up next door stripping, man?" Levi asks before shoving a handful of popcorn in his mouth.

"That's an interesting story."

"Let me guess… Grandma," Ryan says, rolling his eyes.

"That woman," Dean adds, letting the rest of his thought trail off. But I can't help but notice the way each of them smiles and shake their heads, as if recalling some story or situation, which centered around the spunky ol' woman.

"She's something," I confirm. "Why aren't you guys over there with them?" I ask nodding towards the group that they can't take their eyes off.

"Technically, it's sisters' night, which means we're not supposed to be here," Ryan answers.

"But we never leave them by themselves unattended for too long. They seem to find trouble just about anywhere they go," Levi adds. I give them a nod before heading back down to fill an order for a group of couples at one of the back booths.

Just as I start to make my way back towards Levi and the guys, a vision in tight red pants comes up to the bar and throws her arms around Ryan's shoulder. She says something to him that makes him laugh, and watches while he pulls out his wallet.

"I just received word that my fiancée says road-head might be on the menu tonight if I buy the next round," Ryan tells me, an anxious gleam in his eyes. He pulls a twenty from his wallet and sets it on the table. "Six shots of tequila."

"I think she meant more beers, Ry," Lexi tells him with a laugh.

"Yeah, but if road-head is on the table, I want to make good and sure she's tipsy enough to fulfill the offer." Dean and Levi each laugh beside him.

I grab six shot glasses and pour the golden liquid almost to the top of each one. Grabbing a tray, I set each shot, six wedges of lime on a plate, and a saltshaker in the middle. Before I can take his money, Lexi's hand shoots out and stops my movement. One look at her emerald eyes sends lightning bolts of lust straight to my groin. "I need six draft Stellas too, please."

My eyes hold her gaze just a few seconds longer than normal. "Comin' right up," I tell her as I get to work filling the order. The smile is still present on her face, which seems to lighten her mood considerably. "Good day?" I ask, setting the six mugs of beer onto a second tray.

She smiles again and my heart jumps in my chest. "Yeah, it was. You?"

"Can't complain," I say grabbing my towel and holding my hands up around me. "Just another night in paradise," I quip with a smirk and a wink.

"I can see that," she says, shifting her weight from side to side, taking a big drink from the mug closest to her. The conversation seems to be over, but she has yet to move, which makes me smile even more.

"Hey, Lex, you wanna dance?" some needle-dick preppy boy says just over her right shoulder.

"There's no dance floor," she replies, offering him a friendly smile.

"Sure there is," the preppy douche says, nodding towards the area in front of the jukebox with no tables.

"Sorry, Andy. Maybe another time," she says, taking another drink of her beer.

"Aww, come on. One dance ain't gonna kill ya," he pleads, a winning smile pressed firmly against his arrogant face.

"No, but I might," I say, the words flying from my lips before I can stop them.

The asswipe glances from me to Lex repeatedly, the wheels in his head spinning. You can tell he's trying to decide if I'm kidding or not, and I can assure you I am not. I'm not one to resort to violence, unless provoked, but the thought of Lexi dancing with this joker makes me see red.

"Maybe some other time," Lexi reiterates, offering him a small grin.

"Yeah, yeah maybe next time," he replies, while slowly stepping away.

She turns venomous green eyes my direction. "What was that?"

"What? You should thank me. I just saved you from wasting your time with a douchecanoe like that."

"So I can waste my time with a bigger douchecanoe like you?"

"I have a whole list of ways to waste time with you, Firecracker."

Crossing her arms at her chest (which just pushes those gorgeous tits up and on perfect display), she glares at me. "Let's hear it."

"The list?"

"Yeah, the list."

"Well, first, there's making out in the hallway. You seemed to enjoy the hell out of it last time, so I thought we'd give it another go. You know, to waste time. Then, we can move it into your bedroom–or mine. I'm not picky. The list also consists of breakfast the next morning, which is a huge time waster, if you ask me. Especially since we'll be eating in bed, naked, and can get right back to wasting more time–together–under the sheets."

"And then you walk away to waste time with someone else?"

"Fuck no, Firecracker," I say with heat before bending forward and leaning over the bar. "One time, one night, one day with you is never gonna be enough."

She stands up tall, unsure of how to respond. I can see excitement written all over her face, but something still holds her back. Maybe it's the fact that she's still not free from the mega douche she shares a last name with.

"I have to… get back," she says, pointing to her sisters, as one comes up to grab the second tray.

"Come on, Lexi Lou. Time to catch up!"

Lexi glances over her shoulder at me one more time before retreating to her group. I watch her the entire way, enjoying the hell out of the way her hips swing and her red jeans hug her perfect ass. She's a lit stick of dynamite wrapped in a gorgeous package. I already know I'm going to get burned, but know there's no way in fuck I can stay away.

"That was like watching the opening scene in porn," Levi says, saluting me with his beer.

"She didn't cut off your balls and beat you with them, so that's a plus," Ryan says.

"Oh, she likes you for sure," Dean adds.

Instead of answering, I give them a smile before heading down to the far end of the bar to wait on the growing number of customers.

She can deny it for as long as she'd like, but I know the truth. There's an invisible pull that keeps drawing us together. I feel it, and I know she does too. I just have to bide my time until the perfect opportunity presents itself.

Then, game over.

She'll be mine.

Lexi

I'm pleasantly buzzed and ignoring the clock as it slides closer and closer to closing time. Lucky's has started to thin out over the last hour or so, which is good because my group has gotten louder and more drunkier than before. Wait. Is that a word? Of course it is.

It's the shots talking.

"How was your trip to Richmond?" Abby asks, her glassy eyes trying to focus on mine.

"Ahhhhh-mazing! Like better than ahhhhh-mazing! What word is better than ahhhhh-mazing?" I ask my twin as we slide onto empty barstools.

"I don't know. Levi, what word is better than amazing?" Abby hollers at her boyfriend, who's conversing with Dean.

"Abby. That word is definitely more than amazing," he says with this big dopey grin on his face. He looks at her like she hung the moon, and I guess, that's all right. You know, if you're into that sort of thing.

"He says Abby is more amazing," she yell-whispers at me with a giggle.

"What did you find out in Richmond?" Payton asks, moving to stand between Dean's legs and the bar.

"I found out that there is a lot of sperm available for purchase."

"Sperm?" Ryan asks, giving me a curious glance.

"Yep. Tons. And I'm going to buy some," I say, digging out the folder and laying the contents across the top of the bar. My sisters and their significant others gather around, watching and waiting.

"Candidate number one. He's a pharmacist by day, enjoys mountain biking and deep-sea fishing, has blond hair and blue eyes, and a high IQ," I say, pointing to the information on the form.

"Potential sperm donor number two is a computer engineer who designs video games. He has an Italian American heritage with brown hair and eyes, which would be so pretty mixing with our features, especially if it's a girl. Plus, she'd be smarty farty, with cute little glasses. Can you just imagine?" I ask the group as a whole, but don't wait for anyone to answer as I grab the third page.

"Number three is a body builder. He's six two, has light brown hair and hazel eyes. He benches two-ninety and squats Buicks."

"And that's important, why?" Meggy asks.

"It's not, but he sounded nice, so I put him in the keep pile," I tell her before pulling out the fourth and final document.

"And number four. He's my favorite. Donor number four is a member of the Secret Service. He's six-one, weighs one-ninety, and trains for triathlons in his free time. He has black hair and gray eyes and is fluent in three languages. His hobbies include karate, tai chi, and riding his Harley." I stare longingly at the piece of paper as if it were about to propose marriage to me.

"Ummm, Lexi?" Dean asks, pulling my attention away from my intended baby daddy.

"Huh?"

"Why are you looking at sperm donors?" he asks. The fact that he asked tells me my sister didn't inform him of my life-changing decision. And the way the others are looking at me tells me no one actually thought I was serious when I mentioned it earlier in the week.

"Because I'm having a baby. And I don't need Chris or any man to do it. I just need his best swimmers," I tell him with a salute of my half-empty beer mug.

"You're really going through with this?" Payton asks, her hand warm and comforting on my shoulder.

"I am. I'm not letting Chris win."

"What does that mean?" Jaime asks, her arms wrapped around Ryan's waist. I glance over at Abby, the only one who knows the real reason I left and decided to end my marriage. The silent conversation we have with our eyes lets me know she stands beside me and supports me in this decision.

"It means that Chris lied. He didn't want a baby. He told me he did, but didn't. So I'm taking control of my life and doing something I've always wanted to do."

"You've always wanted to get knocked up with a turkey baster?" Ryan asks.

"Not exactly, but it's a little late in the game to be picky."

"So you're doing this?" AJ asks.

"I'm doing this. I'm supposed to call them Monday and let them know which donor I pick. Then, they start the artificial incrimination during my next ovulation."

"Artificial incrimination? How much have you had to drink?" Dean asks before bursting out laughing.

"Po-tay-to po-tah-to. *Insemination.* Anywayyyyy," I continue, drawing out the word. "They'll use the healthy sperm and inject them into my ready and waiting womb. If all goes as planned, I'll be as good as knocked up by first of the year."

Silence surrounds me, but when I glance up, it's not the faces of my family that I see. It's Linkin, and he looks… pissed. What the hell did I do now?

"It's that simple?" Meghan asks.

"Yep," I reply, chugging the rest of my beer. "We should do a shot to celebrate! Won't be long and I won't be able to drink for a while." But the bartender makes no moves for the tequila.

"I'm heading home. I'm exhausted, drunk, and ready to take advantage of my boyfriend," Payton says, sending Dean a sly wink.

"Your boyfriend approves of this plan wholeheartedly," he replies, tossing a few bills on the bar for Linkin. "Anyone need a ride?"

"Me, if you don't mind," Meghan says, pulling a few bucks from her pocket before sticking them under her empty beer mug on the bar.

"Me, too. I'm not far from you guys," AJ adds, setting down her glass. "Plus, at least if I ride with you two, I don't have to worry about witnessing the road-head." We all glance at Jaime who's not even blushing.

"I'd totally wait until you were out of the car, Alison." Jaime punctuates her sentence by sticking out her tongue.

"We're out too. Lex, you ready?" Abby asks, gathering up her jacket and her boyfriend.

"Naw, you two go. I'm gonna stay til close," I say, throwing another five on the bar and sliding my beer mug towards the hottie behind the counter.

"Are you sure?" she asks, glancing over at Linkin.

"I got her. I'll make sure she's home safe," he confirms to my twin.

Abby wraps her arms around me and squeezes. "You're taking control of your life, and I'm so proud of you," she says, pressing her lips to my cheek.

"Love you," I tell her.

"Love you too, Lexi Lou," she says in a singsong voice, a wide smirk spreading across her face. In return, I stick out my tongue and make a very mature, grown-up face, complete with wrinkled nose and duck lips.

When they're gone, I realize I'm alone. With Linkin. And he's staring at me from across the bar. "What?"

Instead of answering with words, he shakes his head and turns to fill up my mug. I watch as he busies himself cleaning dirty glasses, emptying garbage, refilling coolers, and picking up chairs. He moves easily, gracefully even considering his size, as he works, chatting with the other two customers who remain.

I feel myself really relax for the first time. I've been up in arms about my appointment today, worried that I'm rushing into a decision that will impact, not only myself, but a child for the rest of his or her life. But the fact still remains: I want a baby. I've always wanted one, but the older I get, the more I yearn and long for one of my own. I have no plans of getting remarried anytime soon, nor is dating on the horizon, so why not just take matters into my own hands? Or in the hands of the experts who are going to inject the lucky sperm donor's man-juice into my body.

Easy peasy lemon squeezy with vodka and a twist of lime.

Linkin walks the gentlemen to the door, locking it firmly behind them. It's one in the morning and time to head home. I've never seen this side of the business, though I've closed down a few bars in my day. Never have I remained inside the establishment after the doors are locked and the neon beer signs turned off. It's kinda creepy, if you ask me. For some place that was alive and bursting with energy just a short time ago, it looks so sad and lonely now.

I'm well past pleasantly buzzed and leaning more on the side of going to throw up in the morning. My head feels heavy and my brain muddled with slow motion thoughts as I look around the room and zero in on the man who makes my pulse quicken and my body hum. He's bending over, collecting a little trash that was discarded on the floor. His ass looks amazing in his jeans, accented by a tight black tee and a pair of well-worn combat boots.

His colorful ink is on full display, making me want to lick each and every tattoo on his body.

"You okay?" he asks, walking up to me with a towel over his shoulder.

His lips are full and his eyes are dilated as he scans my face. His entire body seems tense, which makes the muscles in his neck bulge. And speaking of bulges, the one in his pants is growing larger as we speak. Licking my lips hungrily, I return my gaze to his face, suddenly wishing he would throw me down on top of the bar and have his wicked way with me.

Yes, please!

"Are you-" he starts, but is cut off by my lips.

I practically leap into his arms, plastering my body to his, and mold my lips to his own. Linkin hesitates, but only for a second. His arms are around me, holding me steady, as his mouth devours mine in a bruising, take-no-prisoners kiss. I grasp his shirt, pulling it from within the waist of his jeans. When my fingers connect with his warm stomach, I groan, loving the way his body feels beneath my fingertips.

"Lexi," he mumbles without removing his lips from my own.

"Yeah?" I pant like the true hussy I am.

"Are you really going to use some jackoff's sperm to get knocked up?" His pained words make me stop my full-on lip assault. Pulling back, I gaze up at him with half-lidded, lustful eyes.

"What?"

"The whole baby thing. Are you serious?" he asks, running his thumbs down my cheeks and around to caress the back of my neck. It's a tender touch that doesn't match the burning in his eyes.

"Uh, yeah. I am."

He nods his head before taking a step back. I feel the draft between us instantly, and it makes me shiver. Linkin reaches down and grabs my hands with his own, pulling me along behind him. "Come on. Let's get you home," he says, leading me towards the back door. He never lets go of my hands as he flips switches, bathing Lucky's in darkness.

Outside, the wind sweeping off the Bay is cooler and tastes of the salty sea. Even though I'm wearing a sweater, a chill races through me, peppering my skin with goose bumps. He doesn't say a word as he leads me towards a blue Blazer with beefy wheels. It's old and well used, but is in decent shape. You can tell he's put some work and time into the old truck.

Without saying a word, he lifts me into the passenger seat and walks around to the driver's side. I can feel the tension filling the truck as he pulls out of the lot and heads towards the apartment building. He doesn't say a word the entire drive, his knuckles turning white as he chokes the steering wheel. I feel like I've done something wrong, but I haven't a clue what.

Was it the kiss? Maybe he didn't want me the way I thought he did. I mean, he was hard in his pants, but maybe that was just a reaction to having a woman crawl all over him. Maybe he realized it was me who was kissing him, and therefore, felt the need to put on the brakes.

Fine. Whatever.

I don't have time for the sex anyway. I'm getting ready to knock myself up with donor number G45629's sperm.

The closer we get to home, the worse I start to feel. Maybe those last few shots weren't my best idea. Closing my eyes, I will my stomach to settle and my mind to stop spinning. With each turn and brake of the truck, I start to wonder if I'll be able to make it to my bathroom before losing what little food I ate on my ride home from Richmond.

Ugh, this is horrible.

The darkness wraps around me, pulling me under, and I welcome it.

My last conscious thought is that I'm never drinking again.

***

The sunlight is peeking through the blinds of my bedroom window, my blankets a tangled mess around my legs. My entire body is heavy and my head pounding as I slowly rouse myself to a somewhat conscious state.

Why in the hell did I drink so much?

Groaning aloud, I rub my sleep-matted eyes and beg the pounding in my head to subside just enough to get a glass of water and some pain killers. When I finally crack open my heavy eyelids, I notice the painting on the wall is missing. What the hell? Did I get robbed and not realize it?

Glancing around, I notice Abby's dresser is missing too! Frantically, I search for any sign of personal belongings and come up empty. I sit up and catch my first glance at navy blue sheets.

Not. My. Sheets.

Holy. Shit.

I'm in someone else's bed.

The shirt I'm wearing isn't my own. It's big and roomy and frankly, smells fucking amazing. No. Wait, Lexi. I could have been abducted by some crazy person who dressed me in his clothes and is going to force me to feed him and his thirty-five cats with my toes, and all I can think about is how great the shirt smells.

Or maybe I had sex last night.

Oh. My. God.

I had sex last night and don't remember it.

Great. My first sexual experience in about six months, and I have no clue who the guy is and if he was any good. It's just my luck, ya know? I couldn't get my husband to sleep with me and the one time I find someone willing to play hide the purple headed mushroom slinger with me, I have no recollection of the entire event. I mean, my luck the guy has an eight-inch shlong and I rode the flesh rocket all night long until I was boneless and spent from too many orgasms.

Then the door opens and a small scream slips from my lips.

"Settle down, Firecracker. You'll wake the neighbors."

Oh. My. God.

I slept with Linkin.

Linkin

10

She looks at me with bright green eyes that show a cross between horror and excitement. Her feet are all tangled up in my sheets (which is a complete turn on, by the way), her makeup is all over the place, kinda like she might have done full drag the night before, and her mouth is hanging open wide enough to catch flies.

And she's fucking gorgeous.

"Here," I say, stepping into my bedroom with a glass of ice water and two Tylenol. She's still looking at me as if she's seeing a ghost, but I guess waking up in a strange place will do that to a girl.

"Thanks," she mumbles, keeping one eye on me while popping the little capsules into her mouth.

"So," I start, glancing at her and feeling like a first class idiot for not really knowing what to say.

"So…" she mimics, looking at me expectantly.

"Sleep okay?"

"Ummm, yeah. I think," she says, rubbing her head.

"That's good," I reply, popping my back. I didn't sleep for shit last night since my couch is about two sizes too small for a guy of my stature. After about three a.m., I went into the twins' room and tried to catch some sleep on the bottom bunk. But those damn things aren't exactly comfortable for a guy six four. So the floor it was until I woke up so stiff and miserable that going back to sleep wasn't gonna happen.

And I'm not even talking about what was happening in my pants.

I watch as she glances around, taking in the sparse decorations and shit in my room. I'm a simple man who doesn't need pictures on the wall or bowls of fake fruit on the table. What's up with that shit anyway?

She pulls her legs up to her chest, revealing the glorious swell of her ass. My dick waves hello. "So. Did we... you know?" she asks boldly, squaring her shoulders and sitting up straight.

"Did we what?" I ask, fighting the grin that threatens to fly.

"You know..."

"I don't," I respond, shaking my head as if confused.

"Don't be obtuse."

"Oh, that's not an act, sweetheart."

"Don't call me sweetheart and just answer the question."

"Did we..." I say, trailing off. I'm making her say it.

"Did we... have sex?" The words trail off as she glares at me.

"You don't know?"

She opens her mouth, but nothing comes out. When she snaps it closed, she continues to glare at me from my bed as if she wants to skin me alive, and then tap dance on my rotting carcass. I'm so fucking turned on right now.

Unable to stand across the room any longer, I make my way to my bed. She tenses, her eyes widening, with each step I take. Coming to stand beside the bed, I reach down and lightly grasp her chin. "Firecracker, if we fucked last night I guarantee you'd remember it in the morning."

Her gasp goes straight to my cock. She seems to try to compose herself, clearing her throat and keeping her eyes locked on mine. "And the shirt?"

"You changed before you passed out," I tell her casually, letting go of her face, even though I want to continue to touch her. Her chin, her cheeks, her naked body. All of it.

I. Want. To. Touch. It.

"And did you at least turn around when I changed?"

"Now, Firecracker, how would that be fair? A naked chest for a naked chest," I say, crossing my arms over my chest and giving her my best smirk. Smoke practically billows from her ears.

"Come on," I tell her, turning and heading towards the door. "Breakfast is almost ready."

And with that, I turn and head out of my bedroom. Not because I want to, but because if I don't leave right now, I'm liable to crawl into bed with her and bury myself so deep inside of her, I'll never want to stop. Because if I know one thing about Lexi Summer, it's that one little taste won't be enough. Like a drug, she'll be my addiction.

And she *will* be mine.

Ten minutes later, Lexi joins me in the kitchen. She's wearing the same red pants and black sweater she wore last night. The same clothes I saw her strip out of last night while she stood in the middle of my room. Yeah, I tried to turn away. She was trashed and I wasn't about to take advantage, but as hard as I tried, my eyes just wouldn't look away. And she knew it, too. She undressed slowly, shaking her hips and ass, knowing that my eyes were glued to her, enjoying the hell out of the show as she went.

"What's that smell?" she asks, taking a seat at the old beat up table in the kitchen.

"French toast. I almost made eggs, but I always crave carbs after a night of drinking, so I took the chance that you'd do the same," I say as I pull the pan of warm French toast from the oven.

"My God, I think I'm in heaven," she says, her mouth practically watering as she gazes at the pan as if it were filled with diamonds.

"Eat up," I tell her, secretly loving how happy she is. My brothers love French toast, which is why it's one of the few things I know how to make.

She douses two pieces of bread in syrup and shovels half a piece into her mouth. She's not a dainty eater, and that thought excites me. I'd rather have a woman who eats real food than one who pretends to get full off garnish.

"I think I love you," she groans with her mouth packed full of food. I can't help the laugh that slips from my lips.

"We should get married then," I tell her casually, but the way she chokes on her food, I'm guessing she doesn't find the humor.

"I don't think so," she says after swallowing. I almost audibly groan as I watch, but I suppress the noise.

"You'll change your mind." Shrugging my shoulders, I go back to eating my food.

"Doubtful," she mumbles.

After breakfast, where we both scarfed down three slices of French toast, I collect the dirty dishes and set them in the sink. I can feel the nerves starting to set in, and I'm not really sure how to take that. I don't get nervous, especially around women, but I find myself almost out of my element with this fiery little woman.

Oh, what do I have to be nervous about?

We're getting to that.

"Thank you for breakfast. I'm gonna head out," she says, pointing towards the door.

"Wait," I say, grabbing her hand before she can run far, far away. That, and I really just like to touch her. Her skin is so soft and smells fucking amazing. "I want to talk to you about something."

Leading her into the living room, we take a seat beside each other on the couch. Our knees touch, but she doesn't pull away, which makes me smile a little on the inside. Of course I don't show it. She'll eat me alive. "What's up?"

Clearing my throat, I just decide to put it all out there. "You want to have a baby, right?"

Alarm clouds her eyes as she gazes over at me. She's on high alert and doesn't say anything. Maybe she doesn't remember telling me last night all about her desire to get knocked up, but there's no way I could forget it. Especially after my idea started to grow roots.

"Yeah," she whispers, her tone defensive and her foot tapping a heavy beat on the carpet.

"Well, I'll give you a baby."

She blinks once, twice, a dozen times. I don't say anything else, but wait for her reply. My heart is pounding and my own desire to tap my foot is strong, but I hold off. Her eyes search my face, looking for something, but I'm not sure what. The she starts laughing. Like full-belly, rolling on the ground, grasping your stomach in side-splitting pain, kinda laughing.

"Oh my God, that was the best joke I've ever heard," she says, wiping tears from under her eyes.

"I'm not joking, Lex." Again, I wait for my words to sink in.

Slowly, her laughter subsides and her eyes change from humorous to serious to disbelief. "Of course you are. That was a joke," she insists.

"Not even a little bit," I confirm, giving her a smile. "You want a baby, and I can give you one." Lexi starts to shake her head and opens her mouth to speak, but I cut her off. "Just wait a second. Hear me out."

Standing up, I drop to my knees in front of her. Her eyes are wide with shock as she stares straight at me. "You need sperm, and well, I have some. Do you really want to have a baby with a turkey baster?"

"It doesn't really matter how I get one," she starts, stuttering.

"Of course it does. We're doing this the old fashioned way, sweetheart."

"We?" she asks, her eyebrows flying into her hair.

"We. You and me."

"I can't have a baby with you," she stutters, spitting out her words and trying to back away from me.

"Of course you can. I'm insanely attractive and you can't keep your hands off my body."

That earns an eye roll. "You're unbelievable."

"I know," I smirk. "Do you know how fucking awesome our kid would be?" I ask, feigning offense. That gets the smallest smile on those sexy lips. "Besides, you don't have to pay for my sperm."

"But we'd have to… you know," she says, pointing back and forth between my chest and hers.

"We would. And I would enjoy the shit out of that part, Firecracker."

"Wait a minute," she says, standing up. "You're telling me that you want to have a baby? With me?"

"Why not?" I ask, shrugging my shoulders.

"Because it's… well, it's just… I don't know what it is exactly, but it shouldn't happen. Oh my God, I can't think straight," she says, dropping her head into her hands. "This is crazy."

"Listen," I start, grabbing her hands and holding them firmly in my own. "You want a baby, right? It's been your dream well before some fucking asshole ripped it away from you. So, let's get you a baby."

"How did you…" she starts, her cheeks staining pink.

"You told me as you were crawling into my bed." That earns a blush.

"But, what am I going to tell my family?"

"Tell them we're dating. Tell them you went to that sperm place. Tell them it was some random stranger who was insanely gorgeous with a massive cock. I don't care." That gets another smile. See? I could spend the rest of my life trying to make this woman smile just like that. It does weird things to my heart (amongst other body parts).

After several minutes where she seems to be lost in thought, she finally speaks. "What do you get out of this?"

"You mean besides the opportunity to take you to bed?" I ask, wiggling my eyebrows suggestively.

"Yes, besides that. Why do this?"

Running my hand along the back of my neck, I turn and face the window. "I guess I'm just at the point in my life where I want to do something for me. I want to live my life under my terms, not someone else's. I'm twenty-six years old and tired of having to deal with crap that has nothing to do with me. *This?* This baby would be my doing, under my terms. A part of me."

"Do you want to be involved?" she asks, her voice quiet.

"Honestly, yeah. I'd love to fucking be involved. I know you planned to go at this alone, but this way, you'd always have someone to help you. A friend, so to speak, to share the load."

"A friend?" she asks, giving me her own smirk.

"A friend who's seen you naked," I reply, getting smacked in the gut.

"You're crazy," she whispers, a small smile playing on her lips.

"Maybe, but I want to do this. If it were anyone else, I'd never offer. But with you? I don't know what it is, but it feels right," I tell her.

"But we barely know each other."

"True, but I trust you not to fuck me over. I hope you feel the same."

She hesitates for only a moment. "I do."

"Then go home and think about it. You said you have to let the clinic know Monday, right?" She nods. "Well, take the day and think about it. If you're not comfortable with it, then go about your original plan. But if you're interested in my super amazing sperm, then it's here, ready to go."

Lexi's laughter fills the living room and she gives me a smile. A big, genuine, makes my heart leap in my chest smile. "I'll think about it," she confirms before heading towards the door. Honestly, that's all I can ask for. At least she didn't run from the apartment screaming, right?

She opens the door and steps into the hall. "I can't believe I'm actually considering this," she mumbles before turning to face me.

"It's the perfect arrangement. You get the baby you've always dreamed about."

"And you get to sleep with me," she mumbles.

"It's inevitable, Firecracker. I'm just giving you your dream along with mine."

She doesn't say anything, but instead heads to her apartment. She has a lot to consider, and I have no clue which way she's leaning.

Last night after she told me she wanted a baby and that her soon-to-be ex-husband stripped that away from her, it got me thinking. The longing mixed with hurt in her eyes was almost too much to bear. Shit, I almost took her right then and tried to knock her up. But I'd never do that to a woman who's only half conscious. When I'm with any woman, she's one hundred percent alert and coherent.

And when I'm finally with Lexi, it'll be because she's begging me to take her.

My life hasn't been my own since even before I left Westville. My legs are chained and a ghost walks with me, but I'm determined to make it better. I'm determined to fix the mistakes of one I love and right the wrongs of the one I despise.

I'm finally taking control of my life.

No, maybe it's not the best time to bring a baby into the family. I'm surrounded by drama and am working two jobs with little or nothing to show for it. This is different than the way I wanted to help my mom fix her mess. That was out of necessity. This is for me. I thought about it from every direction last night, but kept coming back to one thing: I want to help her, and the thought of her with some other dick makes me feel like I'm having a stroke. As I tossed and turned on the bottom bunk of my brothers' bed, the more this idea took shape and I realized I wanted something else too.

A baby.

11

Lexi

"He's crazy."

"Who?" my sister questions as she steps aside and grants me entrance into her and Levi's apartment across the hall.

"Linkin," I grumble as I toss myself down onto their comfy couch.

"Neighbor Linkin?"

"Yes. Did you have sex here?" I ask, tensing and sitting up straight.

"Recently?" Abby asks, blushing a dark shade of fuchsia.

"My God, you two are like rabbits. How recent?"

"I don't know. A week maybe?"

"Gross!" I whine, jumping up and standing in front of the offending furniture.

"Why does that bother you? You sit on the couch in my old apartment all of the time. You don't think we've gotten busy there either?"

"You're as bad as Grandma and Grandpa," I groan.

"So why is Linkin crazy?" she asks, walking into the kitchen and grabbing a pitcher of lemonade.

"Do you have any vodka?"

"Definitely," she replies, reaching above the fridge and grabbing a bottle of the cheap liquor. Before I sit down, I glance at the kitchen chair and give her a look. My twin rolls her eyes. "No, we haven't done it on those chairs."

"Good. I'll never be able to sit on my couch again. All I'll think about is Levi pecker tracks."

That makes my sister giggle. "Pierced pecker tracks," she adds before giving in to a full-belly laugh.

I watch as she pours a bit too much vodka into the lemonade. She doesn't even grab a spoon, but sort of sloshes it around within the pitcher to mix it. She's definitely been hanging out with AJ too much lately. My usually mild sister is turning into a brazen lush.

And I love it.

She's happy. It's written all over her face, radiating from her pores like that pregnancy glow. Oh my God! "You're pregnant!" I holler, stunned that she's pouring such a big glass of the vodka and lemonade.

"What? No I'm not!"

"Why are you glowing?" I demand, waiting to hear that my twin got knocked up by her best friend.

"I don't know. Maybe it was the sex I had about thirty minutes ago," she replies quietly, that ever-present blush creeping up her neck.

"Lucky bitch," I grumble, taking a big drink of the too-strong drink.

"Yes, I am. Levi had to go in early today to cover for someone so I gave him a parting gift."

"You sound like Grandma. Why must you always talk about it every time you have the sex?"

"You brought it up. It's not like I started the conversation with 'Hey, sis! I just got some. Levi does this thing where he rolls his hips and the piercing slides against me in a way that makes me forget my own name.'"

"Really?" I ask, leaning forward, suddenly wanting to hear more.

"Never mind. What's up with you? Why is neighbor Linkin making you crazy?" she asks, taking her own big drink.

"Does it matter that it's like ten in the morning and we're drinking vodka?"

"Call it Hair of the Dog."

"Yep, you've definitely been hanging around AJ too much," I warn her.

"Stop stalling. Talk."

I glance around the kitchen, which has the exact same layout as mine. The few times I'd been in here with Abby before she moved in, were completely different. Sure, the furniture might be the same, but the place is homey. There are pictures of the two of them on the walls, on end tables, and secured to the fridge with magnets. Love lives here, and that makes me smile.

"Well, you know that I stayed behind and rode home with Linkin, right?"

"Yeah. Are you about to tell me you rode *him* home? Or at home?"

"Settle your hormones, Grandma. Do you want to hear this or not?" She waves her hand for me to continue. "Anyway, I drank more shots after you guys left. Apparently, I spilled everything about Chris at some point." Abby's eyebrows rise as she stares straight at me. "I passed out in his bed, but nothing happened," I assure her.

"So this morning, I was all ready to get the hell out of there, but couldn't because he made breakfast."

"Breakfast?"

"French toast so good it was almost orgasmic."

"Damn. Hot *and* can cook," Abby whispers, taking another drink of her special lemonade.

"And wants to give me a baby," I blurt out, my heart pounding in my chest like a jackhammer.

"What!?" she exclaims, spewing a mouthful of her drink all over the floor.

"Exactly! Who offers up his sperm to give a stranger a baby?" I holler.

"Do you know what happens at a sperm bank?" she asks sarcastically.

"Shut up, that's different. I don't know that sperm. I know this sperm. And I don't like it."

She looks at me with confusion written in her emerald eyes. "Wait, you don't like the sperm?"

"No, I don't like *him*."

"Him…"

"Linkin! My God woman, would you keep up?" I howl before chugging the rest of my drink.

"Sooooooo, you like him." It's a statement. Not a question.

"No. I don't."

"Yes. You do."

"You're crazy, just like him."

"So, finish. He wants to give you his sperm?"

"Yes, he wants to make a contribution. The old fashioned way," I whisper. Why am I whispering?

"Nice! Do it, do it! He's so hot, and I would never say this to Levi, but I got an eyeful when he did the striptease for you."

"I can't have his baby, Abby. I don't know him."

"So, get to know him."

"You make it sound so easy," I say, rubbing my aching forehead.

"Well, it's definitely *not* easy. This is as complicated as trying to sneak back into the house when we were sixteen," Abby quips, a smile playing on both of our lips. Ahh, yes. I recall that night very well.

"What do I do?" I plead.

"First off, is this just a donation or does he want to be involved?"

"He wants to be involved. And if I were to actually think about this for a second, which I'm not, I guess it would be really nice to have someone to help me. I mean, I know I could do it solo, but to have someone to share the load is appealing."

"Definitely. If you need a break, you'll have help. Plus, the financial assistance is definitely a plus. Jani struggled for years just to put food on the table for herself because after she paid the bills and bought food and diapers for Elijah, she barely had anything left." Abby's referring to a woman we went to high school with who got pregnant just out of school. The father didn't stick around long enough to see the start of the second trimester, but Jani was determined to do it herself.

The difference between our friend and me is that I have a good, established job with enough income to pay my bills and put a little bit each week into savings. Financially, with a bit of adjustment to accommodate the cost of food, diapers, medical care, childcare, and such, I can make it work. But sharing the financial responsibility definitely goes in the plus category.

"But what about him. I mean, I don't even know him," I tell her, because honestly, that's one of my biggest hang-ups.

"So, get to know him. I mean, you don't have to make this decision right now, correct? You could hold off on the sperm bank purchase for another month, get to know Linkin, and see if you can put up with him in your life for the next eighteen years," she says with a shoulder shrug, like it's so logical.

"I can barely put up with him for eighteen minutes, let alone eighteen years." But even as I say the words, I know they're not true. I know he pushes my buttons, but he does it on purpose. The night I watched the movie and ate pizza with him and his brothers, I actually really enjoyed his company.

Plus, there's the way he treats his brothers. He's a wonderful big brother, I can tell by how happy the boys were with him. They love him, and the thought of bringing a baby into the mix, one that will be right smack dab in the middle of the sword fights, puts a happy little beat in my chest and a smile on my face.

"I think you're right. I can't make this decision today. I need to get to know him and make sure that this is the right thing to do."

"For what it's worth, I've always liked Linkin. Ever since he moved in here six months ago or so, he's been nice and considerate and a good neighbor."

"I know," I reply because I do. He's all of those things with me too.

But a baby?

I just need a little time to think about it.

"Come on. It's almost time to head to the café for lunch. You can ride with me," Abby says as she stands up and stumbles a little.

Giggling, I reach for my phone. "I'll call someone who hasn't been drinking spiked lemonade since ten in the morning," I snort as I try to call up one of my sisters, but the names are dancing on the screen. "How much vodka did you put in that pitcher?"

Abby snorts and laughs at the same time. "Uhhhh, just a little. A little under half the bottle." She starts laughing, which makes me laugh. We both giggle and snort until the tears are rolling and the bellies are hurting.

"Come on. I know where we can get a ride," I tell her as we head towards the front door.

I walk diagonally (not because I can't walk straight, but because that's where I'm going) until I reach the door I'm looking for. Without giving it any ounce of thought, I raise my hand and knock. When he answers the door, his hair wet from a shower, dark jeans hugging his powerful legs, and a shirt that's molded to perfection on those muscular arms, I almost tell him yes.

Yes, I'll take your sperm.

Instead, I say, "Come on. We're going to lunch with my family."

"We?" he asks, crossing those strong arms across his chest, making a little string of drool drip down my chin.

"Yes, we. Me, Abby, and you. You're driving too because some vodka fell into Abby's lemonade and we may have drank it," I tell him.

"You're buzzed? At eleven a.m."

"Don't judge me. An hour ago, you offered to impregnate me just because I want a baby."

"That I did, Firecracker. Let me grab my jacket," he says, turning and heading back into his apartment.

"I can practically see the testosterone rolling off of him, Lexi. You *have* to do it with him. It's practically your duty for women everywhere," Abby whispers beside me, not taking her eyes off Linkin's backside.

"I'm telling Levi you're ogling the neighbor," I fire back at her, causing her eyes to widen in worry.

"You wouldn't!"

"I would. Keep your eyes off the neighbor's ass, hussy."

"You're turning bitchy in your old age," she quips, turning and heading towards the stairs.

"Ready?" Linkin asks, standing behind me and closing his door.

Ready? Is that a trick question? Ready for lunch? Ready to meet my family? Ready to do the horizontal mambo with my Greek God of a neighbor that could result in pregnancy; the one thing I wanted while fighting for my marriage?

Maybe it's the alcohol talking, but there's only one answer to each of those questions.

Yes.

Ready or not, here I come.

The diner is packed with the Sunday lunch crowd and we have to wait a few minutes to get the big table. As soon as we walk through the door, all eyes are on me. Or more accurately, on Linkin.

"What? You've all seen him before. This time he just has more clothes on," I say casually, finding a seat at the table.

"Hey, it's the stripper," Ryan says with a wide smile, extending his hand to Linkin and offering a shake.

"You're really a stripper?" Dean asks. "I thought that was an accident."

"He's not really a stripper. He just stripped for Lexi because Grandma *thought* he was the stripper. But then the stripper showed up and Grandma wanted them to have a strip-off so we could see who was the best stripper," AJ tells the table. You know, at Sunday lunch in a family restaurant.

"Stop saying stripper. It weirds me out," Abby says, taking a sip of her water.

"He'd make a great stripper, though. He's got moves," Payton adds.

"I'd like to see these moves, son," Grandpa hollers from the end of the table. "Maybe you could teach me a few things," he adds with a wink.

"Dear God, can't you all act normal for five seconds? You're gonna make him run away screaming before the waitress hands us the menus," I chastise the table.

It's quiet for a few moments as everyone just stares at Linkin and me. Abby, the traitor, is trying to hide her giggle beside me.

"His abs are pure sin," Grandma says, saluting Linkin and adding a wink for good measure.

"Grandma, you grabbed his butt," Meghan reprimands.

"It was a very nice butt," she rationalizes with an evil grin as she glances over her menu.

"So, Linkin, is it?" my dad asks from the opposite end of the table, clearly uncomfortable with the way the conversations have been going thus far.

"Yes, sir. Linkin Stone," he says with not so much as a hitch in his voice. It's as if my family's brand of crazy doesn't faze him in the least. Interesting.

"Nice to meet you. What is it that you do, exactly? Assuming you're not really a stripper," My dad says, a light blush creeping up his neck.

"I'm a mechanic and body specialist for Stapleton's," Linkin tells my dad and family, casually taking a sip of his ice water.

"Body specialist," Jaime whispers to Payton who makes the Y-chromosomes at the table giggle.

"And you're not a stripper?" AJ asks, seeking confirmation. Her eyes are bright and shining, a mischievous look on her pretty face.

"The only stripping I do is on a car," Linkin tells her with a wink.

"And now I'm picturing him stripping on the hood of a car," AJ mumbles to Meghan, who's sitting to her right. She's not quiet about it, so it shouldn't surprise me that everyone at the table hears her comment. Especially Grandma.

"Oh, me too, AJ. Me too," Grandma says, saluting Linkin with her glass of sweet tea.

Everyone is staring at him as if he's about to stand up and rip off his tear away pants to a Jay-Z song. My palms start to sweat and I brace myself for the letdown. He's about to take one look at my crazy family and run from the restaurant. Why wouldn't he? He's been here less than five minutes and already interrogated for being a stripper.

And maybe I should let him go. He's just as crazy as my family, remember? Offering to help me have a baby.

But something has been blooming in my chest ever since he made his suggestion. Hell, if I'm being honest with myself I've felt something since the first time I yelled at him in the hallway. No, I can't seem to walk away, even though I probably should. The only way to define what I'm feeling is… hope.

I'm hopeful for the first time in I don't know how long. My marriage to Chris was quickly going down the shitter, even before I found that document under our bed. I wasn't happy. I definitely wasn't happy when I found out what he did. But now? I find myself reaching for the olive branch that Linkin has extended to me.

Does that make me a little crazy too?

Probably.

"Linkin and I are dating!" I tell the table before chugging the diet soda set in front of me.

Wide eyes stare back at me. I hear his rushed inhale of breath, but don't look over at him. I'm afraid I won't be able to keep up the ruse. Or that I'll throw myself at him. Either way, probably not the best thing for Sunday lunch.

Instead of speaking, Linkin takes my hand and brings it to his mouth. He places a slow, tender kiss on my knuckles that sends lightning bolts of lust soaring through my blood and striking my nerve endings. Each wave of desire lands squarely between my legs, rendering the panties I changed into before knocking on my sister's door, as useless.

My eyes find his, dark and full of heat. His lips have yet to move from the tender flesh of my hand, and I sorta pray they never do. Unless he wants to use those lips in *other* places.

God, my body is all tingly and hypersensitive.

"You are?" Meghan asks, her surprised, yet happy eyes bouncing between Linkin and me.

Words seem to evade me. As much as I try, with him touching me, I can't make myself speak. Linkin must sense my inability to formulate words and jumps in. "Yes, we are. It's a new development. Right, sweetheart?" he says softly, placing a kiss on my palm this time.

"Right," I answer, my voice gruff and barely above a whisper. My head just keeps repeating over and over the way his deep voice says *sweetheart*.

"Well, I'm so happy for you," Jaime says, offering a smile.

The rest of lunch progresses fine, but I feel completely out of it. I engage in conversation, but I have no idea what I said. Everyone seems to accept Linkin and my decision to date him, even though I'm not divorced yet. Hell, *I* just found out about my decision to date him, and *I'm* not even freaked out. Even if said decision was based on a knee-jerk reaction.

Maybe it's the alcohol talking.

After lunch, we all stand to leave. Outside on the sidewalk, everyone talks over the person next to them as they embrace and say goodbye, as if we hadn't just seen each other last night. Funny, aren't we? We're a close family, one that sticks our noses where they don't belong and teases you mercilessly until you're ready to pee. Or is that tickle? Either way, my family is always there for each other.

"Linkin, it was nice to officially meet you. I heard so much about you after Lexi's divorce party that it was like there was another man in bed with us," Grandpa tells Linkin, not even caring that he tap-danced over the invisible line between acceptable and awkward.

"I'm not divorced yet," I remind my grandpa as I lean forward and graze a kiss over his wrinkled cheek.

"That's because he's dragging his feet like a streetwalker heading to pay her pimp," Grandpa hollers, drawing attention from those around us.

"I'm handling Chris," I tell him softly, touching his arm in a comforting gesture.

"If he doesn't knock off his shit, *I'm* going to be handling him," Linkin adds, arms crossed firmly over his chest in that way that I seem to notice, appreciate, and love.

Before I can say anything, Grandpa turns his full attention to Linkin and says, "You do that, son. Make sure that weasely bastard doesn't hurt my grandbaby again."

I'm stunned silent, trapped in the conversation they have around me. I should be pissed that Linkin's speaking for me, or at least on my behalf, but I'm not. It's shockingly endearing to know that someone has my back and is ready to wage a war in my honor. Warmth spreads through my veins as I gaze up at the man beside me. His short beard seems sexier in the daylight and his brown eyes twinkle with fierceness. He's so tall and strong it's like staring up at a tree.

A tree I want to climb.

"Anyway, it's time for me to go home and nap," I tell my grandpa, leading Linkin away from my family.

"Wait, wait, wait!" Grandma hollers, bursting through my siblings until she's right in front of Linkin. "It was nice to see you again, young man. I wouldn't mind seeing more of you soon." The way she waggles her eyebrows at him tells me she's not casually referring to him joining us at another family luncheon. No, this invite has more to do with him losing more articles of clothing.

A bubble of laughter bursts from Linkin's mouth as he gazes softly down at my pint-sized Grandma. "You're a handful, Miss Emma," he says, bending way down to hug her.

"You have no idea," Grandpa mumbles behind them.

"Oh, Linkin," Grandma coos, hugging him a few extra seconds longer than deemed appropriate. Sighing dramatically, she adds with a devilish smile, "You're quite the handful too." That's when I realize she's grabbing handfuls of Linkin's gloriously taut ass.

"Grandma!"

"What?" she asks coyly, pulling away from the guy I'm dating, but not really dating.

"Let's go, Emmie. If you're good, I'll serve dessert in the red room with that new ball gag we picked up last weekend," my grandpa says lovingly to his wife. He's so sweet and sincere that you almost miss the content of his statement.

Wait.

No.

God no!

"I'm going to throw up," I mumble, unable to look at Linkin.

"They're so cute," he whispers, both of us watching the way Grandpa gently touches the tip of Grandma's nose with his finger. Then she growls and bites at his finger, which makes him thrust his hips forward in a suggestive way that no grandchild ever wants to witness.

"Get me out of here. Now."

Waving goodbye to my family, I follow Linkin over to his old Blazer. Abby is going with Jaime to help pick a color to paint the kitchen, and then Levi will pick her up when he's off work. So it's just him and me heading back to the apartment building.

Suddenly, the inside of the truck cab feels smaller than a two-seater electric car. I can feel his presence, feel his eyes on me as I slide into the truck. I'm engulfed in his scent, wrapped in the heat of his authority, and my body is instantly hyperaware of his nearness. It almost makes me lightheaded.

He turns the key and the old truck fires to life. Linkin pulls from the parking lot and steers the truck towards the place we both live.

"So, dating, huh?" he asks. I can practically hear the cocky smirk in his voice. There's no need to look at him to know that it's plastered on his handsome face.

"Yeah, that was kinda sudden. Just forget I said anything," I say blasé.

"No way, Firecracker. There's no going back after something like that. There's no take-backs when you declare yourself in a relationship with someone in front of your family."

"What are you in the first grade? Of course there is! It's called life."

"Well, *life* has us in a relationship as of about one hour ago."

I keep my eyes focused on the road, determined not to let it show how much he affects me. When I feel his warm fingers brush the back of my neck, I jump in my seat. Obviously, I need to work on my acting skills.

My left leg starts to bounce against the floorboard, my mind goes back to replay our earlier conversation. I've been on the fence, not completely on board but not ready to write off his suggestion either, since he made the big pitch.

"I've been thinking," I start, clearing my throat to buy me a little time to figure out how to say this.

"Yeah?"

"Your offer. It's not off the table yet, but I just keep thinking that I don't really know you. So, I'm giving you a week. One week to get to know you better and for you to convince me that you're the right man for the job."

"Oh, sweetheart, I'm more than ready to show you just how *convincing* I can be." His words draw my eyes to him. Even though that smirk is there, his eyes are ablaze with something dirty and suggestive. My blood actually zips through my veins.

"If I can be candid here, I'm getting ready to start my period this week. I've decided to cancel my appointment tomorrow at the sperm bank, but only long enough to see if your offer is my best choice. If not, I'll call them back and go with donor number four."

"One week, huh?"

"One week. Then I'll have a few days to purchase my sperm before I ovulate," I say, glancing at the light traffic along the Bay.

"You won't be needing that purchase. I'll be making my own donation about that time." His confidence catches me off guard and makes me smile at the same time.

"Don't be so sure," I suggest, trying to calm my racing heart. He makes me so crazy.

Pulling into the parking lot of the apartment building, he throws his truck into park and turns to face me. "So, I get one week to show you that I'm a decent guy and would make a great dad?"

"Yeah. I know it's not a long time," I start, but he cuts me off.

"I'm up to the challenge. Honestly, I don't think you'll need the full week."

I roll my eyes. "You're so full of yourself."

"Maybe," he says with a smile. "Maybe I do it just to get a rise out of you."

"So you like getting under my skin?"

He leans forward until our noses practically touch. His breath fans across my face and I almost reach out and stroke the hair on his face. It looks so soft and sexy right now that my fingers actually twitch to touch it. "You are already under my skin, Lexi. It's only fair that I do the same for you."

"You do," I confess before I can stop the words.

God, if he only knew the extent of how deep he's already under my skin.

I'm in so much trouble.

Linkin

12

"I've met someone."

Mom looks up from the bowl of brownie batter she's mixing to give me *the look.* It's part shocked, part amused, and well, more shocked. She works in an hour at the café that I ate lunch in earlier with the Summer clan. I was bored at home, and since the boys are probably driving her crazy by now, I decided to come see her for a bit before taking the knuckleheads back to my place.

Good thing I did.

Something's up.

Mom only bakes when she's stressed, which lately has been a lot more than usual. Not that her life has been a walk in the park these last six months–hell, last year–but even when her marriage was falling apart and secrets were exposed, she didn't bake like this. She didn't have time. She was too busy putting out fires she didn't start and keeping the mess as far away from the boys as possible.

"Oh?"

"Her name is Lexi. She's actually my neighbor," I tell her, leaning my hip against the counter and tossing an apple into the air and catching it.

"Would this be the woman your brother Jack is planning to marry?" she asks, her lips curling up into a smile. God, I've missed that smile. My mom is gorgeous, but she was dealt a bad hand, and life has slowly sucked the joy right out of her. The only time she smiles anymore is usually reserved for the boys and me. And even then it's rare.

"It would. But in my defense, I kissed her first," I quip with my own smile, recalling Jeff's taunts to kiss her before Jack.

"Tell me about her," she insists as she pours the batter into the pan. I watch as she slides it into the preheated oven. Excitement races through me as I realize I'll be eating hot, gooey, awesome fucking brownies in about thirty minutes.

"She works at a salon uptown. She's the youngest of six and a twin. She's feisty and gorgeous and isn't afraid to go toe-to-toe with me. She's a smart ass to boot."

Mom's quiet so I glance over and see the warm grin. "And you like her."

"Yeah."

"Does she know?" Mom asks quietly, averting her gaze. I know exactly what she's asking.

"No." When she glances up at me, I continue. "I wasn't planning to tell her for a bit. I don't want to bring our shit down on her."

"Link, you can't hide it from her for too long. When secrets lay between you, no one really sleeps."

I get what she's saying. Shit, she lived those secrets; being kept in the dark and finding out too late that the one you love is a dirtbag.

"I know, Mom. I'll tell her, I promise. But I want to wait to see where this thing goes first, you know? I don't like anyone knowing our business." Ain't that the truth. As soon as our dirty laundry started coming out, and the whispers started to get too close to the twins, I pulled them out of town and relocated us all to Jupiter Bay. Here, no one cares what our last name is. No one knows why we up and moved to a new town practically overnight. No one knows the secrets that trail behind us like a shadow.

"I know you like your privacy, Link. Hell, I do too. I haven't told a soul about Arnie." Fuck, I hate it when she says his name. Makes my knuckles twitch to connect with something hard. "But I don't want this mess to come between you and this Lexi. Just the fact that you're telling me about her lets me know that she's special. I trust that when the time is right, you'll tell her what she needs to know."

"I will."

"Good. Now, grab the container on the counter. I cut up some fresh fruit for you to take home with you. The boys should have it for snack."

"Fruit?"

"Yes, fruit. It's one of the basic food groups. You should try it sometime," she quips, snapping the hand towel my direction. "Tell me more about your girl." My girl. Damn, I like the sound of that.

"Well, she's going through a divorce," I state, waiting for the reaction I know is coming.

"She's not divorced yet?" Mom asks, the concern I expect written all over her face.

"Not yet, but it's in the process. The douche she was married to is dragging his feet," I tell her, popping a grape into my mouth.

"You've met him?"

"Unfortunately. He shows up randomly at her place. Both times, I was there to intercept. He doesn't like to be told no."

"Most men don't," Mom whispers, cleaning up her hand mixer and bowl. Turning to face me, she adds, "Just promise me you'll be careful. If she's just coming out of a divorce, she may not be as ready to date as she thought she was."

"No, I'm pretty sure she's ready. She told me a bit about her ex and why she left. She wanted a baby and he wouldn't give it to her. But even before that, she says the marriage was over. He wouldn't ever do anything with her and worked twenty-four seven."

"Hmmm. You've always said you wouldn't marry. And you work two jobs," she reminds me. No, I know she's not trying to upset me, but more like playing devil's advocate. Still, her comments make my gut burn. Yeah, I might have said I wouldn't marry, but that was after watching my mom try to divorce an ungrateful prick who used the fuck out of her and then ran like the fucking coward that he is. And yes, I do work two jobs, no thanks to the ungrateful prick.

"I know I did, but she's different."

Her deep brown eyes, reflecting so much love and hope for me, stare up at me. "I'd like to meet her. It's not right that the boys got to meet her – and kill her, as I was told after I picked them up from school the next day. Promise you'll bring her by soon."

"I promise," I tell my mom, bending over and kissing her forehead. Her brown hair has much more gray in it than it used to, and she refuses to color it. Every bit of extra income is gone and things like hair dye, pedicures, and manicures are things she doesn't indulge in.

Thinking of Lexi, that gives me an idea.

The front door bursts open with a bang and noise follows in the wake of two brown haired little eight-year-olds.

"Linkin!" Jeff hollers as he runs into the room, tossing his book bag onto the middle of the floor and causing Jack to trip over it.

"Hey, dorkface! Pick up your stuff so people don't trip over it," Jack reprimands his twin brother.

"Whatever, peabrain! You leave your Legos all over the room for me to step on," Jeff says, standing right next to me, his arms crossed over his chest, mimicking my own stance.

"Both of you need to be more considerate and pick up after yourselves. One of these days, Mom is going to trip over something that one of you left lying around and she's going to get hurt." I give them both a pointed look, waiting for them to make their next move.

"Sorry," Jeff says, walking over and grabbing his book bag.

"Come on, doofus. Let's go booby-trap the door so the Army guys shoot Linkin when he comes in," Jack suggests as they both take off down the small hallway.

"That went well," I huff, making Mom giggle.

"They're constantly booby-trapping everything. I have to check the toilet seat before I sit down."

"I don't know where they get it," I retort, waiting for her attack.

"Whatever!" she exclaims. "Those boys are the spitting image of their older brother," she adds, snapping the towel again and hitting me in the bicep.

"Fine, they might get it honestly."

After a few minutes of silence–well, silence in the kitchen. You can hear what sounds like a war zone coming from the small bedroom at the back of the house–Mom continues. "Promise me you'll bring her by. I want to meet her."

"I already promised."

"I know you did, but I just wanted to make sure you knew how serious I was."

"I wouldn't have told you about her if I wasn't ready for you to meet her," I whisper, wrapping my arms around the woman who raised me. She's small and frail-like, which pisses me off all over again. Mom has always been full of life and energy, but the king-sized dick sucked it out of her in just eight short years of marriage.

Mom and Arnie hadn't dated long before she got pregnant with the boys. For some reason, she decided to marry him. At first, it seemed all right. I was in high school, working part time at an auto parts store, chasing girls, and drag racing cars, so I'll admit that I didn't pay as much attention to her and him as I should have. Everything seemed fine–at least on the outside–so I went about my teenage life, making money, chasing tail, and getting my own shithole of a place. Things had been going well, until about nine months ago.

Then everything changed.

Everything came crashing down.

I'm a lot more cautious with my own life, but I'm damn sure more aware of her and the boys. I know I'm going to have to tell Lexi about it, but I just hate reliving this bullshit. I don't want her to look at me with pity in those deep green eyes. That would kill me. Because I don't want or need anyone's pity. I'm fixing the mess he created, and that's all anyone needs to know.

When the brownies are done and the bags are loaded into my car, I head towards my place with two mini tornados riding in the backseat. I can't help but wonder what Lexi's doing tonight. If I've only got a week to convince her to let me father her baby, then I'm going to take advantage of every free moment I can get with her.

Starting tonight.

It's time that 'Operation Knock Her Up' commences.

I knock on her door just after five. The television is on, some high-drama reality show crying through the wall. When she opens the door, I'm struck stupid for the second time today. Just looking at her hurts. She's gorgeous. Much shorter than I am, with long sexy legs that beg to wrap around my waist, long brown hair with streaks of copper running through it, the biggest, brightest green eyes I've ever seen, and soft, fragrant, lightly tanned skin. She instantly reduces me to a hard-on.

Always.

"Hey," she whispers, rubbing her eyes.

"Did I wake you?"

"No, I had been up for a bit. I needed a little nap after… I don't usually drink in the mornings on a Sunday, okay. Especially after a night with my sisters."

"Hey, no judgment," I assure her. Nope, not me. I remember my early twenties, when I was living on my own and drinking and partying most of my paychecks away. Sunday morning drinks were a common occurrence for a period of my life.

"Anyway," she starts, but leaves the sentence hanging.

"Oh, so the knuckleheads are over for the night, and I was thinking that since I only have a week to convince you, I'm making dinner. Would you like to come over?" Then I hold my breath, which is crazy because I've never been this excited and nervous for a woman to accept a dinner invitation before. Of course, actual dinner invites haven't been that common either. I'm more of a *meet a girl at a bar and take her home for the night* kinda guy.

At least I was.

"Oh," she says, a hint of nerves laced in her voice.

"I mean, the boys will be there, so you'll have to try to keep your hands to yourself for a night." Just to get a rise out of her, I throw her a smirk.

Lexi just rolls her eyes. "I think I can manage," she sasses, turning and grabbing her keys and phone.

When she steps into the hallway, I'm instantly assaulted by her scent. It's clean with a touch of sweet. I want to lick her. Fuck, I'd lick her like a lollipop until she's moaning and withering beneath my tongue, and then I'd do it some more just to watch the sight of her coming undone all over again.

Discreetly adjusting my crotch, I lead her towards my door. The boys are killing each other in the living room, Jeff standing over Jack, driving his big fake sword into his gut repeatedly. "Boys, knock it off. We have a guest."

"Lexi!" Jack hollers, jumping up and running our way. "Couldn't stay away, huh?" he asks, waggling his eyebrows in a suggestive manner.

I burst into laughter, while Lexi gives me a look, as if she's blaming me for his come-on. I raise my hands in defeat and try to wipe the smile off my face. My little brother is definitely a charmer. "Don't look at me."

"I bet you were just like him when you were younger, always charming the teachers out of no homework and the girls out of their juice boxes."

Leaning forward until our noses are practically touching, I whisper, "Actually, it was their pudding cups." Her eyes dilate with hunger and fire spreads through my veins as I draw out the last two words.

"Oh, I wouldn't doubt it. You're trouble," she states pointedly.

"Naw, I'm a good boy, Firecracker. I just enjoy getting a little bad with the right woman," I tell her with a wink before turning my attention to the pile of ingredients on the counter.

"What are you making?" she asks, leaning her hip against the counter.

"Pasketti," Jeff hollers from the living room.

"Spaghetti," I correct with a smile.

"That's what I said," Jeff grumbles before turning his attention back to the television.

"Hope you're okay with Italian," I say, placing a pot of water on the stove to boil. Next, I grab a cutting board and get to cutting Italian sausage into bite-size pieces.

"That sounds great. Can I help with something?" she offers, looking around at the meager ingredients. Just one glance her way has my blood pumping and my cock stirring. Sure, she could help with something, but I don't think that's what she's offering.

"Well, I'm just using jar sauce, but I usually add some mushrooms to the mix, if you like them. The boys pick them out, but we can definitely leave them out if you're not a fan."

"I love mushrooms," she replies, grabbing the small can of bits and pieces mushrooms and the can opener. "You know, I have a pretty easy spaghetti sauce recipe that my grandma taught all of us. I could show you sometime," she adds casually, her delicate little shoulders shrugging slightly.

Lexi must feel my eyes on her because she glances my way. I offer her a small smile, the prospect of her coming over sometime to share a recipe and help me cook, warming my blood. "That'd be great."

Once the sausage is in the pan and simmering on low, I break the spaghetti noodles in half and throw them into the water. Next, I crank the oven temperature up to four hundred and get the garlic breadsticks ready on a cookie sheet.

Glancing over, I find Lexi at the stove, stirring around the meat so it doesn't scorch. A weird sensation sweeps through my body, and I find myself just staring. She looks so comfortable and so fucking hot standing in my kitchen that my level of contentment stops me in my tracks.

I want this.

This foreign feeling that seems a hell of a lot like happiness.

We work side by side as we finalize dinner, co-existing as if we've been here for years. Neither of us talk, but words aren't needed. Every time I steal a few glances, she's looking at me, a small smile playing on those lips. Yeah, *those lips*. The ones I've been dreaming about kissing again until I'm dizzy with lust and hard enough to jackhammer concrete.

"Spaghetti's ready," I holler at the boys as I move the sauce from the counter to the table.

Before I can even grab a plate, Lexi has a plate in one hand and the other in front of her on the counter, scooping a pile of noodles onto both plates. She moves effortlessly as she adds sauce, meat, and a garlic breadstick to each plate. Then, she delivers them to the table, where my brothers are waiting. Grabbing a pitcher of lemonade that I made earlier, I pour them each a small glass, then two larger ones for us.

"Jeff, use your napkin, not your hand," I advise, grabbing a paper napkin from the pile and setting it beside him.

"My pasketti is the best!" he exclaims, mouth full of half-chewed food.

"Spaghetti," I say.

"That's what I said!"

Smiling, I grab the last plate and pile it high with carbs. Lexi's already sitting at the table, laughing at something Jack is saying, and looks so relaxed, so much younger than her twenty-five years. She looks like she doesn't have a care in the world, as if the stresses of everyday life and those extra ones associated with her douchecanoe ex, no longer exist.

Suddenly, I'm more determined than ever to keep that look on her face.

After dinner, she helps clean up the mess, even though I tell her not to. I can clean up the dishes after she leaves and the boys are in bed. But since she's offering to help, I'm not about to miss a single second of having her in my kitchen, working side by side to complete a chore as simple as washing dishes.

Instead of watching *The Gladiator*, I find a show I like called *Forged in Fire*. Of course the boys are into it since the premise of the show is making knives. Lexi sits beside me on the couch as the boys demonstrate how they'd use each knife made to maim and kill their opponent.

When it gets a little gruesome, I redirect their attention to dessert. Even though they still watch the show, the boys eat ice cream with a chocolate shell that hardens. "Watch, Lex! I'm going to kill my ice cream," Jack says, stabbing the shell with his spoon and breaking it apart into small pieces.

"You better eat it before it melts. Otherwise, I'm going to," she says, smiling fondly down at my brother. They're sitting on the floor in front of the coffee table, eyes wide and riveted as two remaining bladesmiths battle for the title of champion of the episode.

She dips her spoon into her ice cream and scoops up a bit of the hard chocolate shell before slipping it into her mouth. I almost moan out loud as she licks the bottom of the spoon, my pants tightening with each second I watch. Her eyes find mine on her, hot and yearning.

"Do I have some on my face?"

"If you did, I'd just lick it off," I tell her, watching hypnotically as her sexy little tongue slips out and slides along the corner of her mouth.

"Dirty bird," she mumbles.

"You have no idea the things playing through my mind right now." *Like you naked while I suck melted ice cream off your tits.* "If I close my eyes, I'd be watching porn."

She giggles and takes another spoonful of melting ice cream. Her eyes are on mine as she brings it to her mouth and dips her tongue into the sweet, cold mixture, swirling it around and coating the tip of her tongue in white.

My balls start to ache.

"That's not very nice, seductress."

"Do you want a bite?"

"Are we talking about the ice cream or something else? Because yes, I definitely want a bite," I tell her, grabbing her hand and slowly drawing it towards my mouth.

Her eyes are emerald balls of fire as she watches me bring the spoon to my mouth. My tongue darts out, lazily licking the same cream where her tongue just trailed. Her mouth opens and she starts to pant when I slowly slide my tongue along the top of the spoon, parting the ice cream, before wrapping my mouth completely around it and closing. When I swallow, I make sure to do it slowly, my eyes locked on hers the entire time.

Erotic. As. Fuck.

After a moment, she pulls the spoon from my mouth. Clearing her throat, she says, "Okay. We should definitely eat more ice cream."

"Bedtime!" I holler, jumping off the couch as if my ass were on fire.

"No!" Jeff yells, while Jack grabs his sword. "Let's duel this out."

"No duels. No arguing. Bedtime."

The boys say goodnight to Lexi, and I have to practically drag them to their bedroom as if they were off to their deaths. Never mind that it's exactly eight thirty, which is their bedtime, but they're so used to staying up a little past it when they're with me that they're not taking the bedtime enforcement so well.

After they brush their teeth and get in bed, I turn on the nightlight and give them hugs. "Good night, boys," I say as I step back into the hall, leaving the door cracked just a hair.

Lexi's still on one end of the couch, too far away from where I want her.

Which is in my arms.

"Come here," I whisper hoarsely, reaching for her body, needing to feel it against mine. She moves easily, crawling into my lap.

My cock is strained against my pants, but I make no move to adjust it to a comfortable position. I'm afraid that if I move, she'll disappear. Instead, I keep my hands in contact with her soft skin as much as possible. I slide my hands up her arms, reveling in the way goose bumps pepper her flesh. Her eyes blaze with a need, a desire, that I can't describe–can only feel.

Her lips move as she leans forward. They're slightly parted and the sight of them inching closer and closer turns me on like a light switch. Her eyes flutter closed just before our lips connect when we hear, "I need to use the potty."

Cockblocked by an eight-year-old.

Lexi jumps in my lap, pulling back until she practically falls on the floor.

"Were you two kissing?" Jeff giggles while Jack goes into the bathroom.

"No," she gasps at the same time I say, "Yep."

She jumps the rest of the way off my lap, returning to her half of the couch, and curling her legs into her chest. "Come on, knuckleheads. Back to bed," I say, rubbing my hands over my face and willing my hard-on to subside.

They're giggling like girls when I enter the bedroom. "Are we done getting up?"

"You were kissing. K-I-S-S-I-N-G."

"First comes love."

"Then comes marriage."

"That's enough, boys," I interrupt their chanting and tuck them back into their bunks. "Sleep. You have school in the morning."

"I hate school," Jeff grumbles.

"I love it. Miss Hillengoss always wears pretty high heels," Jack smirks.

"You're too young to notice that," I reply, shaking my head. "Goodnight," I add as I step back out of the room, closing the door as I go. I can hear them laughing on the other side.

It's still not quiet when I reach the living room, but I join her on the couch once more. My cock is strained against my pants, begging to come out and play. But he's just gonna have to wait, because that's not happening tonight.

"Are they asleep?" she asks softly, her arms wrapping around my waist once more. The way she's leaning against me brings her dangerously close to my zipper, causing my dick to pound against the restraint in protest.

"Not with you here. They'll probably need to pee again in a few minutes or want a glass of water."

"I should go."

"Probably," I agree, pulling her tighter against my body. Nope, she's not going anywhere yet.

"This doesn't feel like me leaving," she whispers, her small fingers flexing against my shirt, making my abs jump. I'd kill for her touch against my bare skin right now.

"Nope. I can't let you leave yet," I say, picking her up and moving her. She straddles my front, my cock so fucking close to the one place it wants to be more than anything. I'd gladly give up air right now if it meant being inside her.

"Why not?" Her breath hits my face like a caress, and all I want to do is kiss this woman.

So I do.

"Because I haven't told you goodnight yet."

My lips claim hers with a fierceness I've come to associate with only her. She immediately opens her sweet mouth, allowing my tongue to plunder and take. Taste. My tongue moves against hers, stroking and licking, claiming with every second that passes. My hands move to the back of her neck, into her hair, holding her firmly as my mouth devours her. I hold her as if I'm afraid she'll move or leave, and that what I was given won't be enough.

It'll never be enough.

I'll keep craving more.

Her hands grip my shirt as she grinds against my crotch. My cock swells further, every ounce of blood I possess flowing to one concentrated area. I'm lightheaded and dizzy, a feeling I get every time this woman is in my arms.

I need to touch her skin. I need her to touch mine. I need... more.

Quickly, I rip my shirt over my head and toss it somewhere in the room. Her fingers flex against my pecs, branding them with one touch. My mind flashes to the night I danced for her, the way her fingers danced against my body. Electricity charges through me, reckless and destructive, making my hips flex upward, my aching cock seeking out her sweet pussy.

"I need to touch you," I tell her without removing my lips from hers.

"Yes," she groans, moving her hips and driving me wild.

"Back up," I instruct. She instantly shifts back, giving me room to open the button and zipper of her pants.

Once I have access, I pull her back and attack her lips again. They're swollen and wet and just fucking right. My hands go to her shirt, sliding beneath the material and up towards her glorious tits. I've seen some pretty nice ones in my life. Big ones, small ones, fake ones, but none as perfect as hers. They fill my hand as if they were made for my palm.

Lexi mewls as her tongue slides into my mouth, stroking against mine and plunging deep, mimicking to the dirty images in my head of what my cock wants to do to her pussy.

"I want to do so many dirty things to you," I confess, sliding my hand inside of her bra and pinching her nipple.

"God yes. All of it. I want you to do all of it," she gasps, grinding down hard of my dick.

"I will," I tell her, slipping my hand down her stomach, to where her pants are open.

Keeping my eyes locked on hers, I slide my hand between her panties and hot flesh. It's a tight fit, especially with my large mitts, but I manage. The material is already wet and as soon as I come in contact with her warm, soaked pussy, I have to fight the urge to groan.

My fingers immediately slip between her lips, where her clit pulses hard. Her eyes start to glaze over, her eyelids drooping slightly as I apply a little pressure and move my hand. Her hips start to gyrate, her body riding my hand, seeking out the orgasm I'm promising.

"Oh God," she groans quietly, biting down on her bottom lip to keep from crying out.

"I want your hands on me, beautiful," I tell her as I pick up the pace.

Like an electrical current, shockwaves zap through me as her fingers come in contact with my bare chest. She grips my pecs, her nails digging into the tender flesh. Just the thought of her marking me makes me crazed. Fueled. Ravenous.

Her lids flutter closed and I can tell she's getting close. "Keep your eyes open, beautiful. I want to watch you come," I say, slipping my fingers down farther. Her hips buck wildly as I slide a finger inside of her body. She's hot, wet, and tight. So fucking tight it makes my balls throb.

When she tightens around my finger, I realize she's on the brink of coming. My lips find hers as my fingers push her over the edge. I swallow every sound she makes, flexing my fingers and continuing to pump one inside her pussy. She closes her eyes briefly, but only when it seems almost impossible to keep them open any longer. Lexi sags against me, her muscles starting to relax against my fingers.

"Wow," she whispers as I slowly pull from her body. My cock is practically shouting in my pants that it's his turn, but I ignore the horny bastard. Now isn't the time.

"Watching you come might be my favorite thing in the whole world," I confess, pulling my hand out of her panties, and because I'm a dirty bastard like my cock, I bring that lucky finger to my mouth and slip it inside. I can't stop the moan as her scent surrounds me, wrapping around me and soothing my battered soul. She tastes like sex, like desire, like my woman.

And she is.

Mine.

Lexi

13

My body is humming. My mind is blank. My heart is racing.

And I want more.

More of Linkin and his masterful mouth. More of his talented fingers. More of the fire he stirs to life in my soul.

But then reality sets in, and I realize I'm the hussy who just got off to her neighbor's fingers (albeit thick, gifted fingers) on his couch with his twin brothers pretending to sleep down the hall. My entire body goes rigid, much like the erection I've been grinding on like a cat in heat.

"Don't," he whispers, after he pulls his finger from his mouth. Oh, God. That mouth. That finger. Just the thought is enough to make me want to come again.

"Don't?" I pant. "I can't believe we just did that."

"I can't believe we waited so long to do that."

"You're so frustrating," I grumble, maneuvering myself back a bit. For some reason, my brain turns to mush when my body is in contact with his.

"I'm amazing. Stop fighting it," he quips with that smirk I love to hate.

"You're impossible, pushy, and cocky."

"I love it when you say *cock*-y," he says, flexing his hips in a slightly juvenile manner, but for some reason, it makes my palms sweat and my uselessly soaked panties... well, more soaked.

Chuckling, I shake my head at him. It's funny that I was on the verge of an epic freak-out, then he calmed me down just by talking to me. He talked me off the proverbial ledge without even realizing it. He makes what we just did seem like the most natural thing in the world. Being with him, even when it's something as casual as lunch, just seems... right. Easy.

"Go out with me," he says, drawing my attention to bright brown eyes. I open my mouth to speak, when he cuts me off. "Dinner on Thursday. It's my weekend to work, and I've got extra shifts this week to cover for a guy at the bar. I've got Thursday free and I want to take you to dinner."

"Like a date?" I whisper, my throat suddenly turning dry, my tongue heavy with nerves.

Do you know how long it's been since I've been on a date? I've been with Chris since our senior year of high school, and even then, our dates weren't like adult dates. They were juvenile ones with pizza parties and football games. And when I attended cosmetology school and he went to State, our limited time was spent at our apartment, studying or working to cover the bills.

"Yeah, like a date. If I'm going to prove to you that my sperm is perfect for your future baby, I need to spend as much time with you as possible. You gave me a week, and well, unfortunately, I'm busy as hell this week at work. So, I'm going to steal as much time with you as I can, when I can."

I pretend to think it over, but my decision is already made. Truth is, I want to spend time with him too. That thought both terrifies and excites me. It's too soon, right? Yet, I find myself saying the only word I want to say. "Okay."

"Yeah?" he asks, his eyes lighting up and the sexiest little smile crossing his lips.

"Yeah."

I'm lost in his eyes, in the contentment he makes me feel, and the overwhelming excitement of this coming Thursday. Suddenly, he's moving. Or I'm moving. Whatever. Our lips meet in the middle, hungry and savoring, and he kisses me like his life depends on it.

He's really, *really* good at this.

He stops the kiss before it gets out of hand once more. And by that, I mean before he can slip his hands back into my pants, or I can return the favor. Because right now, I'm really wishing I was returning the favor.

"Come on," he says all raspy and breathy. "I'll walk you home."

"Wow, such a noble and chivalrous gesture," I reply, fighting a smile.

"Don't confuse me with nobility, sweetheart. I'm two seconds away from hauling you off to my bedroom and tying you to my bed, where I'd keep you, moaning and screaming my name, all night long."

Yes, please!

He chuckles. "Next time, Firecracker. Definitely, next time."

Linkin helps me off his lap, takes my hand, and leads me to the door. In the hallway, he waits for me to get my key and unlock my own door. When it's open, I turn to face him and almost stumble at the amount of desire radiating from his eyes.

"God, I can't wait to see you again," he whispers. His large hands gently grab my face as he tilts my head slightly, and devours me in another amazing kiss. The way his tongue slides against mine makes my entire body tremble with need.

"I could kiss you all night long," I confess as he trails tender, wet kisses along my jaw.

"I will. It's inevitable, baby. Soon, I'll kiss you all night long. I'll taste and tease you. I'll fuck you. All." Kiss. "Night." Kiss. "Long." Long, tantalizing kiss that leaves my knees weak and my core clenching. His kisses make me completely forget that my pants are still undone.

Then, he's gone.

Linkin pulls away, leaving my body cold and yearning for more. He takes a step back, that knowing smile on his gorgeous face. "I better get back over there before the boys rip the curtains off the walls."

Laughing, I step towards my doorway. "Good night, Linkin."

"Night, Lexi. I'll be in touch," he says, turning and heading towards his own place.

We watch each other, neither of us wanting to be the first to look away. Our eyes remain locked until the last possible second. You know, until you have no choice but to break the contact and close your door. He gives me one final smile before disappearing through his doorway completely.

When I shut my door, it's with a smile on my face and the memories of our couch tryst to keep me company in bed tonight.

"What's going on with you?" Grandma asks from my chair.

I'm spending my Monday afternoon off at the salon, trimming and setting Grandma's hair.

"Nothing," I tell her, placing another roller in her soft, gray hair.

"You can't fool Grandma," she chastises. I can feel her eyes on me through the mirror, and I do everything I can to keep myself from squirming like I used to as a child.

"I don't know what you're talking about," I tell her happily. Probably a little too happily.

"Has that man you were married to signed the papers yet?"

"No." Dammit. Chris is still dragging his feet, even after my earlier call to my attorney. My attorney has made several phone call inquiries to Chris's lawyer, to no avail.

"Maybe I should stop over and see him. I can be very persuasive when necessary," she says sweetly, but the thought makes me shudder.

"Please don't. I'm having enough trouble with him refusing to negotiate the divorce without you getting on his ass. He'll stall even more, just out of spite."

"Humph," she grumbles. "I've never been on his ass, Lexi Lou. It wasn't that nice of an ass to begin with. Not like Linkin's. Now that boy has an ass that would make a nun give up the habit."

I choke on air. "Grandma!"

"What? Tell me what's going on with him. Are you playing hide the salami yet?"

Groaning, I finish placing the last curler in her hair. "We're not playing hide… anything." My face blushes like Abby's; I can feel it.

"Tell me."

I glance at her in the mirror. *No! No, Lexi! Don't make eye contact!*

Before I realize what's happening, my lips are moving. "You know I want to have a baby, right? Well, he offered to help me conceive."

"Conceive?"

"You know. His sperm. My egg."

"You're going to have the sex, right?" she asks, her eyes wide in anticipation.

"Yes."

"I'm glad," she says softly, happiness glistening in her wrinkled eyes. "You haven't been having enough of the sex, and at your age, you should be doing it at least two, three times a day. It's so good for your complexion, you know."

"A day?" I gasp.

"A day, Lexi Lou. That's why I knew that Chris wasn't right for you. You have my blood in you. We're very sexual creatures. Just ask your grandpa."

"I'd rather not," I grumble, helping her stand and walking with her towards the dryer.

"Mark my word, Lex. When you and that beefcake of a man start to have the sex, it'll be two or three times a day."

Why does that prospect excite me? Probably because it's been a long damn time since I had the sex, let alone multiple times a day.

"Anyway, am I crazy? Am I completely off my rocker for even considering this?" I ask, suddenly needing her approval and understanding.

"Absolutely not," she tells me adamantly. "You've wanted a baby since you were old enough to carry around baby dolls. You're an adult; he's an adult."

"He wants to be a part of the baby's life."

"As a real man should," Grandma says, "And that one is all man, Lexi Lou. Hard, chiseled, muscular man. I say do it. Do it a lot. You know, because practice makes perfect." Then she throws me a wink.

Rolling my eyes, I say, "You make it sound so easy."

She shrugs. "Maybe it is. Maybe it doesn't have to be difficult. It's not like you had a one-night stand and got pregnant. You're both prepared and understand what this is going to take going into it. So what if it's not the traditional way to have a baby. Phooey! I say you do what you want to do, and screw everyone else."

I blink at the woman who helped raise me. She makes a valid point, one that, in my heart, I know to be true. It's my life, my decision. And if Linkin is willing to help give me the baby I've always wanted, then why not grab a hold of the dream? Why question and stress about it?

She's right. It's what I want.

And I'm taking it.

"And besides, I bet that man is a stallion in the sack," she whispers with a wide smile, eyes sparkling like diamonds in the sunlight.

"You're horrible," I tell her turning on the dryer and ending the conversation.

But I'm pretty sure she's right. I bet sex with Linkin is going to be way more than I bargain for, in all the right ways. If the man fucks the way he kisses–passionately, deeply, thoroughly–then I have a feeling I'll be left boneless and satisfied, yet yearning for more.

And more will hopefully mean one thing: Knocked up.

At six-thirty on the dot, there's a knock at my door. I've been anxious for tonight, thinking and wondering about what his plans are all day. We've texted daily, sometimes early in the morning after he'd close down the bar. One of his messages last night was a simple request for this evening: wear jeans, sweatshirt, boots, and a jacket.

I've been a mixture of eager and excited all afternoon. My last appointment was at five-thirty, which left me a little bit of time to change and freshen up all the girly bits that need freshening.

Except that Aunt Flo came to visit me last night.

On one hand, I'm saddened because that means I can't expect anymore of Linkin's magic fingers for a few days. On the other, that means that I'm one step closer to ovulation, and that means a baby. So if this deal between Linkin and I is going to proceed, we're already one step closer.

When I open the door, words completely flee my vocabulary. Looking at him in dark jeans that hug his powerful thighs and dangerous hips, a gray Henley under a worn leather jacket that molds to his arms and chest like a second skin, and a smile that makes my panties practically useless, makes my heart try to crawl from my chest. He's breathtaking, if it's okay to say that a man is breathtaking.

But, my God, he is.

"Hi," I squeak out, finally finding a two-lettered word to speak.

He doesn't speak. Instead, he steps inside and drops a big bag on the floor. Then, he gently grabs my right hand, placing a kiss on my knuckles. Without a word, Linkin turns the hand over and kisses my palm. I shudder. And since he's clearly in the mood for a little kissing, he steps forward, grabs my jaw, and places the most perfect kiss on my lips.

Lips that have been missing him for four long days.

"Is it crazy if I tell you I missed you?" he whispers, placing soft, sweet kisses across my lips. He took the words right out of my mouth.

"No. I've missed you too," I confess, feeling lighter for some reason just by stating those words.

"Are you ready?" he asks, taking my hands in his. They're big and warm, and memories of the wicked things they can do to my body flash through my mind.

"Yes."

"Excellent," he says with a naughty grin. Bending down to pick up the bag he dropped, he pulls a small black helmet out and holds it out for me to take.

"Ummm?" I say, extending my hand slowly, as if the helmet were a snake ready to strike me.

"We're going for a ride." Linkin pulls a second helmet from the bag and shoves it in the crook of his arm.

"It's December," I say deadpanned, stunned that I'm even considering this.

"It is. All month, actually. I've been told there's thirty-one days total."

"Smartass," I grumble.

"Listen, if you don't want to go, we don't have to. I just thought that it's a pretty mild night and would be a great time for a ride. But if you don't want to go, we can take my truck."

Actually, I realize quickly that I do want to go. I really, *really* want to. I haven't been on a bike since my wild and crazy days in high school. You know, before Chris. My heart is racing, but it's not from nerves or fear. It's excitement. I feel energized. Free. And even though it's cool, and yes, December, there's only one answer. "Let's go."

With one hand gripping the helmet and the other encompassed by Linkin's, we head down to where his bike is stored. He leads me behind our building, past the lot where we park our cars, and towards a large storage shed. "The manager lets me keep my bike in here for very little extra rent each month," he offers as he unlocks the padlock on the door. Inside, the shed is filled with lawn tools, different things for building maintenance, an old riding lawn mower, and a black motorcycle. I recognize it instantly. He was riding it the day I cut his hair.

Why does the thought of climbing on that with Linkin make me all giddy?

"Ready?" he asks, turning and helping me zip up my coat. When his hands brush my breasts, he smirks and gives me a wink. My blood starts to heat and warmth floods between my legs.

"Did you just feel me up?" I ask, feigning offense.

"Not at all, Firecracker. If I was going to do anything offensive, I'd do this," he says just before his lips plaster to my own. My mouth instantly opens, his hot tongue sweeping inside and stroking my own. His hands wrap around my ass as he gently lifts my feet a few inches off the ground, bringing me flush against his body.

The kiss doesn't last long enough. Not by a long shot. When he puts me down and pulls back, he moves his hands to my face, stroking and caressing my cheeks. "Come on. Let's get you suited up before I decide to forget the ride and take you back to my apartment and ravish you from head to toe."

Yes, please!

Without another word, he reaches for my helmet and places it on my head. It's a tight fit and makes me wonder who exactly this helmet was purchased for.

"Does it fit okay?" he asks, gently slapping the top and making my head shake.

"It's a little tight," I confirm, trying to keep my ears where they're supposed to be.

"It's Jack's. He insisted you wear his because Jeff's smells like cheesy farts," Linkin says with a big smile. My God, that smile. It could disarm nuclear weapons from dangerous foreign countries.

"What?" I gasp with laughter.

"I'm pretty sure it doesn't," he says as he places his own helmet on his head. "At least, I hope not. He just wants the pretty girl to wear his."

Smiling, I watch him slide onto the bike and back it out of the shed. When he has it where he wants it, his long legs holding it up, he extends his hand and helps me climb on. Suddenly, I realize I'm cradling Linkin's large body between my thighs, and I'm about to wrap my arms around his torso and hold on tight.

My Lord, riding a motorcycle is so sexy.

"Ready?" he asks, slipping his helmet onto his head.

"Ready." And I am. Ready for the ride. Ready for whatever is brewing with this sexy, infuriating man. Ready to let go of everything; live in the moment.

My blood starts to hum as he fires the bike to life, giving it a little more gas and revving the powerful engine. Grasping his jacket, I hold on tight, exhilaration sweeping through my body, as he gooses the throttle. A squeal of excitement rips from my throat as I tighten my hold on his large body.

The evening air chills me, but I ignore it. I focus on the way my body vibrates against the machine, my heart races in my chest, and the hum between my legs that has nothing to do with the bike, and everything to do with the proximity of Linkin. I want him, there's no denying that, but I want him more than just in my bed (or his... I'm not picky). I want to spend time with him, get to know him, and see what happens.

Never did I expect to feel this way again, especially so close to leaving my husband. But Linkin brings out a side of me that I haven't seen in a while. He makes me want to be fierce, feisty, and flirty. He makes me want to be daring and ride in the rain. He makes me want to *be* the woman I've always been destined to be; not the woman I've hidden behind Chris's need for perfection.

We ride up the coast for about twenty minutes before pulling off the highway into an old dive-looking building with faded blue paint and a pothole-laden parking lot. It's been years since I've been to this place, and my stomach rumbles at the thought. The Shack is known for their outstanding seafood and not the ambiance. It's an old building with wobbly tables and creaking floorboards. The dim lighting helps cover the fact that the walls are still what's left of the 1970s groovy gold and electric blue colors that were popular back when the building was first built.

Linkin parks the bike in a spot by the door. I climb off slowly, my legs shaky even from the short ride. My fingers fumble with the chinstrap, unable to release the little clasp for some reason. Before I get frustrated, Linkin's there with his big hands and warm fingers. How they're not cold from the ride, I'm not sure, but when they graze against the underside of my chin, heat sparks through my veins and zips through my blood. Of course, maybe it has nothing to do with the temperature of his hands but everything to do with the closeness of his body and his touch.

Yeah, probably that.

When the strap is released, he helps me pull the helmet off my head. My hands instantly go to my hair, flattening the flyaways and taming the helmet-head.

"Don't," he whispers, his voice all husky and deep. It reminds me of sex, and I have to clench my legs together. His hands push my hair from my face, but he keeps those dark eyes locked on mine. They're so expressive and wild, and I can see everything he wants to do to me in those intoxicating orbs. "I like your hair all crazy and free."

"Really?" I ask, thinking about all the times I made sure my hair was perfect so that Chris wouldn't comment.

"Fuck, yes. It reminds me of bed, which then makes me think about sex, and in return does bad things to my body as I picture you naked, hair all wild, and panting my name."

I start to pant. Seriously, I'm suddenly wanting everything he just said, everything I'm now picturing very vividly in my mind. "Sign me up." The words are out of my mouth before I can even think about stopping them.

Linkin gives me a knowing smirk as his hands caress my jaw. "Soon, Firecracker. Very soon. Tonight, I'm going to give you a proper date."

"Somehow, you seem more like a sex-on-the-first-date kinda guy," I quip as we start to walk towards the old red door.

His low chuckle renders my panties useless. "I'm more of a hardly-date-at-all kinda guy."

"So, it's usually just sex?" I ask, stopping in front of the door.

"Usually."

"What makes me different?" I ask, my voice breathy and choppy.

"Everything," he whispers, leaning forward and planting his lips on my own. The kiss is firm and warm and rekindles the blaze in my body that always seems eager and ready to flare to life when Linkin's near. It's the perfect kiss.

"That's kinda cheesy, Mr. Stone," I sass as he nibbles on my swollen bottom lip.

"I've never wanted to have a baby with another woman before in my life," he whispers, his breath fanning across my face. "What does that tell you?"

"That you're horny?"

He chuckles again. "I find myself in a perpetual state of arousal when it comes to you, but no. That's not the answer," he says, leaning back but still holding my jaw.

"What's the answer?" I ask, staring at him, gaging the sincerity of his words.

"I could have a baby with anyone, sweetness, but I've never offered before, nor have I ever really pictured myself as a dad. But with you? I. Want. Everything."

"Everything?"

"Mmmhmmm," he says, rubbing his nose against mine. "I'm going to prove to you that I'm the only baby daddy for your future child. Wanna know why?"

"Why?"

"Because for the first time in my life, I can see myself as a father. But more than that, I can picture myself by your side."

I shudder at his words and the implication. I open my mouth, but no words come out.

"Come on. Let's go inside and eat. We don't have to figure anything out tonight, but I want you to know that I'm serious about this, Lex. I feel something different when I'm with you, and have from the moment I watched you hand Levi his ass in the hallway that morning," he replies with a smile. I chuckle as I recall that morning when I chewed Levi's ass in the hallway of their apartment building for breaking my twin sister's heart. Linkin was there, watching the exchange, and pushing my buttons until I was ready to claw his eyes out as soon as I was finished with Levi.

"I'm starving," I concede, reaching for the door handle.

"Me too," he says as he grabs the door from me and holds it open. His eyes skate down my body and there's no missing the appreciative look in his eyes. "For food too," he adds with a wink and ushers me inside.

I'm pretty sure he just stole a little piece of my heart.

14

Linkin

I've been hard since she opened her front door and it hasn't let up. I haven't ridden with a hard-on since I was eighteen and took the head cheerleader for a ride in the country. And my bike wasn't the only thing she rode.

Lexi heads to the back of the little dive restaurant, finding a booth beneath an old mismatched light. "This okay?" she asks.

"Perfect," I answer, sliding into the bench across from her.

An older woman arrives at our booth a minute later and takes our drink order. I stick with a coke, while Lexi orders a sweet tea. The menu is an old plastic one-sheeter with bent and peeling corners.

"Have you ever eaten here?" she asks, glancing at the options on the menu.

"Nope. I've heard about this place a few times and always wanted to try it. This seemed like the perfect choice."

"I haven't been here in years. Chris didn't like it. If it didn't have cloth napkins and a wine list, he thought it was beneath him," she mumbles, rolling her eyes as she keeps them focused on the menu in her hands.

"But this kinda place is right up your alley," I state. It's not a question. She's given me glances of the real Lexi over the last couple of weeks, and she seems like the type of woman who likes messes and laughter and doesn't mind dirty dishes in the sink.

She glances up at makes eye contact. "Yeah, it is. Sorry to bring him up. That's not very good first date etiquette."

"You're fine. I want to get to know the real you, not the woman you had to become to please someone else."

She stares at me intently, her green eyes searching my face, before nodding her head. "I love waffles with fresh strawberries, wearing no shoes in the yard, and comic books, though I haven't read one in years."

"Comic books, you say?" I lean in closer until my nose is close to hers, I whisper, "I once owned The Amazing Spider-Man number sixteen, signed by Stan Lee, graded 4.5."

Her gasp goes straight to my groan. "September 1964. Not a widely popular version, but signed by the master would bump up the value."

"I got six hundred bucks for it," I tell her.

"Why did you sell it?" she questions, her green eyes searching mine.

I stumble on the words that I need to say, but I fight through it. "Needed the cash."

Ain't that the truth? When my mom found out I sold the one comic book I worked extra shifts at the garage in high school to buy, she was pissed. But I needed to fix the mess we were in more than I needed a signed Spider-Man comic book.

Lexi tsks. "That's too bad."

I just shrug my shoulders and lean back in the booth. My shoulders are tense, so I extend one arm across the back of the booth just to give off a casual appearance. The way her eyes study me, I wonder just how much of my demeanor my fiery little Lexi can read. She gives me a look like she knows I'm anything but relaxed, but thankfully, she doesn't call me on it.

After we both order crab legs with shrimp scampi, I get comfy and just watch her. She's messing with her paper napkin, curling the corners around her finger and then flattening it out again. She looks deep in thought, but there's a hint of a smile playing on the corner of her lips.

"So tell me, have you always wanted to be a hairdresser?"

"Always. When I was a kid, I used to love fiddling with all of my sisters' hair."

"Same with me and the garage. I started tinkering around with car parts, engines and transmissions, at an early age. Gettin' greasy just kinda called to me."

"I like that about you," she says quietly, her eyes locked on mine.

"That I'm a grease monkey?"

"That you don't mind getting your hands dirty."

I have a feeling it has a lot more to do with the fact that her ex received weekly manicures than anything else. The fact that I'm the polar opposite from the douche probably has a lot to do with it.

"Can I stop by sometime?" she asks.

"The shop?" I ask, arching my eyebrows in question.

"Yeah. It's just..." she hesitates like she's embarrassed. Needing to calm her nervousness, and also overcome by the need to touch her skin, I reach forward and grab her hand.

"What?" I hedge.

"It's just... that I like the smell." Her words are almost inaudible.

I might have almost missed her words, but I don't miss the meaning.

And neither does my cock.

"The smell?" I ask, fighting a grin.

"Grease. Dirt. Gas. The smell of fresh rubber just laid on asphalt."

"I think I just came in my pants," I groan, deadpanned. That comment earns me an instant smile.

"Of course you did. You're a total guy."

"Yes, yes I am. But to answer your question, yes, you can come by the shop anytime. Just let me know when so I can make sure I'm extra greasy that day," I quip with a wink.

Our food arrives a few moments later and we continue to engage in small talk. I've discovered that she's very close to her family. Even though I met them all at lunch the other day and witnessed it firsthand, listening to her talk about her sisters over dinner just reinforces the fact that they're tight.

"I can't believe I'm telling you all this," she says, setting her napkin down on her empty plate and pushing it away.

"Uh, your Grandma has had her hands all over my ass. I'm pretty sure that skyrockets me to the front of the line where personal information is concerned."

"True. God, I'm so sorry about that. All of it," she whispers, her face blushing slightly.

"Believe it or not, you don't work at a bar without having a hand or two grope you, though I'd add your grandma is definitely the oldest set of hands on my body."

"Poor Linkin. All the women wanting to touch your ass," she sasses.

"It's a nice ass," I reiterate.

"Ehhhh," she replies with a shrug as if it's no big deal. But I see through her casual front. I don't miss the way her eyes dilate and she nibbles on the corner of her bottom lip. Lexi's looking at me like I'm dessert and she's suddenly famished.

When the check comes, I take care of paying for it, leave a generous tip, and lead her towards my bike. It's probably the last time I'll be able to ride it until spring, though the cold doesn't scare me any. But I don't want Lexi catching a cold because I've got her out on my bike in December.

The ride back to town takes a little extra time, since I actually drive the speed limit the entire way. I don't want this ride to end any sooner than it has to. Besides, I'm totally digging having Lexi wrapped around my back, her body pressed firmly against mine. It's a sensation I could definitely get used to.

I pull the bike into the shed, and swear I hear her sigh in sadness. My little firecracker definitely has a wild streak in her. I knew taking my bike tonight would be right up her alley, and the twinkle I saw in her eyes and the excitement I heard doesn't disappoint. It's been a great first date.

One that would only end even better with a kiss.

Holding the bike steady, Lexi hops off and works on the chinstrap. "Here," I say, pulling my gloves off and tossing them onto the seat. Smiling, I release the little leather strap and let my fingers linger just a few extra seconds.

"I could have gotten it. Why are you grinning like a fool?" she asks, pulling the helmet from her head. My wayward cock takes notice of the way her hair is all tousled and looks like she just crawled out of bed. After sex. With me.

"I know you could have gotten it," I say, sliding my fingers down the chilled skin of her throat and leaning forward until I can feel her breath against my lips. "But I like putting my hands on you," I whisper with a wink.

Her hand slips easily within my big mitt as I gather up the helmets and lock up the shed. We're both quiet as we head into the apartment building and wait for the elevator. It's not uncomfortable, not like I would think, and a big part of that is who I'm with. Everything just seems easy when we're together.

The closer we get to our floor, the quicker my heart starts to beat. Not surprising, I don't want the date to end. Can you believe that? My first date in I don't really recall how long and I'm wishing I could turn back the clock and start our evening all over again, just so I can spend more time with her.

The subtle ding of the elevator alerts me that we've reached our destination. As the door opens, I finally find my voice. "I had a great time."

Those stunning eyes gaze up at me, sparkling as best as they can beneath the dim fluorescent lighting in the hallway. "Me too."

"Are you surprised?" I ask, stepping out into the hallway, her hand still firmly in my own.

"Not really," she says with a smile and I swear to all things holy my chest tightens painfully. My heart is going to burst through my chest. We're both staring at each other smiling like lunatics.

Finally, I pull my attention away from her and towards her door. "Did you order flowers?" I ask, stopping in my tracks.

Lexi bumps into my arm. "Shit," she mumbles, her small hand gripping my much bigger one.

"Friend of yours?" I ask, as we slowly make our way towards the bouquet as if it were a bomb.

"Chris," she whispers, the edge very evident in her voice.

"Ahhh. Should have known."

"I hate them," she grumbles, releasing my hand. I feel the loss instantly.

Lexi holds the large grouping of red roses like they're going to scare her. I'll give it to the douchey fucker, it's an over-the-top display that women generally fawn over. The sweet fragrance fills the entire hallway, and if I had to wager a guess, based on the size of the vase that looks like a bucket, I'd say there's easily four dozen here. But Lexi isn't fawning. No, she looks like she wants to chuck them at the wall, and I'd be lying if I said that didn't make me just a wee bit happy.

"You hate them?" I ask, glancing down at the arrangement.

"Hate," she says with venom, shoving the vase into my hands. *Shit, this is heavier than it looks.* "I even told him that once, but does he listen? Nope. He thinks every woman loves red roses, so *I* must love them," she says, digging her key out of her pocket with a little force. "Well, *I* do *not* love them. I never did. Every time he sent them, I wanted to send them back."

Lexi glances over at me, her eyes wide as her irritation transforms into embarrassment. "Oh my God, I'm so sorry."

"Why?" I ask.

"I can't believe I just went off like that. We're on a date." Her green eyes fall to the floor.

"You don't like these?" I confirm, holding them out as I wait for confirmation. She shakes her head and my feet start to move.

I'm down across from my door before I can even stop myself. I knock and wait. Mrs. Lehman opens the door in her little ol' lady pajamas and robe. "Hey, Mrs. L. These were delivered by mistake to my neighbor's place. She's allergic so she can't bring them into her place. Mind taking them off our hands?"

"Really?" the elderly neighbor says, her eyes lighting up behind crooked wire-rimmed glasses.

"Absolutely. These beauties are all yours," I encourage, nodding towards her table. She steps aside and watches me set the grossly large display in the middle of her table.

"Thank you, dear."

"You're welcome, Mrs. L. Have a great evening." Throwing her a little wave, I make my way back to Lexi in the hallway. "There," I say, throwing her a smile, hoping to soothe the look of uneasiness on her face.

"That was… really nice of you."

"You were just going to throw them away, right?"

"Yeah," she confirms, biting her lip.

"Well, now you've brightened the night of our elderly neighbor. Plus, you don't have to stare at douchey Chris's cheesy flowers."

Lexi gazes up at me, the corner of her lip turning upward. "They are totally cheesy, aren't they?"

"Totally."

She rewards me with another one of her smiles that hits me like a bolt of lightning below the belt. My hand instantly goes to her face, my finger tracing the delicate curve of her jaw. "What's your favorite flower?" I whisper, our eyes locked.

"Lilies. I love the white ones."

"Gorgeous. Just like you."

That sexy little tongue of hers slips out of her mouth and licks her bottom lip. My entire body is alive with want, a live wire of electricity coursing through my blood. It takes every ounce of control I can grab the hell onto to keep from throwing her over my shoulder and carrying her off to my lair, where I'll do all sorts of pleasurable and dirty things to her.

Over and over and over again.

Preferably on her kitchen table.

Or maybe against the wall.

"Would you like to come inside?" she asks, breaking the dirty scene I was working on in my head.

"For a minute," I reply. Even though I'd love to pound weeks' worth of Lexi-induced sexual frustration out on her sweet little body, it won't happen tonight. I promised her a proper date and that doesn't include her bouncing on my cock like a pogo stick.

Lexi opens her apartment door and slips inside ahead of me. After setting her keys on the counter, she turns those hypnotic green eyes my way and my heart skips a beat. "I've been thinking," she starts hesitantly.

"That's never good when a woman starts off a conversation with I've been thinking," I reply lightly with a grin, even though my heart is suddenly jackhammering in my chest. I'm nervous. Fucking nervous of what she's about to say.

"I want to get divorced first. I can't have this mess with Chris hanging over my head while I move forward with my plans for a baby."

"But there are still plans for a baby?" I ask, hopefully sounding light and casual.

"Yes," she confirms with a nod. "I still want a baby, but I need my divorce finalized first. In order to move on to the next chapter in my life, I need to close the book on my relationship with him forever."

Stepping forward, I invade her personal space and stroke the soft skin where her neck meets her jaw. "Divorce first. Sperm donation after."

"Yes," she whispers harshly, a rush of breath hitting me in the chin.

"What about kissing? Can there be kissing?"

"Kissing is good," she adds quickly, that sexy little tongue of hers snaking out to wet her lips expectantly.

"Then we wait to put the next phase of your life into motion," I say as I slide my arms around her back and bring her body against mine. "But we don't wait for the kissing," I confirm.

"No, we don't wait."

That's all I need to hear before my mouth descends on hers. The kiss starts slow, savoring and oh so fucking perfect, but that only lasts a few seconds. As soon as her tongue meets mine, all bets are off. It's like a punch of need hits me square in the gut as all thoughts are consumed with her.

My hands come up to frame her face, which allows me to angle her slightly to deepen the kiss. Our tongues clash and lips devour in what is probably the best fucking kiss of my life. And when her hands grip my back, her nails biting into my flesh. Christ, it takes every ounce of control I possess to not throw her over my shoulder and find the nearest bed.

But I don't.

Instead, I gently slow the kiss down, nipping and licking at her plump lips until we're both breathless. "Oh, there will definitely be more kissing," I mumble against her lips.

"Definitely."

With Herculean strength, I break the connection of our mouths and just stare down at this incredibly beautiful woman. This gorgeous woman who, for some amazing fucking reason, decided she likes me. Me. The dirty mechanic from the wrong side of the tracks, who doesn't trust people very easily because he's been shit on by too many to count. The bartender who's working extra shifts to pay off a debt that isn't his own. The loner who found hope in the prospect of starting a family of his own with a woman who steals his breath every time he sees her.

It's hard to believe it, but she picked me. We're in this together.

"I'm going to head home," I tell her, running the pad of my thumb along her lower lip.

"Okay," she whispers. "Thank you for tonight. I had a great time."

"Me too," I confirm. "I have to work all weekend between Stapleton's and Lucky's, but I'll swing by when I can," I add, taking a step towards the door.

"I'd like that."

She gazes up at me with big, trusting eyes, and suddenly, I can't remember why I should leave. I want to stay and hear her laugh and do some more of that kissing. But I know I shouldn't. We don't have the week deadline anymore, so there's no need to rush this. Our plans to give her a child will move forward, even if they're delayed slightly. Slow and steady is the way to go here.

Except...

My feet move before I can stop them and she's in my arms once again. Lexi wraps her arms around my neck and braces for impact. Instead of allowing my greedy lips to devour her, I keep the kiss soft and gentle. I savor the taste and feel of her, I commit the scent of her to memory so that I have something to keep me company until I can see her again.

She mewls against me, a sound that goes straight to my cock, and I know it's time to end the night. If I don't, it's bound to end up exactly where I want it to: bed.

Placing one last sweet kiss against her lips, I pull away and head towards the door. When I turn back around, her eyes are closed and a soft smile spreads on the lips she's touching with shaky fingers. She opens her eyes and gazes my way, a look that lets me know that she's just as affected by the kiss as I am. I mentally throw my fists in the air victoriously.

"Night, Lexi."

"Good night, Linkin," she whispers.

My body is charged as I slip into the hallway and head towards my door. A cold shower is on the agenda for tonight, that's for sure, but something tells me it still won't help alleviate the throbbing in my pants. Nothing is going to help after that kiss.

I let myself into my apartment with a smile on my face and hope in my chest. I have big plans for Miss Lexi Summer.

But first, I need to have a little *chat* with douchey Chris.

I use my lunch hour to run over to the office building where Chris Jacobson works. It's on the main drag, only a few blocks away from the flower place Lexi's oldest sister runs. Parking my old Blazer on the street, I'm hit with Christmas music piping from speakers beneath the awning of the gift shop as soon as I set foot on the sidewalk.

A bell dings as I step inside the brightly lit office with a tabletop Christmas tree displayed and garland hanging from the ceiling. An old desk is situated in the center of the room and is currently unoccupied. Not waiting to find out where the receptionist is, I head down the hallway, looking for the douche's office. I pass an empty conference room, a supply room with a copy machine, and a small kitchenette.

At the end of the hall, I come to a door that sits ajar and raise my hand to knock. Before my knuckles connect with wood, I hear voices from within the room.

"I'm asking you politely, boy, to reconsider. You're making it worse," an older gentleman says.

"I don't want this." This voice I recognize as Chris's.

"But she does. And you dragging your feet is upsetting her."

"I can fix this, I know it."

"Not anymore, you can't. It's over."

"But..."

"No more buts. She wants out. She deserves to be happy. The only thing standing in the way of that is you." There's a dramatic pause and I find myself holding my breath. "Let her go. Sign the papers."

Suddenly, it all falls into place. Orval is in there with Chris doing, well, the same thing I came to do. But he's doing it the proper way. I was planning on using harsh words and my fists, if necessary.

"I love her." The man who used to belong to Lexi sounds so small, so defeated.

"I know. I do too, and that's why I'm here. She needs this, Chris. Let her go. Set her free to live the life she wants."

"I was giving her everything. We had a home, nice cars. Hell, I was planning a surprise vacation to Fiji. We had everything," Chris says softly.

"Did you really?" There's another pause. "Sign the papers, Chris. Please."

I don't hear anything for several tense seconds over the blood pounding in my ears. And to top it off, I'm probably going to be discovered lurking in the hallway because my own heart is as loud as a fucking snare drum.

"Thank you," Orval says, followed by the scraping of a chair against the tile floor.

Instead of giving them the opportunity to find me, I quickly backtrack to the front door and slip out into the crisp December air. When I reach my truck, I lean against the passenger door, wishing I had a cigarette. And I don't even smoke.

"How much did you hear?" My attention is pulled to the elderly man in front of me with a twinkle in his eye and a sly grin on his face.

"Not much," I answer. "Did he see me?"

"Naw, I distracted him with talk about his latest award on the wall as you slipped out the door," he says, nodding towards the sidewalk.

Without a word, I quickly stand up and fall in line beside him. Orval moves surprisingly fast for a man his age, which only reinforces the stories I've heard from his granddaughters. "I'm down here," he says, nodding towards the new Buick up the block.

After a few moments of silence, he finally speaks again. "So, what brought you to the financial office of Chris Jacobson this afternoon?"

Deciding honesty is probably the best route with this man, I say, "Probably much of the same as you. But with more violence."

That makes him snort. "Oh, believe me, son, I would have loved to have popped him in the mouth a few times over the years, but I learned a long time ago that not everything can be settled with your fists. Chris just needed someone to politely prod him along in this whole divorce mess, and since the happiness of each and every one of my granddaughters means more to me than anything, it was time to make the visit."

"He sent her flowers. I was going to ask him to stop."

"My Emmy got her hair done this morning and Lexi mentioned the flowers. She said Chris is dragging his feet still on signing the divorce papers, and I realized that he would just continue to do it until he got what he wanted."

"And what's that?" I ask, stopping in front of the car.

"Her."

My throat tightens and suddenly it's hard to breathe.

"Not that she would take him back. She wasn't happy. I'm not one hundred percent sure what he did, but they've been on the fritz for a while now. Hell, it could have been a bunch of little things that all piled up. He never came with her to anything, never spent any time with her. The boy worked nonstop. It was sad." I don't tell him what Lexi confided in me that night she was drunk.

"But you, son, you make her happy. I see that sparkle in her eyes that had long dimmed, and for that, I thank you."

I shift my weight from foot to foot, not really knowing what to say. I've never been on the receiving end of too many compliments; let alone what feels like approval from a family member of a girl I'm seeing. "It's my pleasure to make her smile."

Orval nods and walks around to the driver's door. "Be sure that her smile never fades," he says as he opens the door. I get ready to return to my truck when I hear, "Oh, and Linkin? Make sure you keep extra rubbers in your wallet. If she's anything like her grandmother, I couldn't keep enough of those puppies on hand. Ravenous, that woman is. Do you know that one time we actually got it on during a church picnic? Yes sir, the pastor was giving a tour of the new Bible study room when we snuck off to inspect the plumbing in the mechanical room. My Emmy convinced the pastor that we were praying hard in there, which is why the room was filled with her screams of 'Oh God!'"

"Wow, that's... something I probably could have lived without knowing," I mumble, a little overwhelmed at the direction this talk has taken.

"All I'm saying is that when the lady wants it, it's our duty to give it to her."

"I'll keep that in mind," I add, taking a retreating step towards my vehicle.

"Nice seeing you, son," Orval hollers before sliding into his car.

I wave before returning to my truck, a little extra spring in my step. I can only hope Chris will actually take the advice of Lexi's grandpa and quit stalling the divorce, because I'm afraid the next step is a conversation with me.

And I don't think that one will end as friendly.

Lexi

15

I've been home from work for maybe fifteen minutes when a knock sounds at my door. It was a crazy busy Saturday with several walk-ins trying to squeeze in a quick cut, color, or whatever before Christmas. Even though I had a full schedule, I was still able to add two kids' cuts and help a frazzled mom who tried an at-home dye kit the night before.

It didn't turn out so well.

When I open the door, I find the world's ugliest Christmas tree. "What the hell is that?"

Linkin steps inside the entry, forcing me to step aside to let him and his tree in. "It's a Christmas tree."

"That's the ugliest, saddest tree I've ever seen," I retort as I shut the door. "Charlie Brown would even be embarrassed by this tree."

Linkin's inside the living room, positioning the tree, which is already nailed to a wooden stand, in front of the picture window. "Apparently, the selection isn't so great when you wait to buy a tree until the week before Christmas."

"Why did you buy it?" I ask, shaking my head at what can only be described as a small tree with only four branches.

"Because you didn't have one," he states matter-of-factly as he turns the tree to display its best side.

Of which there isn't one.

When he turns, his dark chocolate eyes find mine, raising my blood pressure and making my body hum with excitement. Before I even register that he's moving, Linkin stands before me, towering over me like a giant, and takes me in his arms. I wet my lips without realizing it just before his own lips come down and claim mine. It's a slow, gentle kiss, but I still feel it clear down to my toes.

"Hi," he whispers, pulling back slightly.

"Hey. You bought me a tree."

"I figured you should have one."

"It's kinda ugly," I say with an easy grin.

"True, but she has potential. Here," he says, turning and grabbing the paper bag he had under his arm when he came in.

"What's this? The fire extinguisher for when this bad boy goes up in flames?"

"No, Negative Nelly, it's your decorations," he says, tapping my nose.

"You bought me decorations?" I ask, unable to mask the surprise.

"Actually," he starts before clearing his throat and looking a little sheepish. "No. I couldn't find anything left at the store that wasn't crap, so I made a call."

"You made a call?" ask, reaching for the bag. "Like, to your people?"

"Yeah," he says as I pull homemade construction paper garland out of the bag. "My mom helped my brothers make some ornaments and garland-y stuff to hang from the branches."

I pull the brightly colored chain-linked paper from the bag, smiling widely as I go. When I reach the end of the garland, I pull out several homemade ornaments. There are many paper swords and even a few plastic Army guys tied with string. It melts my heart.

"That's very sweet of you, and them. Thank you," I say, pulling him in for a hug.

"Don't tell anyone. I have a reputation to uphold."

"Your secret is safe with me," I tell him, but suddenly it feels like I'm talking about more than just his soft side. It feels deeper, and even though I don't know much about Linkin, except what he shows on the surface, I feel like I'm safe with him. And I'm not just talking physically.

"Come on," he says. "I have about forty-five minutes before I have to head over to Lucky's. Shouldn't take us longer than," he glances at the sad tree up and down, "five, six minutes tops to decorate this beast of a tree."

I grab the garland and join him in front of the tree. "No lights?"

Linkin shakes his head and lowers his voice to a whisper. "No way. I bet if you even breathe the word match that it would ignite." Standing up tall, he adds, "And since the only thing I plan to ignite is your loins, I figured I'd leave the twinkling Christmas lights off."

His comment makes me roll my eyes. "Such a man," I grumble.

Linkin takes me in his arms again. "All man, baby. One hundred percent, pure... man," he grunts, biting my earlobe and sending a shot of lust racing through my bloodstream.

"Come on, Firecracker. Let's get her decorated before I need to leave. If we hurry, we'll have time for more kissing," he adds with a wink before reaching for the end of the garland rope.

More kissing?

Well, you don't have to tell me twice.

"He brought you a tree?" Jaime asks, a princess doll in one hand and a Cabbage Patch Kid in the other. "Which one?" she adds, directing this question at Payton.

"She has a million dolls," our oldest sister says, giving Jaime a look.

"You're right. I'll get her both," Jaime coos, referring to Dean's daughter, the only child in the family, and places both dolls into her cart. Turning towards me she adds, "Don't ignore the first question. He brought you a Christmas tree?"

"He did," I confirm, dropping a hairdresser play set I found one aisle over into the cart. It'll go great with the apron I found online and had embroidered with her name across the front. I smile just thinking about that purchase; it matches the one I use in the salon.

"Stop buying her more toys!" Payton exclaims. "We're going to have to add onto the house to fit all of her new things."

"That's probably not a bad idea," Jaime adds. "Wait 'til you see what Grandma got her." Jaime smiles mischievously, a wicked little gleam in her eyes brightening her face.

"What do you expect, Pay? She's our first niece," I acknowledge, not even trying to hide the small stuffed cat I just found amongst the display of stuffed dogs.

"I get it," Payton concedes. "I went a little overboard myself. Back to the tree."

"It the barest, ugliest tree I've ever seen," I confirm, unable to hide the smile on my face. "And his little brothers made the ornaments."

"Why don't you have a tree?" Payton asks, trying to steer us away from the toy aisle.

"I left everything at Chris's. Honestly, I didn't really want it. I pretty much left everything except my personal belongings and a few things that were mine before we moved in together."

Following behind my two oldest sisters, I continue, "You know, that's why I don't really understand why he's dragging his feet on the divorce. We waived the mandatory six-month separation. I didn't ask for *anything*. I left him all of the furniture and everything. I took my car, which I pay for, and asked for him to buy me out of my half of the house. We split the checking and savings accounts and the investments that he made on our behalf. Anything in his name is his. It's the cleanest, tidiest divorce. All he needs to do is sign."

"I don't get it," Jaime agrees.

"Anyway, I'm going to ask my attorney to follow up with his once more, but heading into Christmas, it might not be as quickly as I'm hoping."

"At least you can have *the sex* with your hot neighbor until all of this blows over," Payton adds with a wide grin, using the terminology that Grandma uses when referring to sex.

I quickly turn my attention to an aisle end cap, desperate to look anywhere but at my sisters. They'll read me like a book.

"Lexi?" Jaime says slowly. "Tell me you're having *the sex* with your gorgeous neighbor with abs you could lick chocolate syrup off of."

Clearing my throat, I turn to face the two women who helped raise me. "We haven't had sex yet." Yet, being the keyword.

"Seriously?" Jaime exclaims at the same time Payton hollers, "What?"

"How can you not be having *the sex*? The way that man was looking at you that night he stripped, I'm surprised you aren't taking a ride on the bologna pony every day!"

"Would you stop saying *the sex*?" I beg my oldest sister.

"And don't ever say bologna pony again," Jaime adds.

"Sorry," Payton says, waving her hand. "We've had to be careful what we say around Brielle, and I figured asking for a ride on the bologna pony was a hell of a lot better than begging Dean to fuck me against the wall."

"Jeez, that's… descriptive. Anyway, we're just not there yet."

"That's okay, Lex. Not everyone has to be a hobag like Payton here and sleep with the guy on the first night," Jaime chimes in.

"Don't get me started, hussy," Payton retorts goodheartedly.

My sisters continue talking about sex, but my attention falls on the end cap I stopped in front of. I didn't even realize I was looking at the display until this moment. A wide smile crosses my face as I grab two of everything here and throw it in the cart. Jaime glances my way, giving me a questioning look, and I just shrug.

Two little heathens are going to love this stuff.

It's Christmas Eve when my phone rings. I took the afternoon off so I could get ready for dinner at Dad's house tonight. Most of my clients are getting ready for their own Christmas gatherings anyway.

I'm stunned silent as I listen to my attorney share his news, a weird sense of relief washing over me. I don't even remember writing down the information and dates he provides, but after I hang up my cell phone, I look down and find the notes I took. Gazing down at the details, I let out a squeal and hug that piece of paper to my chest.

Grabbing my purse and making sure that I have my keys, I fly out the door, heading towards the door of a big source of comfort and companionship. A sudden pang of sadness fills my gut when I realize that I'm not standing in front of my twin's door. Instead, I'm about to knock on Linkin's apartment, eager to share my good news with the man who is quickly becoming a great friend.

More than a friend.

Is this what Abby felt when she went all-in with Levi? A weird sense of happiness mixed with sadness? I'm excited for this budding new relationship I have (even if it's still in the non-sexual stage), but also a little dejected that my twin sister isn't my go-to person.

In the last week, we've spent every spare minute together. Well, as much as we can in between his two jobs, my job, him helping his mom with his brothers, and pre-holiday gatherings around town, which really isn't that much time. But we've talked on the phone, texted throughout the day, and had a couple of late dinners while he was watching Jeff and Jack.

My knock goes unanswered, and sadness sweeps in. Should I go across the hall? I know Abby is there and would be tickled to hear my news. Hell, she'd probably start pouring the margaritas, ensuring we were heading full-steam ahead into sloshed before Christmas Eve appetizers.

But this is something I want to share with Linkin first.

So with my keys in hand, I head down towards my car. I know he's off tonight from Lucky's, which means he can only be at one place. With my purse thrown onto the passenger seat, I start my car and head out of the parking lot, my foot a little heavy on the gas.

The closed sign is showing as I pull into the parking lot for Stapleton Auto. Disappointment starts to settle into my stomach as I steer my car to the side lot to turn around. But as I round the building, I see his old Blazer parked by a door marked for employees. Without allowing myself any time to reconsider, I park next to his truck and turn off the engine.

The late afternoon air has a salty chill as it blows off the Bay and it has me pulling my sweater a little tighter around my neck. When I reach the door, I contemplate knocking, but decide on just trying the handle, since he could be working on something that's loud. Of course, startling him if he's distracted probably isn't the way to go either.

I opt to try the handle first, deciding to knock if the door is locked. A smile graces my lips when I realize the door is unlocked. As I pull it open, classic rock music filters through the open door, instantly reminding me of the night he stripped to the old Warrant song.

"Hello?" I holler as I step inside, the heavy door slamming shut angrily behind me.

The shop is large with car parts and tools of all sizes scattered around. There's a newer Mustang stripped down to primer in one bay and a Honda Accord with damage to the front end in another. What pulls my attention now is the sleek, sexy, and oh so dangerous Plymouth Hemi Cuda in the center of the room.

I think I'm in love.

"Can I help you?" I hear over the music just before a creeper rolls out from beneath the Cuda.

I'm struck speechless at the sight of him. He looks utterly edible in his tight t-shirt streaked with dirt and grease, well-worn jeans with grimy handprints on the thighs, and a pair of heavy black work boots that look like they've seen better days. But what holds my attention now is that little sliver of stomach that's teasing me, enticing me, with its taut, tanned skin and dark little happy trail.

Oh, that delicious little happy trail.

"Hey," he says, humor laced in his greeting.

"Oh. Hey." I lift my gaze to land on his smiling face, a streak of grease swept across his cheek, just above his beard. Linkin wipes his hands on a red shop towel, that cocky smile ever present. My sights return to the car behind him, my fingers twitch to touch its powerful lines and sexy curves. "She's gorgeous," I say, unable to stop myself as I run my fingers along the hood.

"That she is." Linkin stands up and stretches his arms above his head. I'm rewarded with another mouthwatering and panty-melting view of his stomach. This time, I catch a glimpse of that delectable V that starts at his hips and stretches downward towards his groin.

Oh, how I'd love to get an up-close, maybe even hands-on, view of that V.

"What brings you here on Christmas Eve?" he asks, grabbing a bottle of water from the counter and drinking almost half of it in one long pull. The way his throat muscles work and his Adam's apple bobs lulls me into some sex-crazed frenzy that makes me want to hump his leg like a dog and pant like I'm in heat.

It's embarrassing.

"Lexi?" he asks, his eyebrows shooting skyward, the corner of his lip curving upward.

"Oh! Sorry," I reply, feeling slightly embarrassed. "So, my attorney called me just a bit ago. He had great news and I needed to share it with someone, so I thought I'd stop by and see what you were doing." I hope I sound more casual than I do in my own head. I also don't mention the fact that I bypassed my own sister's apartment just so I could tell my big news to Linkin first.

"Well, you found me working on this beauty," he says, wiping speckles of dust off the headlight.

"She is gorgeous," I answer, unable to stop touching the car. "A 1970 Hemi Cuda with a 440 V-8 big block engine."

"God, you're sexy as fuck when you talk car," he says, his voice deep and dirty. This voice draws my attention and makes me smile.

Suddenly, he's close. I look up and find his hungry eyes devouring me, a look of longing written on his face. The scent of his soap mixed with the greasy environment tickles my senses, a smell that's distinctly associated with Linkin.

He gazes down at me, our bodies mere inches away from each other. I can feel his warm exhale kissing my forehead with each breath he takes. "You were saying? Earlier? The attorney?"

"Oh! Yes, my attorney called me, and guess what?" I don't even wait for him to reply. "Chris signed the papers!" I squeal loudly, grabbing onto his forearms for leverage as I jump up and down.

Or maybe I'm just using it as an excuse to touch him again.

"Hey, that's great," Linkin says moments before wrapping his big arms around me and squeezing. The hug feels amazing, comforting and familiar.

And I never want it to end.

Until his lips are on mine, and suddenly, I never want *this* to end.

My arms wrap around his neck and I hold on tight. When he picks me up and my feet start to dangle, I do the most natural instinctive action I can: wrap my legs around his waist. His tongue is swift and hot as he explores my mouth and strokes my own tongue. I purr like a cat, feeling the groan vibrating in my chest.

Turning, Linkin positions me until I'm sitting on the fender, my legs still wrapped tightly around his waist. "My God, I love kissing you," he whispers against my lips.

"I love it when you kiss me."

"When is it final?" he asks, trailing tantalizing kisses down my throat and towards my collarbone. Shivers of lust rake through my body.

"Huh?" I ask, still focused on the way his lips graze against my skin, leaving a raging fire in its wake.

"The divorce," he whispers, placing opened mouthed kisses down to where my sweater meets my cleavage.

"End of January. We go to... God, that feels so fucking amazing... court. Yeah, we go to court on January twenty-ninth. It'll be final. Finally."

"And I can finally have you," he says, his hand sliding up my side, pushing my sweater as he goes.

"You can have me now," I groan, my body flooded with the amazing sensation of his mouth. It makes me want his mouth *other* places.

But not yet.

Right now, I need one thing.

Ripping his shirt from within his pants, I push it up and grip the taut muscles of his chest, scratching at his skin with my nails to get as close as possible. Linkin grabs his shirt and pulls it over his head, exposing every muscle, ripple, and divot that God gave him. His body is simply amazing.

And I've only seen half of him.

Reaching for his belt, I start to pull at the leather. "What are you doing?" he asks, stalling his kisses and dropping his eyes to where my hands release the brown strap.

"Celebrating," I answer, my green eyes meeting his brown ones. They're dark and hot, and searching for the confirmation to his unspoken question. "Please." My plea comes out just above a whisper, but it might as well have been yelled.

It only takes a few seconds for Linkin to understand. Quickly, he helps me up from the car to stand before him. With swift movements, he slides my sweater up and over my head, exposing my red satin bra. "My God, you are stunning," he groans, rubbing his thumb over my nipples.

Before I can formulate any sort of response, his mouth descends on my chest, his big fingers moving my bra and exposing my sensitive breasts. The flash of cool air is quickly replaced by the warmth and wetness of his mouth. My fingers remove the belt and swiftly work at releasing the button and fly of his jeans.

Our hands are frantic as we help shed each other's clothes. My ankle boots land somewhere in the garage, along with my jeans, panties, and bra. We don't waste time removing his boots. Instead, I slide my hands along his hips, pushing his jeans and boxer briefs down as I go.

His cock is amazing. Long, hard, and throbbing in my hand. Just the way I've pictured it in my dreams. You know the ones where you wake up so wet and aroused you have no choice but to make yourself come in under five seconds? He flexes in my hand, his muscles tightening throughout his body as he releases a torturous groan of pleasure.

In one swift motion, I'm back in his arms and his lips lock on mine once more. The cold metal of the Hemi Cuda is shocking against my ass, but it's nothing compared to the sensation of being possessed by Linkin Stone. My heart hammers in my chest and my body throbs with desire as he steps in close. So close, his cock is sandwiched between us.

His finger slides between my legs. "Fuck, you're so wet," he moans before his tongue delves back into my mouth. Gently, he pushes one finger inside of me, quickly followed by two. The stretch is almost a burn, but the discomfort is nothing compared to the overwhelming need to have him fill me.

"You sure?" he asks, giving me one last chance to stop this.

But there's no way in hell I'm stopping this. If it were to come to an end before we ever really get started, I might actually die. You know, drop dead from lack of orgasm. And something tells me an orgasm administered by the massive cock of Linkin Stone's is something to write romance books about.

"Yes. Very sure. So sure that there's nothing I want more than you, right now." My voice is breathy, my words choppy, but I think he gets my point.

With one thrust, he's there, filling me completely. I cry out in both pleasure and a little in pain. It's been months since I've had sex, and I had started to wonder if maybe AJ was right. If you don't use it, it closes shut.

Linkin stills within me, his breathing labored and the muscles of his back and shoulders tight with tension. "Okay?" he asks, searching my face for signs of my discomfort to ease.

"More," I instruct, the slight burn already turning to incredible pleasure.

You don't have to tell him twice.

He slowly eases out, our gazes locked, as he pistons his hips and slams into me. Again, I cry out, this time in complete pleasure. My ankles are locked around his waist as he sets a bruising pace, filling me wholly, over and over again.

All I can do is hang on and enjoy the ride.

Get it?

Car humor.

I have no time to enjoy my dirty pun because I'm quickly racing towards an orgasm. My nails dig into the hardness on his upper back and I hang on for dear life. Linkin grunts as I leave my mark on his sweaty skin. The orgasm tears through me like a jolt from a live wire, alive and free. I fly over the edge, blinding white light clouding my vision.

Linkin pounds into me once, twice, three more times before stilling. He grunts and groans his release, grinding his pelvis against my throbbing clit. The friction sends me soaring into a second orgasm. Linkin rides out my second release, rubbing and grinding against me until we're a mix of heavy breathing and sweaty limbs.

"Fuck," he groans slowly, running his nose against my neck.

"You could say that again."

"Fuck," he mimes and I feel the smile against my skin.

"Already done that."

He pulls back, gazing down into my eyes. There's a mixture of emotions I'm not ready to diagnose shining back in those dark chocolate eyes. My fingers twitch to touch him, so I take a long, leisurely path of running my hands up his torso, his neck, until I'm caressing his jaw. The beard is prickly, and it makes me wonder what it would feel like on a more sensitive area. My thighs clench.

"What are you thinking about?" he asks, tenderly stroking my neck with the pads of his long fingers.

"Your beard," I answer honestly, loving the feel of it against my hands. "I bet it'll leave marks on my thighs."

Linkin laughs as his lips find mine once more. The kiss is slow, sensual, and starts to spark to life my under-used libido. "That could be arranged," he quips, nibbling on my swollen lower lip.

He pulls back more, looking down to where our bodies are still joined. "Shit, I didn't use anything," he says before meeting my eyes once more.

"It's okay. I'm clean. It's actually been quite a while for me, and I've only been with Chris for seven years." Linkin tenses when I say my soon-to-be ex-husband's name.

"I'm clean too," he confirms. "And I always use condoms."

Our gazes remained locked and I can feel so many unspoken emotions bubbling to the surface. I wasn't expecting to feel *anything* for anyone so quickly after leaving my husband. Is this too soon after coming out of a long-term relationship? Or is there more here?

Linkin slowly eases his body from within mine, warmth and wetness spilling out. He reaches over and grabs a clean shop towel from the pile beside the Cuda. With delicate movements, he tenderly cleans me up before tending to himself.

When he's finished, those dark eyes find mine once more. My heart is pounding in my chest and I can't help but reach for him. I wrap my arms around his neck and pull him against me, skin on skin. My legs encase him, loving the way the scratchy coarseness of his legs feel against the smoothness of mine.

I ease him forward until our lips meet in another slow, tantalizing kiss. He explores my mouth, dipping his tongue into each recess and sliding it gently against mine. "I could kiss you all day," he whispers, barely breaking the kiss.

"That sounds like an amazing day," I reply, my hands sliding over his shoulders and onto his upper back. Linkin winces. "What?" I ask, pulling back.

"I think a tiger got a hold of me," he says with a smile and a wink.

Moving his big body isn't an easy task, especially while sitting atop a classic muscle car, but when I finally get him to turn, I see exactly what he was referring to. "Oh my God, did I do that?" I gasp, taking in the angry red lines that resemble claw marks.

"Fuck yes, you did. I wouldn't trade those war wounds for anything," he chides, spinning back around and wrapping his arms around me. "Those scratches I wear like a badge of honor."

"You're weird."

"Maybe," he says, placing a chaste kiss on my lips. "We should get dressed. I'm pretty sure that door over there isn't locked."

Well, isn't that a pleasant thought. Anyone could have walked in and seen me getting the ride of my life on the hood of a freaking car. Awesome.

Linkin helps me down from the car before lifting his pants, which are still gathered around his ankles. Without even buttoning them, he works quickly to gather my clothes. I'm securing my bra when I feel his eyes on me. He's fully dressed, watching me as I fasten the bra around my chest.

Suddenly, he's moving.

I'm wrapped up in his arms once again, our lips hungry and urgent. The kiss goes on forever, or maybe that's just wishful thinking?

Eventually, I pull back, gasping for air. "We really should get going," I tell him, my hand resting over his chest where I feel his heart pounding and his lungs working frantically to pull in oxygen.

"Where are we going?"

"My dad's. It's Christmas Eve." Linkin stares at me, one dark eyebrow raised high. "I want you to come to my family's dinner tonight. Lots of laughs, some cards, probably some really gross PDA from my grandparents. It'll be fun."

He seems to struggle with saying yes, glancing between the car, his watch, and me. "Mrs. Case is going to be here in about thirty minutes to pick up the car. She bought it for her husband for Christmas."

"Hell of a Christmas gift," I acknowledge.

"It was the car he had when they met, but when money got tight, he sold it. Well, she found the man they originally sold it to, and he agreed to sell it back to her. She had it delivered here yesterday for a tune-up. A friend is supposed to drop her off at four so she can take it home to surprise him."

"That's awesome."

Glancing at his watch once more, he adds, "I'll need about twenty minutes or so at home to shower and change."

"How about I meet you there? I have to finish putting together my dish for dinner, and I could probably use a shower myself," I say, snorting a laugh.

Linkin wraps his arms around my waist. "I kinda like that I made you all dirty."

"Me too," I whisper.

"Okay," he starts, taking a step back. "You better get out of here before I rip your clothes back off you and bend you over the car this time." That piques my interest.

A lot.

"Don't look at me like that," he chastises, knowing exactly where my mind was. "I'll meet you at your place in about an hour."

"Sounds good," I say, stepping forward and reaching for his neck.

Chris wasn't short, but he wasn't exactly tall either. He was just... average. The fact that I have to work to kiss Linkin is actually quite a turn on. And the fact that he always seems willing to kiss me isn't so bad either. Not that Chris didn't want to kiss me, but he wasn't big on random public displays of affection... or those in private either.

With a smile on my face and whisker burn on my neck, I finally bid Linkin farewell and head towards my car. Oh, yes. I definitely made the right choice in tracking down my slightly mysterious and oh so sexy mechanic this afternoon.

I can't wait to see what happens next.

Linkin

I'm nervous as I step up to her door. I've never really done the whole parents thing before.

But what do I have to be nervous about? I've met them all before? She dragged me off to a luncheon with her entire family a few weeks back, so what makes this so different?

Maybe because it's a major fucking holiday and I had my dick inside her less than two hours ago? I swear her dad is going to know that I'm having sex with his daughter and kick me out of his house. And believe it or not, I really want her family to approve of me. If this baby plan goes through, I'm going to be in their lives for a long damn time. I'd hate for it to be uncomfortable.

Before I can knock, she opens the door, a vision in tight red material. "Why are you just standing out here?"

But instead of answering, I just stare.

She's wearing a long sweater dress that hugs every curve of her body, black tights, and short little ankle boots. Her hair is straight and sleek, draping down her back like some Greek goddess. It makes me want to weave my hands in it and pull. While I'm buried to the hilt inside her.

My dick is concrete-hard in point two seconds.

"Wow," I finally say, taking one more appreciative glance before returning to her green eyes. They're smiling and full of mischief.

"Are you done?" she retorts.

"Not yet, but give me a few minutes and I will be," I reply, taking a quick moment to adjust my throbbing cock in my suddenly too-tight jeans.

"Get in here," she says, grabbing my arm and pulling me inside her apartment. It smells sugary sweet with a hint of evergreen.

"Did you bake?" I ask, following her into the kitchen.

"Just some sugar cookies. I bought red frosting and silver and gold sprinkles. I thought Bri could decorate cookies for Santa after dinner."

"That sounds awesome," I say, stepping up behind her, pressing my front to her back. "You smell amazing," I add before placing a kiss on her neck.

"Thank you. You smell pretty delicious yourself," she says, pulling my arms tightly around her front. There's no way to mask my current state of arousal at this point. "And you look nice." She's talking about the long sleeve button-down shirt I found in the back of my closet. I'm pretty sure I've only worn it once or twice, probably to either a wedding or funeral.

She spins in my arms and stands up on her tiptoes. "You trimmed this up," she says, running her cool fingers over my beard.

"I'm not a complete caveman," I tell her with a smile.

"I happen to like your caveman side," she says, reminding me of our tryst in the shop just a little over an hour ago.

"I promise to have a little more finesse next time. Maybe even take you to a bed."

She seems to climb up my chest like I'm a tree, wrapping those fucking boots around the backs of my thighs. "Not that that doesn't sound great, but I happen to really, really like you unhinged. In case you couldn't tell, it sort of turns me on." Lexi slides her sweet pussy against my aching cock, sending every single ounce of blood I possess straight to that one concentrated area. Suddenly, I can't think at all. At least not about anything other than getting her naked.

My hands find her ass, the glorious globes fitting perfectly in my hands. "Firecracker, you gotta stop rubbing against me like that or we're going to be late to your dinner."

She makes a snorting noise. "We're already late," she says as she flexes her pussy against me.

"You're a temptress. You know that, right?"

"Only with you," she whispers before her lips lock on mine, and I'm gone.

Pinning her against the wall, I start to remove all of our clothing, which considering she's still wrapped around me like a steering wheel cover, makes it pretty difficult. Yet I manage to strip us both naked without setting her feet on the floor.

"We've got ten minutes," she whispers, breaking the kiss to position my dick right where it wants to be.

"Not that I'm proud of this, but I'll only need five," I tell her right before I thrust into her warm, wet pussy. "And you'll have no less than two orgasms."

Thrust. "Two? In five minutes?"

"Fuck yes." Thrust, thrust.

"Do your worst," she says, gripping onto my skin and holding on tight.

When we finally leave her apartment fifteen minutes later (so worth being late), I'm smiling big at the three more orgasms I was able to give her, even if that third one took me past the ten-minute mark. She doesn't seem to mind, though. Her grin and flushed cheeks tell me she is just fine with running a little late to her dad's house this evening.

Her hand slips into mine as we make our way down to her car, which is already laden with gifts and treats for this evening. Contentment washes through me as I climb behind the wheel and back her car from the parking spot. It's almost freeing to be with her, as if the secrets and demons of my past aren't still nipping on my heels.

But I push that all aside as I follow the directions to the home she grew up in. Tonight is about us, spending time with each other and getting to know her family. Before I can even think about my words, they're already out of my mouth. "Will you come with me tomorrow to my mom's place? It's not much, but she cooks a mean honey glazed ham."

Lexi glances my way, but I keep my eyes on the road. "You want me to meet your mom? On Christmas?"

"Why not? I've already met your entire family," I remind her.

"I don't have a gift for her."

"She doesn't need a gift, Lex. In fact, she'd probably be mad if you bring one and she doesn't have anything for you," I remind her, knowing that my mom is going to shit a brick when she sees me walk in with my girl.

My girl.

Feels fucking amazing to say it, even if it's only in my head.

"Okay," she says with a shrug and a warm smile. "I'd like to meet your mom."

"You had sex!" AJ exclaims too loudly to Lexi when she greets us at the door.

"Hush!" Lexi whispers harshly, glancing around to see who overheard the declaration.

"Oh, don't be shy. You know just about everyone here had sex before they came. Well, except Meg. And, well, me." AJ shoots her sister a look before turning to face me. "Good to see you again, Linkin. Even if you are wearing your clothes this time."

I bark a laugh, while Lexi hits her sister in the arm. "Stop trying to picture him naked," she chastises.

"Oh, too late for that," AJ snorts, leading us into the living room.

There's a large tree in the center of a picture window and it's overflowing with gifts. Everyone gets up to greet us, while helping to relieve some of the packages I'm holding and placing them wherever there's room near the tree.

"Good to see you again, Linkin," Dean says, extending his hand to shake mine.

"You too," I reply before moving on to the next guy. Soon, I've received welcomes from Ryan, Levi, and Lexi's dad, Brian. Her sisters are all there, wide knowing grins plastered on their faces.

"Oh, look who's here! It's Lexi Lou and her stripper!" Grandma exclaims when she enters the room.

"Grandma, seriously, we've been over this. He's not a stripper," Lexi grumbles as she steps into her grandma's waiting arms.

"Such a shame, though," she replies before turning her attention to me. "Merry Christmas, Linkin," she says, wrapping her surprisingly strong arms around my waist.

"Merry Christmas. Thank you for having me."

Before she replies, I feel a sharp pinch to my right ass cheek. "Oh, believe me, the pleasure is all mine," she says with a wink and saucy grin.

"Stop fondling him. It's Christmas," Lexi rebukes.

"Christmas is the season of giving, Lexi Lou."

"I don't even want to know what pinching his ass is giving you," she grumbles before taking my hand in hers and leading me towards the kitchen.

"Lexi!" Grandpa exclaims from the opposite side of the kitchen island.

"Merry Christmas, Grandpa," Lexi coos while giving the elderly man a big hug. "Your wife is molesting my date again," she adds.

"Link, I apologize," he says, extending his hand towards me. "That woman is hornier than a three peckered billy goat," he adds, shaking his head.

"Stop talking," Lexi begs.

"Anyway, I'm glad you're here. You can be my partner later when we play Euchre."

"Sounds good, sir," I say, wondering when the last time I actually sat down and played cards was.

"You gotta watch out for Dean and Ryan. Those two boys are cheaters," Orval conspiratorially whispers.

"What?" Ryan exclaims as he enters the kitchen. "Dean, Orval's calling us cheaters."

"Are you kidding? This from the man who stuffs Jacks up his sleeves?" Dean enters the room, joining the conversation.

"Those were extras. I had no idea they were there."

"Sure you didn't," Levi chimes in as he joins us in the kitchen.

All able hands, which surprisingly turns out to be the male hands of the family, make quick work of whipping boiled potatoes into creamy mashed potatoes, carving the turkey that smells devine, and pulling pans from the oven. Levi, actually, looks surprisingly at home in the kitchen, and seems to be telling everyone else what to do. I help where needed, which right now appears to be buttering steamy rolls and placing them in a fancy breadbasket.

When the food is ready, we gather around the table, hands folded in prayer.

"Lord, bless this food we are able to receive on this glorious Christmas Eve. I'm thankful that my son-in-law, six granddaughters, great granddaughter Brielle, and others could join us for this meal. I'm also grateful for the love of a good woman, my wife, Emma. Without her, I'd be lost in this world." For some reason, my throat burns with emotion. I've never thought it possible to love someone the way Orval appears to love his wife. They smile at each other, even through prayer, and the prospect makes me yearn.

Yearn for more in life.

I feel Lexi's hand wrap around my wrist, as if we're being pulled together by some invisible, magical force. Just the feel of her fingers on my skin calms me and brings me comfort.

"Please continue to watch over us, guiding us each day. Continue to watch over our Meggy, giving her extra comfort and strength, as she continues to learn to live her life without Josh." There's a sniffle somewhere in the room, but I don't dare look up to find the source. Something tells me I already know where it came from.

"And continue to bless our family with love and laughter. In your name we pray, Amen."

"Amen," we all say in unison.

When I glance down at the woman standing next to me, she gives me a sad smile, her gorgeous green eyes filled with unshed tears. A louder cry comes from the corner, and Brian is there, comforting and holding is daughter.

"It's her first Christmas without him," Lexi whispers, watching her dad hold Meghan.

"The pain will never go away, but over time, it'll lessen a little more."

Lexi nods her head, and pulls me towards the kitchen. We fall in line and fill our plates with more food than I've eaten in the last week. Even as Meghan joins us at the table, chatter and small talk commences. We eat and laugh and enjoy each other's company. There's teasing and loving glances and maybe a few wandering hands beneath the table.

Even through the sadness and heartache, you can still feel the love, the happiness, the unity.

Life goes on.

"I can't believe all those toys," I say, steering Lexi's car towards the apartment building. "Where in the hell are they going to put them?"

She laughs as she replies, "I don't know, but that's their problem."

"I think Dean almost had a heart attack when he realized most of the gifts under that tree were for his daughter."

"She's the first niece, first grandchild, and first great-grandchild. What do they expect?"

"Help renting the U-Haul?" I offer with a laugh.

When we pull into the parking lot, I quickly help gather up all of Lexi's goodies. She got a few new sweaters and scented lotion-y stuff from her sisters, a new smock with her name embroidered on the front, and a gift certificate to Adam & Eve from her grandparents. The looks on the girls' faces when they all opened the gift certificates to the online sex toy retailer may have been one of my favorite moments of the night.

"This is what holidays will be like when we have a baby, won't it." I didn't realize I say the words out loud until Lexi stops and turns to face me.

"What do you mean?" she asks, questions written on her beautiful face.

"A loving family who spoil and worry and stick their noses into each other's business. Our child won't want for anything."

"Probably not," Lexi confirms softly.

Not used to dealing with so much emotion in one day, I offer her a genuine smile. "Good."

We're quiet as we head up to the third floor. I bypass my own door and head down the hall towards hers. Our arms are laden with gift bags, but I manage to slip her key into the handle and unlock the door. When I walk in, the first thing I notice is the scent of pine.

"Is that the tree?" I ask, depositing all of her bags onto the kitchen table.

"What?" she asks, and I don't fail to notice that she locks the door behind us.

"It smells like pine in here."

"Oh, that. No, that's not the tree. I bought a pine scented candle to cover up the scent of your dead, rotting evergreen."

Laughing, I step forward and wrap my arms around her. "It didn't smell that bad."

"Even the critters vacated it. They couldn't take the stench of death," she quips with a smile.

"Oh, my little firecracker. Whatever will I do with you?" I ask, nuzzling her neck like some poor lovesick sap.

"I can think of a few things," she purrs, her hands slipping under my button-down and skimming up my abs.

"I like the way you think," I say, placing a chaste kiss squarely on her lips. "Let's get this stuff put away so I can defile you in front of the dead tree."

"Oh, that won't take much. I'm the naughty sister," she says, turning and grabbing the leftovers and putting them in the fridge.

"Oh, I believe it." To punctuate my statement, I give her a quick slap on the ass.

We make quick work of putting away all the food and stacking the opened gifts in the corner of the living room. They're all things she'll have to put away after I leave. But when she comes into the living room with two mugs of homemade eggnog, something tells me I won't be heading out anytime soon. Instead, I pop back into the kitchen, grab the leftover cream puffs Levi made for dessert, and join her on the couch.

"That was very stealthy of you to stick the cream puffs into our bowl when no one was looking," she says, the corner of her lip curving upward.

"These little fuckers are delicious." I should probably savor it and take bites, but instead find myself shoving the entire treat into my mouth and chewing.

"They are," she says, reaching for one. Before she can grab one, I move the bowl just out of her reach.

"Hey," she says, leaning forward and chasing the bowl.

Shaking my head, I take one of the treats and hold it up to her mouth. I'm transfixed on her movement as she slowly leans forward, her eyes locked on mine, and takes a bite of the puff. My heart thunders in my chest as her little tongue slips out of her mouth and licks away traces of white cream off her lips.

I almost groan.

Lexi leans forward, taking the rest of the cream puff into her mouth, and moreover, my fingers as well. Her eyes dilate as she sucks the sweetness off my fingers. How in the fuck can something as simple as eating dessert turn so erotic?

"Can I ask you something?" she says, leaning into the cradle of my arm and kicking her legs up onto the couch.

"Sure."

"What was your childhood like? You kind of alluded tonight that it wasn't so great."

Sighing, I knew this question was coming. "I have an awesome mom. Got pregnant with me young, while she was still in high school, and my sperm donor ran off before she had a chance to tell him. It was tough, very tough. Money was tight, but she made it work with what little we had. Then she met Larry, married him, and had the twins. Everything seemed great for a while, but it didn't last. He's gone too, like my father."

"I'm sorry," she says soothingly, rubbing her hand along my arm as she snuggles into my embrace.

"Nothing for you to be sorry about," I say, my hand sliding along her outer thigh and underneath the dress. Slowly bringing my hand to her front, I can feel the heat radiating off her sweet pussy. It makes me so hard just thinking about how mind-blowing it feels to be inside her.

"Are you trying to distract me?" she mewls, arching her back and my hand slips into her tights.

"Is it working?"

"Definitely."

Maneuvering us until she's beneath me, I position myself in what is quickly becoming my favorite place to be: between her thighs. Pushing up her red sweater, I expose her fit abdomen and red bra. Gently, I push aside the cups, revealing two perfect little nipples. They're tight little buds, begging for my mouth.

And who am I to deny?

My mouth descends, first licking and sucking on one, and then the other. I'm rewarded with a soft moan. "You know," I start, as I alternate between licking, sucking, and nipping at her perfect tits. "We never really discussed the real issue with the condoms."

"I told you I'm clean," she gasps.

"Not that. The other issue. The baby." This time I bite down on her nipple until she hollers in pleasure.

"I can't think when you do that," she whispers.

"You mean this?" I ask, leaning down and latching on to one nipple, while my fingers tweak and pinch the other.

"Yes. That."

"Should I stop?"

"Yes. No. Wait. I can't... No, definitely don't stop."

"Lexi? I haven't worn a condom the previous two times we've had sex," I remind her, even though I'm not sure she's even paying attention to my words right now.

"So?"

"Are you okay with that?" I ask, looking for confirmation.

"That I might get pregnant? That's kinda the point," she reminds me.

"It is, yes. But I know you're not completely divorced."

"Potato po-tah-toe. He signed the papers. It'll be final when we see the judge on January twenty-ninth."

"So if it happens before your court date, you'd be okay with that?"

"Soooooo fucking okay," she groans, grinding her sweet pussy against the bulge in my jeans.

"We should get rid of these clothes."

"Yes, get rid of them. Gone."

I get up and remove all of my clothes, while she does the same. Once we're both naked again, I take her in my arms and carry her towards the bathroom. I'm feeling like getting a little dirty, so we might as well kill two birds with one stone.

"I feel like getting a little wet," I tell her as I turn on the water, waiting until steam starts to fill the small space before stepping under the spray.

Lexi squeals as the hot water hits her back, so I quickly turn so that the majority of the water is pelting me. Reaching down, I turn on a little more cold until it's a bit more manageable. When the water temperature is right, I pin her naked body against the shower wall. My lips savor the flavor, the scent, and the texture of her skin. She's quickly becoming an addiction I'll be powerless to fight.

Not that I want to.

"Please," she begs, her legs wrapped tightly around my waist for the umpteenth time today. I crave her.

Instead of thrusting into her waiting pussy, I peel her body off mine. Lexi whimpers her protest, but I have other things in mind for my little firecracker. "Turn around," I demand.

She moves, giving me the most luscious view of her ass and the arch of her back. My hands grip her hips as I position myself behind her. "Hang on, Firecracker," I warn, taking my throbbing cock in my hand and giving it a squeeze. A tinge of pain sweeps through my groin, but I revel in the discomfort. The last thing I need is to fire my gun too soon. Lord knows this woman makes me lose every bit of finesse I thought I possessed, replacing it with a ravishing fever to consume and own her.

Lexi glances over her shoulder as she places her hands on the shower wall. Her mouth is slightly agape, her breathing choppy with anticipation. Our gazes locked, I gently slide into her wet, hot pussy. Collective moans of pure ecstasy mix with the humidity clouding the bathroom. It's fucking heaven.

I keep my strokes slow and long as I continually fill her over and over again. She glances over her shoulder once more, her lips swollen and gorgeous face flushed. My grip on her hips tightens as I watch her eyes glaze over.

Suddenly, she moves, standing up and arching her back so that her sweet ass is pressed firmly into my groin. She lifts her arms, extending them over her head and wrapping them around the back of my neck.

Jesus.

One hand slides to her sexy stomach before slipping down to stroke her clit. It's hard and begs for my fingers. I give it a gentle pinch causing her to call out my name. Mother fucking hell, I'm not going to last. I'm like a sixteen-year-old boy again, unable to last more than a few minutes. She just makes me lose any semblance of control.

While I play with her wet clit, I continue to piston my hips forward. Her tits are pushed skyward, begging to be touched. My fingers find one perfect little nipple, as I lightly pinch and pull on it until it's hard.

Lexi turns her head, giving me access to her mouth. My tongue dips inside, licking and tasting every square inch of her delicious mouth. Keeping the connection, I tweak her clit once more at the same time as I pinch her nipple. She bucks against me, wild and with abandon. I know she's getting close, I can feel her pussy starting to milk my cock, tightening and gripping me for all I'm worth.

"Fuck, you feel so fucking amazing," I tell her, my lips hovering over hers.

"So fucking good," she chimes, gasping as I continue to work her clit and nipple.

"Do you want to come?" I ask, slowing my strokes until I'm buried completely inside her.

"Yes. Please."

"Hang on, baby," I tell her before pulling out and slamming inside her. I pinch both fingers at the same time, right when I know I'm hitting that sweet spot deep within.

"Oh, God!" she hollers, clamping down on my dick so hard I see stars.

Her body spasms against mine as she rides out her release, which triggers my own. Her pussy squeezes my cock as I slam into her body. "Fuck," I groan, releasing everything I have inside of her.

When the aftershocks finally subside and our breathing has somewhat returned to normal, I rest my head on the back of her neck, burying my nose into her soft skin. Her hands are still extended over her head, wrapped around me. Placing tender kisses, I lick away the water, tasting the saltiness of sweat. It's erotic as hell.

Feeling her start to sag against me, I reach around and grab the bar of soap. My cock pulls from her body, limp and overused from three rounds of fucking in the last several hours. Yet, give me a few minutes and I'd bet my Harley I'd be ready to go once more.

As long as it's Lexi I'm with.

No words are spoken as she turns around and watches me wash her skin. I lather up my own body while she starts to wash her hair, a mundane task that I have the sudden desire to assist with. So, I do. She doesn't say anything when my hands start to scrub her scalp, working the suds around in her shiny dark hair.

We rinse together, a few stolen kisses here and there, before declaring our shower complete. She grabs two fuzzy towels from the cabinet beside the tub, handing one to me before wrapping one around her body.

I follow her into her room, not really sure if I should run to the living room and grab my clothes or not. I'm not really sure what she's thinking, where we go from here. I know what I'm hoping for, but I make no assumptions when it comes to Lexi. If it were up to me, I'd climb into bed, pull her in close, and fall asleep beside her.

Keeping my towel fastened around my hips, I sit on her bed and watch her get ready for bed. She uses some face stuff and removes eye makeup, and then some other girly moisturizer on the rest of her face. She brushes her long brown hair until it's smooth and glossy. Then she turns my way.

And drops her towel.

Slowly, she makes her way towards me, stepping between my legs. "I'm not sure what your plans are, but you can stay." She clears her throat, maybe looking for a little courage to keep going. "I'd really like you to stay."

Sliding my hands up her outer thighs to her hips, I answer honestly. "There's no place I'd rather be." I'm rewarded with one of those smiles that makes my heart beat faster and my gut tighten.

Lexi slips out of the bedroom, turning off lights left on in the other room, and verifying the apartment is secured for the night. When she comes back into the room, still naked and curves on full display, my tongue practically dangling on my chin, she gives me one of those sassy little grins that I can only associate with my feisty little firecracker.

She flips off the light before slipping into her bed. Dropping my own towel, I climb in on the opposite side, but quickly move to the middle. Her skin is warm as I cradle her body against mine, spooning her close and secure.

"Good night," she whispers, glancing over her shoulder at me.

"'Night, Lexi," I reply before placing one more kiss on her waiting lips.

As I drift off to sleep, probably more comfortable than I've ever been in my life, I can't help but smile. I have a beautiful woman in my arms and more possibility on the horizon than ever before.

Life is good.

17

Lexi

Something tickles my nose, pulling me from a deep sleep. I swipe it away, but it returns moments later. "Wake up, beautiful. Merry Christmas."

Linkin.

My body starts to heat when I recall how easily he pushed me over the edge into multiple orgasms on multiple occasions. Just the thought of how easily he played my body, especially last night in the shower, has me on edge and probably embarrassingly wet.

"Stop smiling like that, Firecracker, or we'll never make it out of this bed."

Cracking open my eyes, I'm overcome with this weird giddiness that I've never experienced before. It's part hope, part elation, part anticipation, all wrapped up in a naked package.

"I made pancakes," he whispers conspiratorially with a wide grin and sparkle in his dark eyes. "And coffee."

"Oh, coffee and carbs. You're a wicked, wicked man," I chide back.

"I am. It's one of the many things you love about me," he adds, pulling back the covers. "Get up and throw on a shirt before I say fuck breakfast and fuck Christmas and keep you tied to the bed all day."

"That doesn't sound so bad," I reply, standing up and stretching before taking the shirt directly off Linkin's back. He helps, of course, lifting his arms so I can remove the fresh white t-shirt he must have retrieved from his apartment. "This one will do," I say as I bring the material over my head, inhaling the manly, musky scent that is pure Linkin.

"That one's mine," he quips with a smirk.

"Was..." I say, singsong, letting the word trail off as I turn into his chest. "Merry Christmas," I say softly, wrapping my arms around his naked chest.

"Merry Christmas," he replies, kissing the top of my head as he holds me close.

"Okay," I start, slowly pulling back. "It's carbs and coffee time."

"Are you sure? Because it kinda feels like I want to get you naked and do dirty things with my hard-on time," he pleas, following me into the kitchen.

"Maybe if you're a good boy and stuff me full of fluffy pancakes." Reaching into the cabinet, I pull down two coffee cups.

"Oh, I'll stuff you, all right," he quips with a smile before filling our mugs, leaving room at the top for me to add my flavored creamer.

My ears start to burn, probably a rosy shade of pink like my cheeks. I've never blushed, yet ever since Linkin stripped his way into my life, I find myself turning into a pool of hormonal girly mush more often than not.

"Eat. If you're a good girl, I'll give you a present."

"Present?" That perks me right up.

"Only if you're good."

"Oh, I'm definitely good," I say, batting my eyelashes and piling big, fluffy pancakes onto my plate.

An hour later, we're dressed and ready for lunch with his mom. Well, technically, Linkin was already ready since he slipped home and showered and changed while I was sleeping. He returned with a small red box with gold ribbon. It's been sitting below the Charlie Brown Christmas tree, enticing me to open it.

And now it's time.

"You first," I say, handing Linkin the large flat box with his name on it.

Linkin rips the paper off like a kid. He uses his pocket knife to cut through the package tape, and slowly pulls the gift from the packaging.

"Wow, that's amazing," he says, his eyes twinkling like Christmas lights and wide with excitement.

"You like it?"

"Like? I fucking love it," he replies, running two fingers over the painted canvas.

"I'm glad. I mean it was either the '57 Chevy Bel-Air or the sunflower fields at sunset."

"Well, as much as I like sunflowers and sunset, this car is a classic. It's like the T-Bird or the Mustang. It's an icon. Thank you," he says, setting the painting that I found at a craft show aside, and kissing me square on the lips.

"I thought it was time to add something to your walls," I quip, referring to the fact that his walls next door are still completely naked.

"Your turn," he says, handing me the small box that I've had my eye on since I noticed it sitting beneath the tree.

I waste no time pulling the ribbon and paper off the box. It's a white jewelry box, the name of the designer on the front unfamiliar. Gently, I open the lid, a soft gasp seeping from my open lips. "This is… stunning," I choke, air not moving to my lungs the way it should.

He doesn't speak, but instead, reaches for the box. Linkin pulls the necklace from within and grips the clasp. Moving my hair to the side, I turn until he's at my back. The metal is cool as it hits my neck, the small pendant almost reaching my cleavage.

When he has it securely in place, I grab the pendant and take a closer look. It's a pair of scissors with a diamond in the middle. It's simple and stunning and so very… me. Tears cloud my eyes as I continue to stare down at my beautiful new necklace.

"Do you like it?" he asks.

"I love it," I confirm, moving to my knees in front of him and placing a kiss on his lips. "It's the best gift I've ever received."

"I'm not so sure about that, but I'm glad you like it."

"No, really," I say, looking back down at the necklace. "Chris wasn't really a fan of my career. In fact, he wouldn't even acknowledge it as a career. He always referred to it as my hobby."

"Mega douche," he says, shaking his head.

"That he is. But it's Christmas and I'm not going to give him even one more second of my thoughts today," I say, smiling and holding onto the charm.

"I've got an idea," he says, an ornery gleam shining in his chocolate eyes. "Why don't I do the dishes real quick and you gather up your things. We'll slip next door and you can help me hang that picture, probably in my bedroom. And since we'll already be in there, you can show me those dark blue panties I caught a glimpse of while you were dressing earlier."

"You were being a Peeping Tom?"

"Fuck yes, I was."

Shaking my head, I stand up, offering him my hand to help him stand with me. "Deal," I say, leading him towards the kitchen.

"Oh, and Linkin?" I ask, catching his attention. "They're actually purple. And lace. And a thong."

His groan is the last thing I hear as I slip back into the living room to gather up the final two presents for the day.

I follow Linkin up the front steps of a small white house, stepping over a big tank with what could possibly be millions of army guys scattered all over the porch. "Dammit," he grumbles, sweeping his foot to the side to move the little army men from our path.

Before I can comment, the front door flies open. "Linkin!" one of the twins hollers before launching himself out the door and around his brother's leg. He's quickly followed by a second tornado, who mirrors his twin's actions and wraps himself around Linkin's other leg.

"Why are the army guys spread out all over the porch? Mom could have come out here and slipped and fell," Linkin chastises softly.

"Sorry. We were at war but then the maiden made us come in and take showers. She said we smelled like death," one of the twins says, I think Jack.

"Yeah, we smelled like death. Isn't that cool?!" Jeff exclaims proudly.

"Not really. That's an expression that means you smell horribly and need to find a bar of soap and water. Do you remember Lexi?" Linkin asks, walking like a robot through the front door with one boy attached to each leg.

"Of course, I do! Hello, beautiful," Jack coos, waggling his eyebrows at me. I can't help but laugh.

"Merry Christmas," I say to no one in particular.

"Merry Christmas," I hear in a woman's voice as I enter the house. She enters the room, her steps faltering when she sees me. Her graying brown hair is pulled up in a messy bun and she looks a little tired. But her eyes sparkle like chocolate diamonds, just like her son's. "Oh. Hi," she says, stepping forward and offering me a genuine smile. "I wasn't expecting a guest."

"Yeah, sorry, Mom. This is my friend, Lexi," Linkin says, trying to shake the boys off his legs. "Lexi, this is my mom, Karen."

"So very nice to finally meet you, dear," Karen says before wrapping her small arms around my back and squeezing. She's surprisingly strong for such a little thing.

"Nice to meet you too," I reply as she lets go and casually gives me a look over. "Sorry to crash your party," I add.

"Nonsense. I've been dying to meet you ever since Linkin mentioned you." Leaning in, she says, "It's not every day that my son talks about a girl, let alone brings one home."

"Mom," he says, warning edging his voice.

"Anyway, I'm very happy you're here. Come in and take your jacket off. I'm sorry the place is such a mess. The boys here seem to scatter toys mere seconds after they're picked up and put away," Karen says, shaking her head at the two boys who are now carrying plastic swords.

"Come play with us! You can be on my side, Link," Jeff says, handing his older brother a sword.

"That means I get Lexi," Jack chimes in, again, wiggling his eyebrows and making us all laugh.

"Yeah, I'm not so sure I trust you with my girl, Jack. You'll probably kill me and make off with my maiden," Linkin says.

"It's war, Linkin. Whatever happens, happens," Jack says casually, shrugging his shoulder.

"Let me put all of our stuff down and you can try to kill me in a bit," Linkin says, grabbing the two large presents that we brought in from the floor and taking them to the small Christmas tree.

"Can I help in the kitchen?" I ask Karen.

"Everything's almost ready, but I'd love for you to join me," she replies, smiling sweetly. My gut tells me I'm in for a bit of an inquisition about my relationship with her oldest son.

"Merry Christmas, Mom," Linkin says, leaning in and placing a gentle kiss on her cheek as he comes back into the room.

I can't help but grin at the exchange. He clearly loves his mom and helps her out whenever needed. That thought alone warms my heart a bit. Beneath the rough and tough exterior, Linkin's a good guy with a loving heart. He worships his brothers and his one parent who raised him, and if I'm being honest, I think you could add me to that category. I might not be ranked as highly as his family, but when we're together, Linkin makes me feel like something special. Something treasured. Something real.

"What can I help with?" I ask Karen as I follow her into the tiny, yet tidy kitchen. It smells of warm bread and honey glazed ham.

"There's nothing left to do but set the table," she says, pulling the ham from the oven.

"Let me," I say, taking the small stack of plates from the counter and placing them on the table. I notice right away that we're one short, thanks to my surprise visit.

"The cabinet beside the fridge," Karen says, as if reading my mind. I find mismatched plates, bowls, and plastic cups, and finish setting the table. We work in tandem to finish preparing the meal, but it's not uncomfortable. In fact, it's so easy, it's as if we had been doing it for years.

"Be kind to him," she finally says, standing beside me and transferring the ham from the roasting pan to the platter. "I'm not sure what all he's told you, but he hasn't had an easy life. He grew up way before he had to because it was just the two of us and he had no choice but to step up and help. But that's just the kind of person he is. He's a good man," she says, her kind eyes staring over at me.

"He is," I confirm with an affirmative head nod. And that's the God's honest truth. Everything I've seen about Linkin is that he's a decent, sincere, giving man, even if he is, at times, a smug jerk who likes to push my buttons, just for the sake of pushing them.

But then I think about our situation, or the one that we might be in very soon.

A baby.

We haven't been using protection, knowing good and well that a baby could be the result. In fact, that's the hope, at least for me. Linkin volunteered to father my baby. A stranger. A friend, yes, but that's more of a recent development. The man's surely a little loco.

Even then, I still consider him more friend than stranger. So what does that make me?

Yeah, a little crazy too.

"He's been a great friend to me through the tough events in my own life, and I'm very grateful for that. I hope he considers me as much of a friend as I do of him."

"Oh, Lexi," she says with a humorous chuckle. "Don't you get it? You *are*. But you're… more. The fact that you're even here, with me and his brothers, tells me that." She takes a moment to place the bowls on the counter. "Can I ask you a personal question?"

I give her my full attention, my gut churning with uneasiness. Words don't come, so I nod my head in reply.

"He mentioned that you're separated, getting divorced." She doesn't continue, nor does she ask the question I know is coming.

"I am," I confirm. "I separated from my husband in October, and am pleased that he signed the divorce papers this last week. It'll be finalized at the end of January."

Karen nods her head. "Good. I'll be honest, I was a little worried about him getting into a relationship with you with your divorce still pending."

"I get that. I'm looking forward to nothing more than closing that chapter in my life and moving on. And," I says, picking at the corner of a napkin, "I really hope that Linkin is part of that."

She doesn't say anything else, but gives me a warm, sincere smile and wraps her arms around me again. I feel like I just passed some big test where his mom is concerned, which makes the tightness in my chest loosen just a little more.

"I'm hungry!" Jack says, running into the kitchen, waving his sword.

"Me too!" Jeff exclaims, following on his brother's heels.

"Me three!" Linkin adds with a wide smile as he brings up the rear.

And boy, oh boy, what a rear it is.

"You didn't have to buy them anything," Linkin says as we head back to our building.

"I know, but when I saw it all, I just knew I needed to get it for them."

Of course, he's referring to the gifts I found for the boys when I was Christmas shopping with Jaime and Payton. Not only did I find lighted swords, but daggers, shields, and armor too. It was a huge hit amongst the little gladiators, and we had to act out several death scenes before Linkin and I were able to leave for the evening.

Well, Linkin kept dying thanks to Jack's sword.

I believe his words were, "She's mine!" He would always yell it right before slamming the plastic weapon into his brother's chest.

"I'd say it was a huge hit. Thank you," he says, taking my hand and bringing it up to his mouth. The kiss is tender, his lips warm as he keeps his eyes on the road.

And I struggle to keep from crawling over the console and riding him like a carousel pony.

"You're welcome. Seeing their faces when they opened them was worth it," I answer, my breathing a bit more shallow now that his lips are drawing lazy lines across my knuckles.

"I'm pretty sure my bruised ribs would disagree." He rubs his sore abdomen just to punctuate his point.

"You'll live."

"I'm not so sure about that. I might need a little TLC," he says, flashing me a dirty smile.

"TLC?" I ask, playing along a bit, even though I'm already feeling squirmy in my seat.

"You know, mouth to mouth."

That gets a bark of laughter. "Mouth to mouth? Or... mouth to *other* body parts," I say, my voice dropping seductively, my eyes falling to his lap.

"Mouth to cock. I like it." He's already getting hard. I can see the outline of his cock through his jeans, and it makes my blood boil with excitement. I can't believe I'm this ravenous for him. I'm like a horny teenager, craving him in a way I've never experienced before.

And that's completely true. In the seven years I was with Chris, I never felt like this. As much as I loved him and enjoyed sex with him, what I'm experiencing with Linkin isn't even in the same ballpark. They're apples and oranges, night and day, whiskey and beer. Chris is all organized, schedules, and pressed Oxford dress shirts, while Linkin is, well, everything Chris isn't.

I'm not saying that to be mean, but it's true. Linkin is dangerous and thrilling. He's smudges of grease on a pair of worn jeans and hair that's standing straight up. But those things are what makes him... *him*. Sexy. Desirable. Magnetic. I'm drawn to him for who he is and how he makes me feel, which right now, is a little like I'm freefalling into the unknown. I may not know what's coming, but I know it'll be worth the ride.

Pulling into the parking lot, Linkin parks his truck, grabs the few small gifts he received from his mom, and comes around to help me out. Before we hit the sidewalk, I turn into his chest, reaching around and grabbing his ass.

Sliding my hand around to grab his front, I give him a saucy grin and ask, "Now, what was it you said about mouth to cock?"

18

Linkin

I'm definitely working tonight. It's New Year's Eve, and Lucky's is packed! They're lined up two deep at the bar, and I'm doing everything I can just to keep my half of the bar satisfied and with alcohol.

A band is playing country music, which isn't exactly my taste, but it's got a good beat. And the residents of Jupiter Bay have come out in droves to celebrate the end of one year and the start of another. Party hats and those fucking blow horns are everywhere, but it doesn't distract me from keeping the beers flowing and the mixed drinks pouring.

Yet somehow, in the midst of chaos, I seem to be able to spot my girl. She's in a small group with her sisters and their significant others, drinking beer and laughing. I catch her watching me every so often, but only because I'm seeking her out so I can watch her. She's my addiction. My drug.

They decided to celebrate their monthly sisters' night a week early since New Year's Eve gave them the perfect opportunity to celebrate. For me, this night should produce the rest of the cash flow I need to pay off debts for good. Between the extra tips during the holidays and a cash bonus from Ernie, partnered with what I've been able to save over the last few months, that last payment can be made sooner than expected.

Good. I'm ready to be done with this shit.

I could pick up on her laugh a mile away. She's dragging Meghan and AJ out onto the dance floor where the band is singing about country girls shaking it. I'll admit, it's a great fucking view. Lexi wearing those ass-huggin' jeans and a tight sweater any other day is hard-on inducing, but tonight? Paired with my favorite fucking boots, her hair teased a little wild, making her look freshly fucked, and a wide carefree smile? She's a fucking walking orgasm. A wet dream.

My wet dream.

Our eyes meet from across the bar as she moves her hips to the beat of the music. I can spot at least three dicks watching her dance, and that thought irritates the shit out of me. I've never been a jealous man, mostly because I haven't cared about anyone enough to ever get green-eyed, but with her, I want to throw her over my shoulder like a caveman. I want to lift my leg and pee to mark my territory. I want to walk out there, kiss the shit out of her, and declare loudly that she's mine.

But I can't.

I won't.

Lexi would have my balls if I ever did anything remotely close to that.

The other sisters join her on the dance floor. Catching movement off to the right, I notice that the guys – Dean, Ryan, and Levi – are paying very close attention to their ladies. There's no way any dick would be stupid enough to try to get close to any of those girls. Not with those three waiting and watching.

It's weird that it calms me a bit knowing that they'll watch out for her, but at the same time, it should be me. I'm the one who should be standing on the sidelines while she has a great time, celebrating with her sisters. I'm the one who should be stepping in when some fuck gets too close. There's a lot that I *should* be doing, but one thing I *know* I'll be doing.

I'm the one taking her home.

"Take a break," Lucky says, stepping up beside me and grabbing my shoulder.

"Too busy for a break tonight, man."

"Yeah, well, I think I can hold down the fort for a few minutes. Besides, you've poured that beer three times and still haven't delivered it to the guy," he says, taking the overflowing mug of draft beer from my hand and handing it to the guy standing in front of me. "Go dance with your girl," he adds, nodding towards the dance floor where a slow song is just starting.

You don't have to tell me twice.

I'm moving, sliding under the lift-top at the end of the bar, and intercepting my girl as she exits the dance floor only seconds later. As I wrap my arms around her waist, halting her progress, she spins around, fire dancing in her eyes and a hand raised, ready to strike. When she sees it's me, her features relax and I'm rewarded with a smile.

"I thought you were someone else. I was about to knock your head off," she says, slipping into my embrace.

"Well, I'm glad you wouldn't just let any asshole paw all over you."

"Nope. You're definitely the only asshole I want pawing me," she quips with a wink.

"Dance with me, beautiful."

"But you're working," she says, glancing over at the busy bar.

"I'm on break. I get five minutes to dance with my girl," I reply, pulling her back onto the dance floor.

Her smile is instantaneous as warm, familiar arms wrap around my neck, pressing her tits firmly against my chest. This is fucking heaven right here. I pull her in even closer, staking my claim for anyone and everyone to see. She doesn't even know it, but I'm making a declaration to every jackhole in the joint that she's mine.

And she is.

My heartbeat kicks into overdrive at the thought.

Me, Linkin Stone, self-proclaimed bachelor and confirmed bad boy, is tossing all of those stupid titles right out the proverbial window and grabbing onto a relationship like it's the very air I need to breathe. Because that's what she's quickly become.

My air.

Without saying anything, she leans forward and rests her head against my chest. She's the perfect height, and I wonder, as she puts her ear to my heart, if she can hear the drum solo in my chest. It's pounding so hard I swear everyone in the bar can hear it.

"Having fun?" I ask, my hands dangerously low on her hips as we sway in time with the beat.

"Mmhmm," she murmurs, the vibration of her hum shooting straight through my chest and landing on my dick.

The song doesn't last nearly long enough, and before I know it, it's about time for me to get back behind the bar. "You're staying until close, right?" I ask, hopeful and anxious to take her home for the night.

"I am," she confirms, tightening her grip around my waist until it feels like a hug. I stop moving and just hold her close. Her hair smells like jasmine, a scent that is pure Lexi.

When the song ends and a fast, upbeat one begins, I glance up, noticing the lines at the bar. Definitely time for me to get back to work. Her sisters are around us, well those that aren't single. Ryan and Jaime, Dean and Payton, and Levi and Abby walk off the dance floor, smiling brightly as they pass by.

That's when I notice the remaining two sisters, each off to the side of the room. AJ is chatting it up with a group of guys I've seen in here several times before, while Meghan chats with a guy dressed a little too nicely for Lucky's. I watch as she offers him a friendly smile, listening intently on whatever he's saying.

"Hey, who's that?" I ask, drawing Lexi's attention towards her sister.

"Oh, that's Nick, her boss."

"He's awfully dressed up for a night a Lucky's," I say, noticing the way the man's body is turned towards Meghan. He smiles easily back at her, his arms crossed casually at his chest. They look comfortable, and if she's his employee, well, that would make sense. I know it's not someone I need to keep a close eye on.

"His sister got married tonight. She's a teacher with AJ at the junior high."

A loud noise pulls my attention towards the bar, where I see Lucky's grandson, Brant, dumping the full garbage can behind the bar into a much larger one on wheels. That's my cue that my break's over. "I gotta go, Firecracker. The boss is drowning behind the bar."

Turning towards me, she threads her thin fingers into my hair and plants her lips on mine. It's a short kiss, one that I'd love to continue – in private – but duty calls. Reluctantly, I pull back and give her a wink. "Have fun with your sisters," I say, pivoting to head back up front.

Lexi grabs my hand, halting me and causing me to turn around quickly, fearing something is wrong. "I'm going home with you tonight," she whispers, placing another kiss to my lips.

Catcalls and hollers erupt around me, letting me know her sisters are witnessing the kiss, which makes us both smile against each other's lips. "Damn right, you are," I reply before finally breaking away and getting back to work.

Three hours until close.

Until I get to take her home, to my bed.

Until she's naked and beneath me.

Three hours until she's mine.

Lexi

The New Year celebration came and went, and January is already nearing an end. And more importantly, so is my marriage.

My anxiety for today is at an all-time high. Higher than when I was supposed to start my period two weeks ago. Especially high the day it actually came. Right on cue. Twenty-eight days exactly from the last time I started one. It was a sad day, one that reminded me that even if things are going well, sometimes you get knocked back a few steps.

I'm not exactly sure why I was so sad, especially because we hadn't really been trying. I mean, we weren't preventing, but we weren't actually doing the deed with the purpose of creating life. Maybe it's because I had months – hell, years – of disappointment where having a baby was concerned.

Linkin was surprisingly solemn that day, too. He was quiet in a way I didn't expect, and held me extra tight that night when we fell asleep in my bed together. I don't know if it was because I was so down and upset or if he really was feeling blue too, but I like to think it's the latter.

Speaking of bedding together, oh we've done quite a bit of that. On the nights he doesn't work at Lucky's, we alternate between his bed and mine. On those nights he's working late, I get a surprise visitor sometime around midnight. Of course, it's not exactly a surprise, per se, since I gave him a key for his late night booty calls.

But booty calls isn't exactly what I'd call this. I mean, there's sex – and a lot of it – but it's more than that. I feel it, and I think he does too. When we're together, I get his full attention, which is a nice change from when my soon-to-be ex-husband was around. If he weren't staring at his phone, I would have thought something was wrong with him.

There's something almost magical in the way Linkin wraps his arms around me and pulls me close. It's as if I'm the only woman in the world, and he's afraid I'm going to get away if he doesn't hold on tight enough. Our friendship has definitely blossomed into something bigger, though we haven't discussed exactly what that is yet.

Right now, we're just riding the high, spending time together, and having *the sex* as much as humanly possible.

Seriously, I had no idea a person could crave another as much as we do each other.

Is this what Abby was talking about? And Jaime? And Payton? And even Meghan, before her life was ripped apart by an unexpected landmine.

I feel it, deep in my heart, when we're lying together in bed or we're cooking dinner for the twins. I feel it when my phone notifies me that I have a text and I get all giddy excited that it might be from him.

Who would have thought? That annoyingly cocky smartass from next door has wormed his way into my life, and more importantly, my heart.

Today is the day.

I'm dressing in a soft blue sweater and skinny jeans, and Linkin's favorite boots. I call them his favorite because he has made me put them back on after more than one occasion, after stripping me naked and doing dirty things to my body. The man has incredible stamina when it comes to positions you'd think weren't possible, but Linkin proves me wrong every damn time.

Anyway, back to the reason for today.

D-Day.

The day I go before the judge, who will grant the conclusion of my marriage, essentially allowing me to move forward one hundred percent with the next phase of my life.

I arrive fifteen minutes early to meet with my attorney one final time before we're scheduled to appear in court. I'm pleasantly surprised when I see my grandparents waiting just outside the courtroom.

"What are you guys doing here?" I ask, the small heels of my boots echoing in the nearly vacant hallway in front of the courtroom.

"We thought we'd come show you support as you dissolve your marriage," Grandpa says, with an extra sparkle in his eyes. It makes me wonder why he's so vested in today's court date. Is it more than just showing me support? Something seems fishy.

"We needed to make sure that man doesn't try any last minute funny business," Grandma says proudly, confirming what I was starting to speculate.

"I see. I appreciate your support, but I don't think he has a leg to stand on when it comes to funny business."

"You never know when dealing with a man scorned," Grandpa adds solemnly, the hairs on the back of my neck raising.

"Besides, I want to see this over so you can finally bed that totally doable hunk of a man you brought to Christmas Eve," Grandma adds loudly, happily, and somewhat proudly on my behalf. Of course, I don't have the heart to tell her I've already been bedding that totally doable hunk of a man since Christmas Eve.

It's as if she can read my mind, just like when we were kids. "Oh, don't worry, Lexi Lou. I totally know you've been bumping uglies since Christmas Eve. You have that constant *I just got screwed by a massive man love sword* glow on your face."

"What!?" I ask, mortification gripping me, pulling me under and drowning me in humiliation.

"Oh, did you think you were hiding that? Grandma knows all about the joys of riding a flesh rocket, Lexi Lou. In fact, I encourage it. I was just trying to be politically correct."

"When have you ever worried about being politically correct, my love?" Grandpa asks, bringing her aged hand up to his mouth and placing a gentle kiss on the top.

"I'm not, but Chris is standing right behind Lexi listening to everything we're saying so I thought I'd try to keep the fact that Lexi and that gorgeous man, Linkin, have been doing the nasty for weeks now from his delicate little ears."

Gasping, I whip around, surprised to find the man I was once married to standing directly behind me. Chris's face is an ugly shade of red, a look of anger mixed with embarrassment written all over the face I used to love. "Chris," I choke out. I feel horrible for him overhearing that conversation. Not because he knows that I've moved on, but because even though I'm angry and hurt by his betrayal, I don't want to rub his nose in anything, let alone what is turning into my own happiness.

"Alexis," he bites out as if my name were a nasty taste of something gross.

"They're ready for us," my attorney says, stepping up beside me, essentially cutting off any further communication.

The courtroom isn't large. Nothing like those you see on TV. In fact, the small room is surprisingly disappointing in regards to what I was expecting. There are a handful of chairs along the back wall, two small tables in the middle of the room, and a judge's desk up front. Besides the American flag and a printed photo of the Constitution behind the judge, there's no other décor or markings.

"This is the family courtroom," my attorney says, leading me to the table to the right. Chris and his attorney take their positions at the table to the left, and we all wait for the judge to enter. Grandma and Grandpa quietly sit behind me, their support having a calming effect on me.

The rest of my time in the courtroom passes in a blur. The judge reads the terms of our divorce, making no amendments to the agreement already signed between Chris and myself. He signs his name on the paper and passes it off to the recorder, who stamps and notarizes the documents that end my marriage.

When we're dismissed, a new sense of freedom washes over me.

And the first thing I think?

I can't wait to find Linkin.

"Alexis," Chris says beside me, his voice quiet and… sad. I'm not prepared for the look of devastation written all over his face. It's like a kick to the gut, leaving me gasping for breath and dizzy.

I open my mouth to respond, but he holds up his hand.

"I granted you your divorce. I get it. I messed up. But Alexis?" he asks, stepping forward and invading my personal space. Before I can take a step back, he lifts his hand and touches my cheek. "This isn't over. I love you."

I'm rendered completely speechless and my grandparents step up beside me. Chris drops his hand, smiles sadly, and turns and walks away.

But is he really walking away?

Uncertainty churns in my stomach like bad Chinese, and I wonder if this is really over. Will he let me go the way I expect him to?

"Ready?" Grandpa asks, placing his familiar hand on my arm.

"Ready," I choke out before clearing my throat. "Let's go."

I'm eager to see Linkin.

The drive towards Stapleton's is a quick one and it only takes a few minutes before I find myself pulling into the lot. One of the bay doors is open, a flurry of movement coming from the inside of the shop. When I step out of my car, the sounds of an impact wrench and rock music follows me to the glass door. This time, since it's during business hours, I'm using the front entrance.

Inside, a man sits behind the counter, a warm smile on his face. I recognize him as the owner, Ernie Stapleton. "How can I help you?"

Maybe this wasn't such a good idea. What was I thinking coming here during his work hours?

"Miss?"

"Actually, I was hoping I can speak with Linkin for a quick second," I say quickly.

"Sure, sure. Wait right here and I'll grab him," he replies, hopping up off the stool and walking through the door behind him and into the shop area. "Link! You have a visitor!" he hollers over the tools and music.

I watch as all heads in the garage turn and glance my way. Everyone has seemed to have stopped working and is watching Linkin as he ducks out from under the hood of a car and looks my way. When our eyes meet, even from afar, I feel that same strong, sexual current I always feel. A slow, sexy smile spreads across his gorgeous face, making my dirty mind conjure up all sorts of repeat scenarios starring him and me in that greasy garage.

The sound of his boots as he walks across the concrete floor, along with the beat of my heart, echoes in my ears. The music fades, the murmurs of his coworkers and their judgmental eyes fades, even the gentle hum of the heat in the front office, it all simply withers away the moment he starts to walk my direction. Our gazes are locked, fiery hot with desire, and there's only one thing I want to do.

No, one thing I *need* to do.

As soon as he crosses the threshold into the office, I'm moving, plastering myself against his body, throwing my arms around his neck, and pressing my lips firmly to his. The kiss catches him by surprise, but his delay is only a fraction of a second. His tongue pushes against my lips, seeking entrance, as he devours my mouth as if he were a starved man. The kiss is electric, and probably a little bit inappropriate, considering we're standing in the middle of a business. And thanks to the kiss to end all kisses, I'm too caught up in the moment to even care that I'm making out with Linkin in front of his boss and coworkers.

Eventually, the need to come up for air becomes too great. Just as he starts to pull his lips from my own, a throat clears behind me, followed by chuckling. "Damn, I don't recall there ever being a day when a beautiful woman came to the shop and kissed the daylights out of me," Ernie says, humor laced in his voice.

Embarrassment starts to set in.

"No? I would have thought all the pretty ladies would have been lined up back in the day, Ern," Linkin says without removing his eyes from mine.

That makes his boss laugh. "Well, my Bonnie was there with her rolling pin and cowboy boots, making sure they all stayed away," he says, slapping Linkin on the back. "I'm gonna slip into my office and make a call for a few minutes, give you two a bit to talk."

When the door closes, I finally snap out of my mortification stupor. "I can't believe I just did that," I mumble.

"You're completely irresistible to my charms."

I snort. "I see you're still as modest as ever."

"You wouldn't want me any other way," he whispers, wrapping his big hands around my waist one more time. "I take it today went well?"

Oh. Yeah. The divorce. The reason I'm here.

"It went very well. In fact, you're looking at a freshly divorced woman on a mission," I tell him, trailing my fingers down his chest. Have I told you what this tight t-shirt, smeared with grease and grime does to me? I'm totally a grease monkey bunny.

"A mission, huh? How can I help you complete your mission?" he asks, his head bends down and his lips dangerously close to that place right behind my ear that drives me wild.

"I have ideas. They don't involve your pants."

"I love it when I don't have pants."

And I love you.

Wait.

What?

Did I really just think that? There's no way I'm in love with him. I mean, we haven't known each other that long, and can you really count the first few encounters? I wanted to claw his eyes out with a nail file. For God's sake, I just got divorced! Literally, like an hour ago!

I can't be in love with him. He's infuriating and arrogant and… amazing.

He's smart and kind and sexy in a way he probably doesn't even realize. Or maybe he does. But I really like the person he is, not just the pretty face and hard body on the outside. He's so good with his brothers, helpful with his mom, and a great friend to me. But this is more than friends. These feelings I'm having are definitely *not* friendly. They're lustful and carnal. I feel cherished, yet taken in a way I've never expected, nor wanted.

But I do want this.

"Everything okay?" he asks, pulling my attention.

"Fine, yes, thank you."

"So these plans that don't involve my pants, should I bring dinner home tonight?"

Pushing all thoughts of the L word out of my mind, I focus on the here and now. "Definitely. I have a feeling you're going to need your energy later this evening," I tell him, glancing around the room to make sure we're alone before tapping the place where his dick is hard and secured in his pants.

Linkin's eyes dilate and darken, and I can almost see his dirty thoughts. "I'll bring pizza, but leave my pants at the door."

"Sounds perfect," I say, noticing a younger guy walking up to the office door. "I better leave you to it."

He reaches out and grabs my arm before I can get too far away. "What? No goodbye kiss?"

Stepping into his arms, I whisper, "I'm not sure I'll be able to stop at one more kiss…"

Linkin's groan fills the front office as the door opens and a customer enters. Our alone time has officially ended, and my guy is needed, reminding me once again that he's, in fact, at work. "I'll see you later," I say, slowly turning and heading towards the door. Before I slip outside, I glance back over my shoulder, catching Linkin's eyes firmly following my ass.

When he glances back up, he offers me a smug little grin and walks to the door. He places a too-quick kiss on my lips before whispers, "One hour, and you're mine."

Oh, I already am, Linkin.

I already am.

By the time he knocks on my door, I'm an anxious ball of overactive hormones, ready to pounce. I'm honestly afraid I may jump him and hump his leg like a dog the moment he enters my apartment. He lets himself in with his key, and my heart starts to pound with excitement.

I smell the pizza first, followed by the man. He smells musky, mixed with gasoline and grease. Call me weird, but the combination drives me wild.

Linkin sets the pizza box down on the counter and turns his dark eyes on me.

Then they drop to my outfit.

Or lack thereof.

"Jesus," he mumbles, his wide eyes still staring at my chest.

"You know," I start, slowly walking towards him, my legs crisscrossing and the red heels clicking against the cheap vinyl floor. "I saw this outfit online a few weeks ago, and I just had to have it."

Stopping in front of him, I pop my hip, my right leg out a little and my hands resting on my hips. "See, I used to *love* wearing sexy lingerie. But over the years, my efforts weren't fully appreciated, so I stopped." Taking another step forward, I run one fire engine red painted fingertip down the bust of the black leather corset. "But you seem like the type of man who would appreciate the effort."

"I'm having a heart attack," he mumbles, his eyes following the line my finger traces down to where the corset meets the black lace panties.

"Do you want me to put on something else?" I ask, my fingers toying with the ties holding the panties together at my hips.

"Fuck no," he growls, finally seeming to snap out of his trance. "I appreciate the ever-loving fuck out of your efforts right now," he confirms with a smirk.

"I figured you'd be the man for the job," I say, slowly releasing one side of the panties.

Linkin reaches out and halts my hand, keeping the ties from completely releasing. "I'm the *only* man for the job, Firecracker." His gaze burns my skin as he takes in my outfit one more time. "Now," he starts, pulling me into his arms, "let's go to the bed so I can appreciate the hell out of you."

Quickly, he bends down and lifts me into his arms. His lips are on mine a second later, hot, bruising, and branding, as he walks blindly into my bedroom. His tongue is fierce as it probes my mouth, claiming me.

The bed is soft beneath me, but there's a hardness to his voice when he speaks. "Get on your knees with your legs spread." Doing as I'm told, I kneel on my bed, my legs spread shoulder width apart, and my heart beating a furious song in my chest. It's exhilarating. Freeing.

I watch as he stands beside the bed, slowly removing his black leather belt. My pussy quivers at the thought of him using it on me. He doesn't though, and drops the belt to the floor. Slowly, he removes his work boots and tosses them off to the side, before ripping off his t-shirt and unbuckling his jeans. My eyes are glued to his fingers as he slides the zipper down, the bite of the teeth echoing in the room. He's seducing me merely by undressing.

His jeans are left hanging open as he approaches. "I haven't even gotten a look at the back," he says, walking around to the side of my bed. His appreciative groan tells me all I need to know about my purchase.

Yeah, well worth the ninety dollars.

I startle when his hands touch my bare ass. He grips my cheeks firmly, but not enough to hurt. In fact, his possessive hold does the opposite: it excites me. When I feel the light slap on my right butt cheek, I moan.

"You like that?" he asks, crawling onto the bed with me and wrapping his body around my back. "You like to be spanked?"

"Apparently," I say, breathlessly.

"Mmmm," he mumbles, running his nose around my shoulder and inhaling sharply. "I'll have to remember that."

Linkin grips my hips. "Lean forward and place your hands on the bed."

I get on all fours and wait for whatever he has planned next. I don't have to wait long before his big hands run from the backs of my thighs, up and grip my ass once again. "Seeing your ass all rosy is making me hard as fuckin' concrete," he groans, kneading the globes of my ass with his warm hands.

Groaning, I push back into his hold and I find myself on the verge of begging. Begging for him to touch me, take me. I've never felt this wild, this out of control, as I do right now, right here with him.

"I need to taste you," he says before squatting behind me. His big finger grabs the string of my thong, brushing against my swollen, soaked center as he does. Again, I'm unable to control the moan of pleasure.

"You're so wet," he says, sliding his fingers between my folds. "So fucking wet for me. Do you want me to taste you, Lexi? Do you want me to lick your sweet pussy?"

Whimpering, I try to make myself speak words, but I just can't seem to do it. My brain is officially nonfunctional, so I let my body speak for me. Pushing back against his finger, I feel the tip penetrate me.

"Is that what you want?" he asks, slipping one big finger into my center. I mumble some sort of garbled acknowledgement. Linkin slides his finger in and out, a slow, torturous movement that serves as an accelerant to the already burning fire within me.

"How about this?" he asks moments before his finger is gone. It's quickly replaced with warm breath and a hot tongue.

Linkin swipes his tongue through my pussy, licking and tasting me. His hold on my ass cheeks tenses, driving me closer to the edge. As he probes me with his tongue, I start to shake, my arms and legs weakening as my body is strung even tighter. It's too much, yet not enough all at the same time.

"Let go," he grumbles without removing his mouth. The vibrations from his words, combined with his possessive grip on my ass, push me over the edge. Blinding white light fills my vision as I gasp and wither against his face. Linkin draws every ounce of pleasure out of my orgasm with his tongue, until I'm ready to collapse in exhaustion.

"I'm not done with you, sugar," he says from somewhere behind me.

I hear the sound of him removing his jeans, but I don't have the strength to turn and watch. Instead, I wait, there on my bed on my hands and knees. I wait for his command.

Fortunately, the wait is short-lived. He climbs onto the bed with me, positioning himself at my rear. Pressing his hard chest against my back, he reaches around and gently releases my breasts from the cups of the corset. Linkin plays with my nipples, the sensitive nubs hard little buds of nerves.

When he's satisfied with the state of my nipples, he switches his focus to my panties. I feel the tug of the second tie before it's pulled away completely from my body. I'm just about to beg him to hurry when I feel the head of his large cock slide through the wetness. He moves it around, coating himself with my moisture.

"Please. Hurry." My words are choppy. A plea.

"Patience, Firecracker," he says, sliding his dick up and moving it around my ass. I tense, not really sure how I feel about him being in the no-fly zone. "Relax, baby. I won't do that. Yet." He punctuates that one word by nipping at the back of my shoulder.

Moaning, I try to stay still, try to control my breathing.

It's a lost cause.

Especially when I feel him start to push inside of me.

My pussy stretches around him, taking everything he gives. He's seated all the way in moments later, a loud sigh of pleasure ripping from my throat. "Fuck, you are so hot and wet and tight." Pulling back, he pushes back inside with a little more force this time. "I could do this every day." Out and slamming back in. "Over and over." With each word, he thrusts his hips, crashing into my body in perfect rhythm.

"Yes, yes," I chant as he continues to plunge.

I can feel a fine sheen of sweat on my overly sensitive body. Linkin continues to grip my hips tightly, surely leaving bruises with his fingers, as he pounds into my body. "Yes," I groan, arching my back and changing up the angle of his cock. And that's when it hits that wonderful place inside of me, that leaves me panting like a dog and crying out in pleasure.

Linkin slides one hand up my back, tracing the dimples and divots of my spine with his fingers. The other hand continues to hold me hostage, his hips pounding against my butt as he leads me headfirst into another orgasm. I can feel it coming, my body quaking and gripping his massive erection. His hand moves up my back and grips my shoulder, making me arch perfectly.

My release sweeps in, overwhelming and all-consuming. I bear down on him, grasping him tightly with my internal muscles, milking him dry. Linkin follows me into paradise, vocalizing his release with non-intelligent words.

When he's finally still, our bodies sated and spent, he tucks himself into the crook of my back and turns us into the bed. We're lying back to front, his body still buried within my own. He holds me firmly against his sweaty body. The only sound is our joint pants as we try to get our breathing under control.

It's perfect.

"I'd say I made the right choice in lingerie," I whisper, my lips and tongue suddenly dry.

"I'd say. Though, if you're not quite convinced, I could do a little more convincing in about an hour or so."

"An hour? I thought young twenty-six year old men had better stamina than that," I quip, intentionally trying to get a rise out of him.

"Baby, I think I've proved moreover that my *stamina* is just fine," he says, wrapping his body around mine tighter. I can actually feel his cock flex inside of me.

"How about a shower?" I ask.

"The pizza's probably cold," he adds, placing a kiss on my bare shoulder.

"Shower first, reheated pizza after," I suggest.

"Then I'm going to show you more of my stamina," he says, turning me in his arms and dislodging himself from my body.

Linkin grazes his lips over the tops of mine, slowly and savoring. A sigh of contentment slips from my throat as something bursts true in my chest.

Love.

What I feel for this man is so much deeper and more real than anything I've ever felt before, and I'm no longer scared of it. It's time to embrace it, revel in it.

It's time to live.

Linkin

20

There's an extra pep to my step as I make my way to the dive Mexican restaurant in Westville. I haven't been here in months, not since my last payment. And after today, this'll be the last fucking time I'm here.

I walk inside, anxious to get this little meeting over with.

The restaurant is dimly lit with Mexican music piping through the speakers. I bypass the hostess stand, keeping my head down as I head straight to the back of the room. There, sitting at the same table as always, is the man who took everything from my family.

No, that's not exactly true.

He was the facilitator.

My piece of shit stepfather, wherever the fuck he is, is the reason. This man just helped.

I slide into the bench across from Hector. He doesn't even look up as he shovels forkfuls of refried beans into his open trap.

Without saying a word, I reach into the inside jacket pocket and pull out an envelope.

"Two?" he asks, glancing up only to look at the envelope on the table.

"All of it," I say, no emotion in my voice.

That gets his attention.

Setting his fork down, he wipes his mouth with a tattered napkin and reaches for the envelope. Without removing the bills, he counts out five thousand. Hector glances up at me, his dark eyebrows raised into his shaggy hair. "You rob a bank?"

"How I got the money isn't your business. That's the final payment. We're done."

"Done," he confirms, shoving the money into his pocket.

"Call my mom. Tell her that her last payment was it." My tone is to the point and emotionless, but inside, I'm a ball of fucking energy.

Hector whips out his phone and dials. "Karen, my love, how are you?" I swear I almost fly across the table. My fists ball up under the table, and it takes every ounce of control I have not to react. "Good news, the debt is paid. Your last payment covered it." He listens for a moment before adding, "If you ever need any help with money, you call," but before he can say his name, I'm ripping the phone from his hand and hanging up.

With one swift swipe of my finger, I delete my mom's contact info from the dirtbag's phone. "That's enough. Don't ever contact my mom again. You're paid in full."

"I am," he says, taking his phone back from me. "If you ever see your daddy again, tell him his line of credit has been restored."

"He ain't my daddy," I growl menacingly. "Don't contact us again. We're done," I say, sliding out of the bench.

"We're done," he confirms, nodding his head. A look of respect washes over his face. "You're a good man, Linkin. It wasn't your mess, but you cleaned it up. Take care of your mom," he adds before I turn towards the door and walk out.

The sunlight is almost blinding as I step out of the restaurant, but I feel weightless. Relieved.

We're free.

I'm not sure what has me pulling into this particular parking lot as I arrive back at Jupiter Bay, but I don't question it. I climb out of my old Blazer and head inside the brick building.

My hands are stuffed into my pockets as I approach the receptionist's desk. It's tall and imposing and sort of hides the pleasant woman on the other side. "Can I help you?" she asks, beaming a bright white smile and friendly disposition.

"Uh, yeah. Is Dean here? Dean McIntire?" I ask nervously, which makes her smile falter.

"Is he expecting you?"

"No, I don't have an appointment. Can you tell him Linkin Stone is here to see him?"

She nods her head politely and heads down the hallway. She returns a few moments later, Dean hot on her heels. "Linkin," he says, offering me a smile as he pushes up his glasses to perch higher on his nose. "Everything okay?"

"Yeah, sure. Actually, I was wondering if you had a few minutes? I'm sure you're busy since it's tax season and all. I promise not to take up too much of your time." Again, I feel nervous and rock on the balls of my feet to keep moving.

"Sure," he says before turning to the receptionist. "Hold my calls."

I follow Dean into a large office. He offers me a chair, but doesn't go around to sit on the opposite side of the desk. Instead, he takes the seat beside me, which instantly puts me a bit at ease. The last time I was on this side of a large desk, I was in the principal's office for skipping school.

"What can I help you with?" he asks, giving me his full attention.

"I know you're not a financial advisor, or whatever in the hell they're called, but I was hoping you might help me get some things squared away for the future. Or at least give a direction on how to start."

"What are you thinking?" he asks, leaning forward and looking me straight in the eye. His interest is definitely piqued.

The next thing I know, I'm telling him my entire story. Everything about my mom and brothers, the reason we left Westville, and the debt I just paid. I even go as far as to tell him about Lexi and my offer to help her conceive. He's officially the only person I've ever told about my past, without glossing over the big things, but there's something I like about Dean. He seems genuine and trustworthy, which isn't something I'm accustomed to.

Except where Lexi and her family is concerned.

We spend the next thirty minutes going over my finances, or lack thereof. I'm starting with nothing, but I have a thousand reasons to improve that situation. By this time next week, I'll have a savings account, checking account, and something called an IRA. Whatever the fuck that means.

But if it's going to help me protect my future – a future I want with Lexi and any potential unborn children I may be fortunate to have – I'm all in. But I can't exactly offer her nothing, so it's time to get my ducks in a fucking row. That starts today.

***

"Get in the shower," I tell Jack for the third time in the last fifteen minutes.

The knuckleheads are running around in their underwear and the new armor Lexi got them for Christmas. I'm not sure what the hell is going on, but they're wound the fuck up tight tonight, and they're both grating on my last nerve.

"Jack!" I holler over the dying in the living room. When I enter the room, I trip over a wire strung about six inches off the floor and fall.

"Dammit, Jeff!" I growl, picking myself up off the floor.

"Dammit, Jeff!" Jack mimics in a pretty good impression of my no-nonsense voice. If I weren't so pissed off, I'd find it funny.

But I don't.

"Jack, don't say that!"

"Jack, don't say that!" he copycats, swinging his sword around and almost knocking his twin's head off.

"I swear to God," I start, but my threat is cut off by a knock at the door.

Tripping over a remote control car, I throw open the door, surprised to see Emma there. "Hey," I say, stepping aside as she pushes her way in.

"I was just over at Abby and Levi's, dropping off a pecan pie and a vibrating butt plug, and thought I'd stop by and say hello," she says so casually, I almost miss what the hell she just said.

"What?"

"Oh, don't act like you've never heard of a vibrating butt plug. It was a free gift with my last purchase at Adam & Eve. I already have three, so I shared it with sweet little Abby. Anyway, I thought I'd stop by and see what you were up to. Oh, look at this!" she exclaims, walking into my living room. "You're having a party! I love parties."

I follow behind the little ol' lady who's already grabbing a sword and hoisting it high above her head. "Grandma loves a good, hard sword! Can I play?" she asks my brothers, who stare at the crazy old woman like she has two heads.

"You want to play gladiators with us?" Jeff asks, surprised, yet hopeful.

"Damn right, I do!" she exclaims, smiling widely as she kills my little brother.

"Oh! She got me!" Jack stumbles around, drawing out and overacting his untimely death.

"I'm better with the flesh sword, you know, but this will do just fine," Emma mumbles to me, an ornery smirk on her face, before she proceeds to dance around my living room like a banshee and stalks after my other brother.

"Could I, uh, get you a glass of tea? Or water?" I ask, scratching my head and watching her interact with my brothers.

"Maybe some water, son," she says, swinging the sword around with a battle cry. I run off to my kitchen.

A few minutes later, Emma joins me in the kitchen, a satisfied look on her face. "So those are the brothers?"

"They are. Sorry they're a little wound up tonight," I apologize, handing her a glass of water.

"Don't worry about it. I helped raise six girls. You don't know what chaos is until they're all trying to use the bathroom at the same time." I snort a laugh, picturing Lexi and her sisters all fighting to get into the bathroom to get ready for school.

"It's awfully quiet in there. I should go check on them."

"Oh, don't worry about that. Jack is in the shower and Jeff is reading a book."

I blink once, twice, multiple times, trying to process what she just said. "Excuse me? You got Jack in the shower? And Jeff to... read?"

"Of course, Grandma did!" She takes a few steps until she's standing practically right in front of me. She glances around conspiratorially before whispering, "The key is to make them think it was their idea. I asked the boys what they were supposed to do before bed, and the next thing you know, they're offering to read and shower."

Rubbing my head, I reply, "I have so much to learn."

"You'll do just fine," she says, patting my hand. The knowing look in her eyes makes me wonder if maybe she knows about Lexi's and my arrangement. And that would make sense. Lexi's very close to her family, so why wouldn't she discuss having a baby with me?

"Would you like to stay for a bit?" I ask as she heads towards the door.

"No, my Orvie is waiting on me. He took one of his little blue pills, so I'm on the clock to get home," she adds, checking her watch.

I follow her to the door, and hold it open. "Thanks for stopping by."

She gazes up at me with kind, smiling eyes. "Link, you're a good man. Keep making my granddaughter happy and everything will fall into place." She reaches up, grabs me around the neck, and pulls me down towards her lips. I think she's going to place one of those grandmotherly kisses on the cheek, but no. Not Emma.

Lexi's grandma presses her lips against mine, rendering me completely speechless and immobile. She pulls away quickly, a satisfied smirk on her face before throwing me a wave over her shoulder. "Tata!"

Then she's gone, leaving behind the scent of sugar cookies and mothballs.

I shake my head, trying to get the image of Emma's liplock out of my head. It was innocent, sure, but still. It's my girl's eighty-one-year-old grandma. Not exactly something I want to think about. Ever.

Instead, I take a quick moment to enjoy the silence and check my phone. There's a message from Lexi, who is working late tonight at the salon.

> **Lexi:** A client just asked me to trim his nose hairs. They were so long, they looked like they were climbing out of his nose and waving at me.
>
> **Linkin:** Makes note to grow out nose hairs. It drives Lexi wild.
>
> **Lexi:** You know it. *smiley winky face*

And before I can reply, she sends me another message.

> **Lexi:** I'll be done in fifteen. I'm getting ready to blow dry my last appointment.
>
> **Linkin:** And you're coming here?

Lexi:	Are the boys there?
Linkin:	Are you using me to get close to the boys?
Lexi:	Definitely. It's not every day a boy professes his love before slaying his brother with a sword.
Linkin:	True. Jack has me beat there. Maybe I need a better sword.
Lexi:	No, you're sword is pretty amazing. It's my favorite of all swords.
Linkin:	Good to know. My sword will be very excited to see you.
Lexi:	Thirty minutes.
Linkin:	Make it twenty-five and there might be a reward.
Lexi:	Will it involve pizza? I'm starving.
Linkin:	You know me well.
Lexi:	Gotta go. See you soon.

I smile as I set my phone down, ready for Lexi to come home. Home. This place is small and lifeless without her. Sure, my brothers turn it upside down and make the walls shake, but it's not the same thing. This isn't their home. They just stay here when my mom needs help.

But when Lexi's here, everything is alive. The sounds, the smells, the lifeless walls. She makes this small, dingy little apartment a home. My home. Our home.

How in the hell did this happen? I went from a guy not wanting any of this to a man wanting all of it.

As I check on my brother in the shower and make sure the other finished reading his required chapters, I throw some leftover pizza in the microwave and wait for my girl to get here. Because even when I was surrounded by noise, I was alone. I floated through life, aimlessly and recklessly, doing what I had to, trying to get by.

But now I want to stop running. I want to settle down. I want Lexi.

And it's time to tell her.

Lexi

"We need more penises!" Grandma bellows, clapping her hands victoriously.

"Seriously? There's more cock in this place than a Chippendales Show," Levi says, shoving another blow-up penis onto the end of the bar.

"Actually, back in the day, the first male dancers weren't Chippendales. There was a group known as the Petal Teasers who had the ladies lined up with their quarters."

"Petal Teasers?" Payton asks, moving the penis streamers hanging in front of her face.

"Lesser known, obviously. And their name could have used a little work. I tried to tell Ross that when he started the club, but you know men. They never listen to a woman."

"Club?" I ask at the same time Jaime asks, "Ross?"

"Anyway," Grandma says, waving her hand. "The boys couldn't get along, each one wanting the spotlighted feature, which resulted in one of them leaving. Hence, the Chippendales."

"Are you saying you know the people who started the Chippendales?" Dean asks, removing the blow-up cock from his mouth. Wait. That didn't come out right. He was blowing it up, not blowing-

Nevermind.

"Knew them? Honey, who do you think taught them their trademarked hip thrusts?"

I swear you could hear a pin drop in Lucky's. Everyone setting up for the joint bachelor and bachelorette party this evening is silent as we wait for her to elaborate. Or not. Maybe it's best we don't know the rest of this story.

"Anyway, what I learned a long time ago, kids, is that there can never be enough penises, especially when celebrating the pending nuptials of two crazy kids who enjoy getting their freak on."

"Please don't say *getting their freak on*," I beg.

"At least she didn't call it *the sex*," Abby chimes in beside me.

"Oh, there will definitely be *the sex* going on," Grandma adds. "We were right beside them at that bed and breakfast two summers ago. I think that stallion was capable of breaking the bed, if given enough time."

"My ears are starting to bleed," Meghan whimpers, shoving little rubber dicks into her ears like earbuds.

"That's why they're so perfect for each other. Two sexual creatures, destined to spend the rest of their lives together, procreating and lusting after one another," she says, looking out into the room with some weird far-off dream look on her face.

"Gross," AJ groans. "Stop referring to our sister – your *granddaughter* – as a sexual creature. It's not normal."

"Sex is normal, AJ. It's healthy, and if you have the right dancing partner, the horizontal tango is a serious health benefit! I mean, how do you think your grandpa and I have lived such a long, healthy life? Regular sex is a big part of life longevity,"

Grandma says, causing several faces to turn a weird shade of green.

"What time is the happy couple arriving?" Dad asks, breaking up the nightmare-inducing conversation from only moments ago.

"Seven. They're having dinner uptown and coming by for drinks," Meghan adds, helping Linkin hang a few more streamers (these sans penises) from the ceiling. "We have thirty minutes."

"She thinks it's for our monthly sisters' night that we delayed two weeks and Ryan is just going to drop her off," I say. No one brings up the reason for the delay, but I was told it was because of Meghan's fiancé who passed away a year before, earlier in the month.

Grandma sticks her head beside mine, making me jump. "I still think we could have benefited from a couples dress-up theme."

"Not everyone is a couple, Grandma," I reply quietly, concerned about Meghan overhearing.

"Yeah," AJ chimes in, a look of annoyance on her face.

"But I had my Christian and Ana costumes ready to go, Alison Jane. I suppose there's still time to change. I could go put it on."

"For the love of all things holy, don't you dare dress up as Anastasia Steele tonight," I beg her. As I turn, I'm hypnotized by the way Linkin moves on the bar as he's hanging the rest of the blue streamers. His customary black t-shirt rides up, exposing a few inches of toned, sexy happy trail, which causes my overactive hormones to spark to life.

In fact, these pesky hormones have been so over-the-top lately. It all started earlier in the week with my boobs hurting and my sex drive revving up to a gazillion RPMs. In the last few years, I've been obsessed with conceiving enough to know what these symptoms point to. But I held strong, trying not to give in to my feverish desire to run to the drug store and purchase fifteen different pregnancy tests. Not until I was late.

Today, I was late.

And I have a secret; one that I can't wait to share.

"Speaking of procreating," Grandma starts, snapping my thoughts from my libido, as she gets right in my face. "You're positively... glowing tonight," she says with a wicked smile.

"Thank you," I reply, dropping my eyes and my voice.

"Does he know?"

I glance up, shocked, yet not really surprised in the least. "No. I just found out."

"He's going to be so excited," she whispers.

"He is," I confirm, glancing back to the bar area where Linkin is talking with my dad and Levi.

"When are you going to tell him?"

"I was trying to figure out a clever way to tell him, but all I keep coming back to is just shouting it out."

"Oh, Lexi Lou, you don't need some creative baby announcement. When you're ready just say the words and sit back and watch his face light up. I promise you, you won't want to miss that part. I remember the look on your grandpa's face when I told him I was pregnant with Trish," she says softly, her green eyes filling with tears. Hearing the emotion in her voice is enough to send my crazy-sensitive emotional status teetering on hysterics.

"I wish I had more time with her," I whisper, the words choking the air out of me.

"We all do, sweetie. She was an amazing woman, but more than that, she was an amazing mother." I fight the tears. "And do you know what?" she asks, giving me her full attention. It's as if we're the only two in the room. "I have no doubt in my mind that you, Alexis Summer, will be just as wonderful to this child." Before I realize what's happening, she has her hand gently resting on my stomach.

The tears fall unchecked. I glance around, and notice no one paying us any attention, which is probably a good thing, considering I'm crying and my grandma has her hand on my belly.

But then my glaze shifts and lands on Linkin. Concern fills his eyes as he takes in my tear-streaked face. He's moving before I can even offer him an *I'm okay* smile.

"Tell him when you're ready, child. He'll be over the moon with excitement... just like the rest of us." Grandma offers me a wink before disappearing.

"What's wrong? Are you okay?" he asks, looking me up and down for any signs of problems.

"I'm fine," I say, clearing my throat. "She got me a little emotional, is all."

"That's it?" he asks, looking like he's ready to defend my honor and sleigh the dragons.

"Yeah. She talked a bit about my mother," I say softly, feeling sad for all that I – and my sisters – have lost, but so incredibly blessed to have had her for the handful of years we did.

Linkin wraps his arms around me, pulling me tightly into his chest. His hug is warm and comforting as I breathe in the familiarity. How can someone I've known mere months mean more to me than anyone else ever has?

Because I love him.

And it's so much more consuming than anything I've ever experienced. He's the wind in my sails as he helps guide me through oceans. He's the sun as it rises high in the sky, lighting up my day. He's the air I breathe, the comfort I call home.

He's everything.

I almost tell him right there, but then I hear Payton holler. "They're here!"

Instead, I grab his hand and pull him towards the center of the room with the rest of my family. There's a few regulars sitting at the bar, smiling and watching the chaos, while Lucky pours drinks behind the counter. We picked this particular location because there's a band performing at The Beaver, therefore we'd have this place mostly to ourselves.

So far, the plan has worked.

"I can't believe she was staring at you like that. Seriously, I was sitting right there! It's not like she couldn't see me! I was the one with my hand down your pants while she was flirting with you, and I'll be the one with your tongue between my-" Jaime gripes, stopping when she enters the bar, Ryan hot on her heels. "What's this?"

"Surprise!" we all answer together.

"What the…" she yells, a happy-surprise look on her face.

"Why are there dicks all over the bar?" Ryan asks, glancing around at the obscene amount of penises in the room.

"Grandma was in charge of decorations," Meghan answers.

"That explains it," Ryan says, shrugging off his jacket and taking Jaime's from her arm.

"You guys," Jaime calls before running into our waiting arms. We're a big mess of twelve arms all gripping and hugging each other. I love our group hugs, though I'll admit, most of them happen at the end of the evening after the alcohol has been flowing and all that's left is talk about road-head.

"It's a surprise bachelor and bachelorette party," Abby says, connecting all of the dots for our sister.

"Thank you so much," she says, tears swimming in her matching emerald green eyes. "I can't believe you did all of this. *And* were able to keep it a secret," she adds with a laugh. Truth is, we're not the best with secrets. Each of us came equipped with a sister lie detector system which is able to scope out a sister's secret at fifty paces.

"Anything for you," Payton says, turning and grabbing the drinks off the tray Dean is holding beside her.

She hands shot glasses to each of us, careful not to spill any of the amber liquid from within. I hold the small glass in my hand, suddenly fearful of spilling my secret. All eyes will be on me – Lexi, the wild one – as I refuse to take the shot. They'll know. They'll figure out my secret before I've had a chance to tell Linkin. And let's be honest, I've imagined telling him about being pregnant fifty thousand ways, but in a bar was never one of them.

On top of that, it's Jaime and Ryan's big night. The last thing I want to do is steal their thunder and make tonight all about me. That would be very uncool little sister of me, and I'd never want to do that to my sister.

"What's wrong? You're staring at that shot like it's about to tell you Victoria's secret," Linkin says softly beside me.

"Oh, I was just thinking that I haven't eaten much today. Doing a shot before I eat probably isn't the brightest idea."

"Ahh," he says with that trademarked smirk. "Fear not, fair maiden, I shall take the shot on your behalf and no one will be the wiser." This time, I get that sexy little wink. "And maybe when you're feelin' like drinkin', I'll talk you into sharing the secret."

My body tenses with fear. "Secret?" I ask, my throat suddenly dry and my heart trying to claw its way from my chest.

"Yeah, you know… Victoria's secret? I'd love to get an up close, personal view later this evening of what treasures and secrets Lexi has beneath that sweater," he whispers, his deep voice dripping with sex.

"Oh. That secret." God! I'm such an idiot. I'm going to give away the secret completely on my own and will have no one to blame but myself. Quickly trying to draw attention away, I slide against his hard, unforgiving body and practically purr. "I'll definitely let you in on *that* secret later tonight."

"Attention, everyone!" Payton hollers over the jukebox in the corner and the Summer girls' giggles. "Tonight, we're here to celebrate the upcoming wedding of our sister Jaime to Ryan. Jaime, we couldn't be happier that you've finally found your happily ever after." Jaime turns and snuggles into Ryan's side, her smile wide and full of happiness. "And Ryan, thanks for not running away screaming after you met our crazy family. In fact, we think you fit in nicely, and we're blessed to have you become a part of it in a few weeks."

"To Ryan and Jaime," my dad says proudly, lifting his shot glass high in the air.

"To Ryan and Jaime," everyone echoes before taking their shot of hard liquor.

I can feel Grandma's eyes on me, but I don't look over to confirm. I know if I do, I'll blurt it out right here and now. I keep my eyes on the floor, careful not to make eye contact with anyone in the room.

Suddenly, I feel the glass pulled from my fingers and replaced quickly with an empty one. Linkin throws back the second shot before anyone is the wiser. A sigh of relief slips from my lips as my eyes connect with his dark chocolate ones. They're shining with mischief and maybe the start of a little buzz.

Grandpa steps forward, a second round of shots ready to go.

"Uh, Grandpa, I'm not sure that's a good idea. I need to eat something," Meghan says, a concerned look on her pretty face.

"Oh, come on Meggy Pie! How often does your granddaughter get married?" she asks, then suddenly freezes. "Well, that other time doesn't count," Grandma quickly adds, referring to the first engagement Jaime had. Gavin left her the week of her wedding because he realized he was gay.

"Anyway, to our beautiful Jaime," Grandpa says, choking a bit on his emotions. "It has been a joy watching you grow into the superb, compassionate woman you are today. I know you'll make Ryan very happy."

"To Jaime and Ryan," Grandma adds, raising another shot above her head.

"To Jaime and Ryan," we all cheer.

Before Grandma throws back her drink, she loudly declares, "To road-head!"

And the room falls silent once more.

Linkin

22

The party has been in full swing for the last hour. Lucky was kind enough to let us take over the place, without charging us any sort of rental – even though we offered. Instead, I told him I'd help clean up afterwards and even offered to help behind the bar. Of course, with The Beaver hosting a band tonight, the place is pretty empty, which is why he was fine with us having the party here. He's making more money off the Summer family than he would have without them.

"I brought you all something," Orval says as he takes a seat at the table where Levi, Dean, Ryan, and myself are seated. We've been watching the girls with their dad and Grandma shooting pool, darts, and trash talking better than most guys I've met over my time tending bar.

"Did you make those?" Dean asks Levi, who is sort of the resident Betty Crocker. The dude can cook and bake just about anything. I'd give him a good ribbing over it, but the fact is his shit is good so I keep my mouth shut. That way, he keeps making stuff for us.

"Nope," Levi says, glancing down at the plate of chocolate brownies.

"I made them," Grandpa declares proudly. "My Emma was off getting her hair done earlier at the salon with Lexi, so I thought I'd whip up a batch of my famous double chocolate brownies. They're delicious! Try one," he encourages, shoving the plate in Dean's face.

"Fine," he says, taking one from the plate. We all watch as he slowly takes a small bite, chewing carefully.

"Wow, not bad," Deans says with a shrug before taking a much bigger bite.

"What, did you think I was going to poison ya?" Grandpa asks, laughing, as he holds the plate out for Ryan and me to each grab one.

"I don't know, Orval, would you?" Levi asks with a cheeky grin.

"Poison ya? Naw, that's not my style," he says, eyes sparkling under the fluorescent lighting and neon beer signs.

My mouth waters when I take my first bite. These were the type of treats that were rare when I was growing up, but when Mom would make something, it was chocolate brownies. They're one of my favorites. "These are damn good," I tell Orval, polishing off one brownie and diving in for a second. Doesn't matter that I just ate a plate full of appetizers and other junk food that the girls brought.

They're brownies.

And they're fucking good.

It doesn't take long before the four of us polish off the small plate of brownies. Orval smiles proudly as he looks down at the empty tray. There's nothing left but crumbs. Hell, I think Levi even licked the crumbs.

We're all chatting loudly and telling stories, yet still keeping our eyes on the girls. It's my first taste of sitting on this side of the bar, shooting the shit with people who I'm starting to consider my family. Warmth spreads through my chest as I seek out my girl. She's standing with her twin, who may look similar in physical features, but is night and day different in personality. Abby has that whole sweet and innocent thing going on, and Lexi is, well, not. Not saying she isn't sweet or innocent, but Lexi has a wild streak begging to come out and a feisty side that I love to rile up.

When she looks up, our gazes clash and I feel it like a punch to my gut. The wind is knocked out of me the moment she smiles, which suddenly is stirring up other things below the belt. It's a heady feeling to love someone, yet fearful of fucking it all up at the same time. She's far too good for me, but I'd be damned lucky if I had the chance to spend the rest of my life making her happy.

Standing up, I make my way to the middle of the room to meet her, since she's already heading my direction. "Dance with me," I instruct, since it's not really a question.

Her eyebrow shoots skyward and a tiny smirk crosses her lips, but she doesn't call me out on my rudeness. Instead, she links her hand in mine and follows behind to the center of the makeshift dance floor. The old karaoke machine is fired up, though no one has used it tonight. Together, we slow dance to some old country tune about finding everlasting love.

Ironic, right?

"The party is a success," I tell her, boastful of the amount of work Lexi and her sisters put into the party.

"It is. Jaime was totally surprised, and is well on her way to being happily drunk. Ryan is sure to get road-head tonight."

"Road-head, huh?" I ask, waggling my eyebrows at her and giving her my best dirty smirk.

"Maybe if you're a good boy," she replies sweetly.

"I have it on good authority that you prefer me when I'm bad." That gets the familiar sparkle back in to her eyes. She was looking a little tired and rundown earlier, and I've been trying to keep a close eye on her. I'm glad we have no plans for tomorrow so she can sleep in and hopefully catch up on some much needed rest.

Well, that's if my wayward cock doesn't decide to be a dick and wake her up too early. You know him, all needy and hard for her all the damn time. I'm like a walking hard-on. *Kinda like now*, I think, casually adjusting myself.

We finish up the song, but the discomfort in my pants is starting to really piss me off, so I excuse myself to head to the john. Lexi's off to throw darts with her dad, which gives me a few minutes to get my cock under control. I mean, I know she's hot and he's super excited for later tonight, but this is a bit excessive, even for him. It's like I'm a teenager all over again and the hot cheerleader just walked into class.

Hoping that using the head will help alleviate the hardness in my pants is fruitless. In fact, it's fucking difficult as hell. Have you ever tried to piss with a hard-on? No? Well, it's not comfortable, my friend, not to mention the fact that things are pointed straight up, but you're trying to piss down. Fun times.

Levi comes in a few seconds later and approaches the urinal next to mine. He's kinda grumbling under his breath, but I don't comment. I mean, we're not exactly in the right situation or place to ask if everything is all right, ya know?

"Jesus," he mumbles, clearly having some sort of issue over there. I don't care how good of a friend the guy is I'm still not asking questions.

When my deed is finally done, I head over and wash my hands. It seems to take Levi a few extra seconds to piss, like me. Not that I'm noticing or anything. Shit. This is weird. And wrong.

So very wrong.

Is it hot in here? I'm suddenly sweating.

As I'm drying my hands, anxious to get out of the sweatbox of a bathroom, Levi joins me at the sink. "Hey, man," he says, his voice seeming a little strained.

Like mine.

"Uh, hey," I mirror, shooting the paper towel into the basket like a pro baller. Before I can make my escape, the door opens and Dean comes in.

"Oh, uh, hey," he says, turning his back to us and sliding over to a urinal.

"Hey," Levi and I mirror.

"I'm just gonna…" Dean says, his voice trailing off as he slips past the urinals and goes into the stall.

I have my back to the room as I try to conceal the gun suddenly ready to fire in my pants. What the hell is wrong with me? Even if I were sporting wood while holding my girl on the dance floor (even if her talking about later tonight got me revved up to six thousand RPMs), there's no way I'd still be chubby after visiting the bathroom with other dudes in it. It's time to get the hell out of this bathroom.

The bar is still dimly lit, with very few customers. Well, other than the Summer clan. "Presents!" Payton hollers from the back of the room. She's standing next to a table of gifts, presumably for the bride and groom.

I slowly make my way over to where Lexi is standing, careful to use her as cover for my raging boner. Slipping behind her, I wrap my arms around her waist and kiss the back of her head. She smells like flowers and some other girly shit that smells amazing. Of course, the cock banging against the inside of my zipper would completely agree.

"I'm almost a little afraid," Jaime says, her speech a bit slurred, as she takes one of the chairs up front. Yet, there's no hiding the smile on her face. When Ryan joins her, he seems… off. A little sweaty, maybe? His cheeks are a bit flushed. I'm not sure what the deal is. Ryan, like me and the rest of the guys, stopped drinking quite a while ago after a beer or two, so he shouldn't be buzzed up. Yet, he looks like he's as uncomfortable as a nun in a strip club.

"Don't you worry, Jaime, we have you all covered for the honeymoon!" Emma exclaims, loud and proud, to the entire bar. Probably a good thing there aren't many people in here.

"That's what I was afraid of," she mumbles, reaching for the first gift bag that's handed to her.

She carefully opens the gift, removing a small card. "May all your nights be kinky, love Payton and Dean." Jaime slowly eases a box from the bag. Ryan helps hold it, placing the box in his lap, while his fiancée removes the lid.

"Woooo," Meghan declares, fanning her face, when Jaime holds up some sexy little white outfit. It's lacy and sheer and will barely cover her. In fact, I'm not sure much of her will be covered at all. Ryan seems to appreciate it, though, grinning like the cat that ate the damn canary.

"Someone's gonna get lucky," AJ proclaims loudly.

"That's the point," Payton adds.

Jaime and Ryan open several gifts with lingerie ranging from sweet and innocent to scantily clad and illegal, as well as some sex toys that make her blush. I've never seen this side of a bachelorette party before. I mean, I've been to a handful of bachelor parties over the last few of years, which usually just consists of beer and maybe a stripper. This is my first experience with vibrators and floggers (those came from Emma and Orval).

"One left," Payton says, handing Jaime the large gift.

Jaime opens the box, and whatever is in it, makes her cry. Ryan gazes in the box before wrapping his arm around his fiancée, pulling her close to his chest.

"What is it?" AJ asks, the sisters all leaning forward to catch a glimpse of the gift.

She doesn't speak, instead pulling it from the box and flipping it around to show the crowd. It's a framed piece with three photos. Across the top it reads Generations of Love. Beneath it is three photos, two wedding photos and one casual one of the bride and groom-to-be.

"Oh my God," Lexi whispers beside me. "That's my grandparents… and mom and dad on their wedding day."

"Who's it from?" AJ asks, kneeling in front of the picture and lightly touching the photo of their parents.

Jaime reaches into the box and pulls out the card. She starts to read silently before bursting into tears. She hands the note to Ryan before burying her face in his chest. He glances down at the card, reading it to himself, before hugging the crying woman tighter against him. "It's from Meghan." His voice is soft as he glances up and locks his eyes with hers. The smile he gives her is laced with pain, but shows just how much he appreciates whatever the note said.

Not a lot is said after that. There are hugs and tears and everyone raises whatever glass they're holding. Brian says a toast as we all raise our hands in the air in memory of a man I never knew, but suspect I would have really liked.

"Thank you for this," Meghan says with tears glistening in her green eyes, holding her glass. "But that's not why we're here. We're here tonight to celebrate Jaime and Ryan. What you share is an unbreakable, forever kinda love that we have watched grow over their time together. Josh loved you guys and he would want us to celebrate, not cry. So, let's drink to love. Love is real, love is alive, and love is forever."

"Love is forever," they cheer around me, downing the water I switched to.

A bit later, the party is winding down. Orval and Emma left just a few minutes ago, with Brian in tow. He made us (us being Dean, Levi, and myself) promise that we'd get everyone home safely. Especially Meghan. He's more concerned about her. She's put on a brave face tonight, but no one could miss the far-off looks on her face or the tears in her eyes.

The girls are pleasantly plastered. They're singing karaoke (horribly, I might add) and dancing around on the small stage up front. The regulars left a bit ago, leaving just us in the bar with Lucky. The guys and I have been drinking water, flushing that last shot from our system, and picking up the penises. Seriously, they're everywhere. After a final rendition of "Pour Some Sugar On Me," they finally set the mics down and come help clean up.

My eyes have been on Lexi the entire time. She's glowing, probably from excitement and alcohol, and I'm getting a little more than anxious to get her home and into bed. Of course, my cock has been on board with this plan since we were dancing. He's still hard and raring to go, which is a bit alarming.

I'm just about to make my way over to where she's at and claim those bee-stung lips when the front door opens. A few of the regulars have come and gone all night, but this one stands out like a sore dick. He's wearing pressed Oxford pants and a button-down shirt. His shoes probably cost more than I make in a month slinging beers at the bar. His stylish hair is combed perfectly and his eyes laser sharp as they seek out the one woman I'd come to blows over.

Chris mother-fucking-douchebag Jacobson.

23

Lexi

I don't see him come in the bar, but can feel the change in the air. My eyes are on Linkin, so it isn't hard to miss the way he visibly tenses and sort of snarls at the door. When I glance over, I am shocked to find Chris standing there, scanning the room. Then his eyes find me, and my stomach lurches.

He's moving towards me, a warm smile on his face. My stomach twists again with uneasiness and uncertainty as he comes to stand before me. "Alexis," he says, his voice low and soft.

"Chris," I reply without any emotion. "What are you doing here?"

"I came for you," he says sweetly, another friendly smile on his face.

Before I can reply, there's a presence behind me. I don't have to turn to know who has stepped up behind me. I can smell his soap and feel the invisible pulses that vibrate between us.

"For me?" I ask, annoyance and stubbornness sweeping through my blood.

"Everything okay?" Linkin asks, stepping beside me and crossing his arms over his expansive chest.

"Everything will be just as it should be shortly," Chris snarls at Linkin.

"Yeah, with you out of here," he replies, not fazed in the least by Chris's presence.

"I don't think so, Linkin. In fact, I'm willing to bet that once Alexis hears what I have to say, it'll be *you* who will be vacating the building."

"You think so?" Linkin taunts, that cocky grin spreading across his face.

"I know so," he growls, turning his attention back to me. "Alexis," he starts, but I cut him off.

"It's Lexi."

"Lexi," Chris tries again, rolling his eyes at what he probably considers my immaturity. He knows I hate to be called Alexis. It's too formal, too stuffy, and frankly, I just don't like it after years of him calling me *only* by my birth name.

"How well do you know this man?" Chris asks, bringing my thoughts back to his interruption.

"Excuse me?" I ask.

"I'm willing to bet you don't know much about this man at all. He has a past, Ale- Lexi, and he's hiding it from you."

"What are you talking about?" I ask, frustration and exhaustion setting in.

"He's a gambler! He has connections to some very questionable people back in Westville, and has been giving them large sums of money on a regular basis!" Chris proclaims before opening a manila folder he had tucked under his arm. Inside are pictures of Linkin sitting at a table, handing over an envelope that appears to be full of cash. And if I were looking for confirmation, the next picture is of the greasy man looking in the envelope, counting the cash. "You see? He's a con man, a criminal," he declares, pointing down to the photos I hold in my hand.

And then he says the one thing that almost brings me to my knees. "And this is who you chose to have a baby with."

I gasp, glaring up at him. "You have no right to judge me or the choices I make!"

"We can fix this. Together," he begs, reaching for my hand.

"Fix this? You had a vasectomy! There's no fixing that!" I yell, not even caring who hears. Gasps fill the room, reminding me that I never confessed to my sisters as to why I left Chris. Well, no one but Abby.

"That was a mistake," he says quietly.

"A mistake? A fucking mistake!?"

He blanches at my unsavory adjective. "Ale- Lexi, look, we all make mistakes. I want you. I want us."

"There *is* no us."

"But there could be," he begs, taking another step forward. Linkin growls loudly behind me, making Chris's steps falter. "I've made an appointment at the clinic in Richmond to have it reversed. We can work past this."

"No." There's conviction in my voice and I feel it all the way to my toes. Even if Linkin isn't who he says he is, there's no way I'm going back to Chris. My heart is no longer his, if it really ever was.

"No?" he asks, glancing over at Linkin. "But, he's-"

"Whatever he is isn't your concern, Chris. We're over. Even if you hadn't gone and had the vasectomy, things weren't going well. I was alone all the time, and I wasn't happy."

"But I was working hard to give you everything you could have dreamed of," he whines in that tone that has always grated on my nerves.

"Except, you didn't. You denied me the one thing I wanted more than anything, and not the baby. I wanted your time, Chris, and you never gave it to me. I was second to everything else in your life, and it was finally enough. Finding that paper under our bed was the straw that broke the camel's back." Taking a step forward, I place my hand on his arm. "It's over."

Chris looks completely forlorn, and his sadness breaks my heart. Not because I love him, but because I don't anymore. Because whatever I felt for him is gone, and getting to this point was still painful. It hurt when I realized my marriage was over, even if I masked that hurt with anger.

"But him? He's trouble," Chris says, pointing to Linkin.

"And I can explain everything in those pictures," Linkin says casually, his arms still crossed over his chest as if he doesn't have a care in the world.

"Well? Let's hear it," Chris encourages, his tone sarcastic and impatient, as he crosses his arms trying to mimic Linkin. There's no comparison in size, and definitely not in muscle volume.

Linkin turns, giving my ex-husband his back and giving me his full attention. "Hi, baby," he says, offering me that smirk that does weird things to my panties. "I was planning on telling you all of this, but wanted to wait until it was over to spill the details.

"My stepfather was a gambler. He was a lousy piece of shit who lost everything my mother worked for. He was barely around, and when he was, he was usually drunk. He owed a shit-ton of money to bad people, and when they came to collect, he ran, like the chicken-shit coward he is." Linkin's features are tight as he tells me more about his past than he ever has.

"My mom was losing everything. She owed a lot of money, but couldn't make ends meet. Everyone in town was talking and it started to get back to the boys at school. Jeff got into a fight when some kid called him a loser like his dad, and I knew it was time to move.

"Mom agreed easily, and we decided on Jupiter Bay because it was far enough that not everyone knew the details of her husband's transgressions, but close enough that we could make the payments needed to pay off the money owed."

"But it wasn't hers or your debt," I say.

"No, it wasn't. The man you see in that picture came to me and said my stepfather owed him fifteen grand and he was gonna take it from my mom if I didn't pay the money, and he didn't mean it nicely."

"He can't do that!" AJ says, causing us to all glance to the small circle around us.

"Legally, no, but I wasn't exactly looking to go to the cops with this shit. So, I stepped up and paid."

"You paid the fifteen thousand dollar debt?" Meghan asks.

"Well, not all of it. Hector, the man in the photo, told my mom the debt was two grand. Over the last nine months, she has been paying what she could and still get by raising my brothers," he adds.

"You told her it was a two thousand dollar debt," I figure out. "You didn't tell her about the rest owed." It's not a question, but a statement.

Linkin shakes his head. "She didn't need the stress of wondering how she was going to pay the other thirteen grand."

"You paid it." The realization is heady and sends me reeling. "And you never told her." Linkin doesn't need to confirm. I already know the answer.

I already know what kind of man he is.

"That picture was me paying the final five grand. And, before you ask, I made that money legally. I work two jobs and every tip, every bonus received at Christmas went to pay off that man. I needed his hold on my family, on my mom, gone forever."

My heart is pounding in my chest and I'm unable to keep myself back. I need to have his arms around me, I need him to know I understand. I launch myself at his chest and he easily catches me, holding me tightly against him. My lips seek his, needing the feel, the coarseness, the closeness of his lips on mine.

He's not expecting my kiss, but recovers quickly, swiping his tongue along the seam of my mouth and delving in urgently. The kiss is vital to my very being, a burning sensation spreading through my body, taking over my lips. I'm practically climbing him like a tree, my body wrapped around his much bigger, much taller, much firmer one.

"You're amazing," I tell him without removing my mouth.

"I'm not really. Not as amazing as you are, Lexi," he says, tightening his hold on me. I can feel his hard-on pressed exactly where I want it – well, with far less clothes.

"I love you," I blurt out, not able to keep the words contained any longer.

If Linkin is shocked by my confession, he doesn't show it. Instead, he smiles brightly; you know that ornery smile that makes me wet and wanton. "That's actually pretty fucking great because I'm in love with you too," he says.

"Oh my God, that's the sweetest ever!" Jaime proclaims beside us, clapping her hands. When I turn and look, everyone seems to have those big dopey smiles on their faces. Well, everyone but Chris.

I untangle myself from the man I love and turn to face my ex. "I'm sorry, Chris."

He nods. "Me too," he says, his eyes filled with his sadness, as he turns and heads towards the front door.

"So…" AJ says, not really sure what to say.

"A vasectomy?" Jaime asks, shaking her head.

"I knew there was something up with you not being able to get pregnant," Meghan says.

"I was worried it was you," Payton confesses. "You know, like with me." She's referring to her diagnosis of PCOS, or polycystic ovarian syndrome and the effects it has on her ability to conceive.

"No, definitely not me. I'm actually very much able to conceive," I say without thinking.

Payton stares at me hard, her all-knowing little eyes focused on my every move, her brilliant mind working to decipher my words. "What does that mean?"

"What?" I ask, fretting ignorance.

"You know exactly what. Are you…" she asks, leaving her question completely open.

"What? No."

"She didn't drink tonight," AJ adds, causing me to look at her. "What? You didn't think I'd notice? You drank clear liquid but I'm guessing it was water or Sprite. You also didn't take the shots. Linkin did." She smiles smugly and shrugs her shoulder.

"You're pregnant?" Jaime asks, surprised, yet very excited.

"Pregnant?" Linkin says, turning and facing me. A look I can't read on his face.

"I'm… well, I was… it's not the right… fine. I'm pregnant."

My frantic eyes collide with his wide brown ones. They're filled with so much hope and enthusiasm that it makes me smile. "Really?" he asks, stepping forward and reaching for me.

"Really," I confirm as he wraps his arms around me and lifts. Before I know it, I'm being spun around in circles and laughing uncontrollably.

"We're having a baby?" he whispers against my ear, his hot breath short-circuiting my brain. "We're having a baby," he states a bit louder. "We're having a baby!" he hollers at the room, making me giggle.

Carefully, he sets me down in front of him and grabs the sides of my face. "You're knocked up."

"I am."

His lips are firm against mine as he places a chaste kiss on my lips. "Fuck, I never thought hearing those words would feel as amazing as it does hearing them come from your lips."

I feel the strength and validation of his words as he gazes down at me, holding my head with his hands. They're rough and strong, yet so soft and tender at the same time. Much like this man.

"I love you," he says and it's all I need to hear.

Linkin 24

"I love you too," she says sweetly in return, my heart pounding a heavy rhythm in my chest.

I never knew saying, and hearing those words, would feel as good as it does to say them with Lexi. She's smiling up at me, her emerald eyes shining with unshed tears, and I feel complete. Everything I've endured, all the dues I've paid, every moment has come to this.

To her.

And our baby.

My hands drop to her stomach as I touch the place my son or daughter is nestled snuggly. She grins down, putting her hands over the top of mine and linking our fingers.

"I can't believe this," Meghan says happily, wrapping her arms around both Lexi and me.

I've been hugged more times tonight than ever before, and it doesn't look to be slowing anytime soon. I'm almost kinda glad Lexi's grandma isn't here right now as I'm hugged by each of her sisters and given those one shoulder bro-hugs from the guys.

"Sorry about the disruption," Lexi says to the group.

"Are you kidding? I haven't been this entertained since Grandma thought Linkin was a stripper," AJ replies.

Reaching over, I grab my girl and pull her to me. She nestles into my front perfectly, and it doesn't take her long to discover what's going on in my pants. Hell, what's been going on in my pants for over an hour. "Really?" she asks, moving her ass against my cock, almost making me come on the spot.

"You have no idea," I groan. "I've been hard since we danced. I'm starting to think something's wrong," I tell her chuckling, but to be honest, I'm not really joking. I'm a little concerned. I mean, I just stood beside my girl while she went toe-to-toe with her ex-husband, not to mention the fact that I just spilled the details of my past. In front of an audience.

And I did it all with a woody.

Lexi turns her head and gives me a look over her shoulder. "Really? We should go do something about that," she says, flexing her ass and wiggling it against my engorged groin.

"Stop that or we won't even make it out of the bar," I practically growl.

She opens her mouth to speak, probably something sassy that'll turn me on even further, when she's interrupted by Jaime. "Are you kidding me? How can you even be hard right now?"

Ryan glances around before looking down at his fiancée. "I don't know but I've been hard for the past hour!"

"Dude, are you really talking about your hard-on right now?" AJ asks, slurping up the last of her mixed drink.

Levi comes up behind Abby, interrupting Ryan before he can answer. "We need to go. Now."

"Are you okay? Why are you all sweaty?" she asks, concerned as she checks over her boyfriend.

"I'm fine, I'm just..." he glances around and whispers, "I'm fucking harder than concrete right now and it's starting to hurt."

"What?" she asks loudly, glancing down at Levi's crotch, which he adjusts.

"Yeah, if we could go now, that'd be great, Pay," Dean says while holding a jacket over his front.

"Not that I'm not super excited to get that out and play with it, but is something going on here?" she asks Dean, looking around to the others.

"Something is definitely going on. I'm two seconds away from jacking off, but even then I'm not sure it would help. This hard-on is fucking intense," I add. I make sure to hold Lexi still to keep her from sliding her delectable ass against me. It's torture and making my balls bluer than a cobalt crayon.

"I agree. I couldn't even pee earlier." Ryan moves his hips and continues to adjust himself.

"Oh my God, this is great! It's like you got into some of Grandpa's Viagra or something," AJ chirps.

Her words seem to hit everyone at the same time and the light bulbs start turning on.

"Orval!" Levi says, immediately followed by Dean. "The brownies!"

"You ate Grandpa's brownies?" Meghan asks, concern mixing with humor. "Last time he made them they were laced with pot."

"He said he made them while Emma was getting her hair done," Ryan groans.

The girls all start laughing. "Let me get this straight, you all ate Grandpa's brownies, and now you're sporting more wood than a baseball dugout?" Payton pants through laughter.

"Pretty much," Dean grumbles.

"He made Viagra brownies. Who does that?" I ask.

"Grandpa!" everyone hollers.

"We need to go. I'm going to explode," Ryan says, grabbing Jaime and throwing her over his shoulder like a sack of potatoes.

"You guys got this?" he asks, not even bothering to hear our answers. He's heading towards the door so fast, his shoes are practically smoking.

"Road-head!" Jaime hollers, smacking him on the ass while he grabs their coats off the table and is out the door.

"Not fair," I grumble, glancing around at all the clean-up we still have to do.

"What an asshole," Levi says, watching them leave.

"Good thing it's his party or I'd hate him a little right now." This from Dean.

"Pshhh. I do hate him," Lexi says. "He better not make me waste a perfectly good erection because I'm cleaning up the four thousand dicks Grandma bought as party decorations."

"I've got an idea. How about I see if we can get in here first thing in the morning before Lucky opens up," I offer.

"What are you waiting for?" Lexi exclaims, pushing me lightly towards the bar.

It takes me approximately one minute to ask my boss if we can just come in before we open and clean up the mess. He agrees, as long as every sign of the plethora of penises is gone before the neon beer signs go on in the window.

"Done," I say, returning to the group of eager beavers.

Literally.

They all scramble to grab their jackets as Lucky starts to turn off the lights and secure the building. "Meet here at ten a.m. We'll clean up the joint and deliver the gifts to their place," I instruct, reaching for my girl.

"They can make us breakfast as a thank you for their cockblocking," Levi agrees, grabbing Abby's hand and practically dragging her to the door.

Dean and Payton are making a beeline for the door themselves, leaving me and Lexi… and Meghan and AJ behind. "Well, looks like you ladies are with us," I say to the two remaining sisters.

I think my dick is going to fall off. Think I'm joking? I've had a hard-on for so long, I'm afraid there might be some sort of long-term permanent damage at this point. It doesn't help that Lexi keeps teasing the shit out of me, showing me little peeks of cleavage or eye-fucking me while I'm trying to drive her car to take her sisters home.

But now we're home.

Now she's mine.

As soon as we step inside the elevator, I'm all over her. She's pinned between the wall and my hard body, our mouths clashing in a frenzy of urgent lips and frantic tongues. She fits perfectly against me, her smaller frame lining up so fucking seamlessly with mine. It's like she was made just for me.

"God, I love you," I tell her once more, the bell indicating we've arrived on the third floor. I don't put her down as I grab her ass, hold her tight against my body, and slip out of the elevator before the door closes.

"Do you have my keys?" she asks, attacking my neck with her mouth. My brain short-circuits with every swipe of her tongue and graze of her lips against my sensitive skin. "God, I love this beard," she says, running her hands against the abrasiveness.

"I love seeing the marks it leaves on your thighs," I say, unlocking her door and slamming the door behind us.

"Yes, that. Leave marks." She's breathless and panting already and I haven't even gotten her naked yet.

"My pleasure."

I carry her to her room and set her on the floor. My lips only leave hers long enough to pull her sweater over her head and do the same with my t-shirt. She kicks off those little black ankle boots that I fucking love and starts working on the belt around my waist. I leave her to it and decide to feast on those glorious tits of hers. They're covered by ivory lace, her nipples poking into the material and begging for my mouth.

And who am I to deny?

Moving the lace aside, I audibly groan as my lips feast on one tight little bud, then the other. Her hands grip my head, threading into my hair, and giving it little tugs while I suck and nip with gentle teeth.

Her hands drop back to my pants, ripping them open and diving her soft fingers inside. She grabs my hard cock, wrapping those fingers around my hardness and giving it a not-so-gentle squeeze. "Fuck," I moan, fighting against my body's desire to thrust into her hand. Instead, I grab her hands and pull them from cock. It practically starts to cry, but I ignore him.

"Come here," I tell her, practically tossing her on the bed. I pull those tight jeans from her legs, catching my first glimpse of the ivory lace hidden within.

I waste no time. Starting at the inside of her knee, I drag my tongue all the way up to her sweet pussy. She's wet. I can see the way the light lace between her legs darkens a bit. But also I can smell it. There's nothing sexier than the scent of a woman who's turned the fuck on.

Swiping my tongue over the panties, we both groan as her taste hits my tongue. Instead of moving those panties to the side and diving in, I start over on the other leg, sliding my tongue from her knee to her pussy. This time, I don't deny either of us the pleasure. I move that little scrap of material aside and run my tongue from the bottom to the top.

Her moan is music to my ears.

Using one hand to grip the panties and keep them out of my way, I use the other to tease. I coat my pointer finger in her wetness, paying a little extra attention to her clit. I have to rest my arm across her gyrating hips as I lick and suck and devour her. Using a single finger, I gently push inside her body. She's already clenching, pulsing around me, a prime indication that she's so close to coming. When she comes, it'll be with my mouth all over her.

I slide a second finger inside of her and keep licking her clit. She's getting so damn close. Her legs wrap tightly around my head before falling open and riding my face. My cock is like steel, weeping as I continue to ignore his needs. Once I get her off, I'll bury myself so far inside her she'll feel me for days to come.

And speaking of come, it's time for her to do just that.

My tongue work turns into lip work as I latch onto that tight little bud and suck hard. At the same time, I slide a third finger into her pussy. The grip is almost unbearable as her muscles squeeze and pulse around me. Lexi's panting and begging, riding my face and chasing her orgasm.

When it starts, I feel it clear down to my own toes. My balls tighten as her internal muscles squeeze the hell out of my fingers, milking and pulling them in farther. "God, yes!" she screams, rotating her hips at a frenzied pace.

She falls limp against the bed, her body sated and sweaty. I can already see the red burn on her thighs and the sight makes my cock jump in my pants. Unable to deny him any further, I get rid of my boots, socks, and jeans. My boxer briefs quickly follow until I'm standing before her completely naked, aching cock seeping with pre-come.

Gazing down at her gorgeous body, my sights fall to her still-flat stomach. The place my child grows. Her eyes are on me as I kneel between her legs, but my mouth goes to her belly. I rain tender, open-mouthed kisses on her skin, hoping that baby inside can feel the love I'm sending him or her. Jesus, my heart practically hurts it's so full.

When my eyes gaze back up at her, there are tears swimming there, but I don't need to ask; I already know these are the good ones. A single tear slips from her eye and falls into her hair, my thumb there, wiping away the residual moisture.

"Do you know what this means to me?" I ask, my hands holding her waist, my thumbs rubbing circles on her skin.

She doesn't speak, but shakes her head.

"This baby, *our* baby, is already my entire fucking world. You and this child are everything," I confess, my vision suddenly blurry.

More tears fall from her eyes as she reaches for me, pulling me up her body. Our lips meet in a slow, passionate kiss. I feel everything she's telling me, everything she's giving me. I rip the panties from her body, careful not to hurt her. Her legs wrap around my waist, lining up her pussy with my cock. In one long thrust, I'm there, wrapped in pure heaven and breathing her in.

She's tight, her body still riding high from the previous orgasm. As I slowly move within her, I commit everything to memory: the feel of her body, the scent of her skin, the taste of her lips. The love I feel in the way she holds me against her, moves with me, is something I'll never forget.

Lexi arches her back, allowing me to get even deeper. I can't stop touching her. I trace her jaw, her neck, and her arms. My eyes devour her movements as she grips my back, hanging on as her sweet pussy starts to tighten its hold. There's no fight left in me as my own release starts to barrel down. My spine tingles and my balls tighten. After hours of being hard and worked up, there's just no stopping this release.

"Don't stop," she begs, her legs wrapping around my waist once more. She hangs on tight as I give us both what we want and need. My hips piston forward, driving into her body with enough force to shake the bed.

"I never want to stop this, Lex. I will always want to fuck you," I'm panting, my words a rush of emotions. "Forever. It will always be you, baby," I add, thrusting once more and pushing her over the edge into pure bliss.

"Yes!" she screams, the bite of her nails piercing my flesh and the vise-tight grip on my cock thrusting me straight into an orgasm. It seems to never end as I move, releasing everything I have into her warm, wet body.

My limbs fail me as I slump against her body, gasping and sweating. Brown hair is plastered to her neck, but that doesn't stop my lips from finding soft skin. Her fingers caress my back, her legs still wrapped around my waist, and my happy cock still buried inside her pussy. This is fucking heaven.

She turns her head, our lips meeting softly. We're both breathing hard in the aftermath of our epic sex, as our lips caress and tongues dance.

Knowing that she's being crushed by my weight, I slip to the side, my dick falling from her body, and pull her with me. She fits perfectly in my arms, her small body nestled against my side.

We both take a few minutes to recoup. My hand traces tender circles over her shoulder while her fingers toy with the hair on my chest. If I could feel this contentment for the rest of my days, I'd die a happy man.

"I'm sorry I didn't tell you about Hector and the debt I was paying." As much as I tried to hide that ugliness from her, I know that it was ultimately hurting us by keeping that piece of info in the dark.

"I get why you didn't tell me, but you need to know that I don't care about your past or where you come from. That's not important to me, but what is important to me is trust. I trusted before and it blew up in my face."

"I get that, baby, and I'm sorry. I do trust you, and I hope you trust me."

She moves until she's straddling me, my drugged dick suddenly perked back up and ready for another round. "I do, Linkin. That's why I'm here."

"I won't ever take that for granted and I'll never give you reason to question me," I reply through slightly gritted teeth as she circles her hips and teases my cock.

Lexi leans forward and takes my lips with her own. "So Viagra, huh?" she asks, that feisty look I fell in love with filling her emerald eyes.

"Apparently," I groan as she scratches her nails down my chest and sits on my groin.

"Hmmmm," she says, fire dancing in her eyes. "We can't let that go to waste," she adds, moving up on my hips and taking my cock in her hand. I can feel the wetness from earlier as she sinks down, taking all of me in one fluid motion.

"Oh, God," she groans, her body already tightening around me. "You know," she starts as she moves up and down, "they say that pregnancy hormones make you horny." She lifts up and slams back down.

Yep, she's going to kill me.

"You don't say?" I say, or think I say, but my words might have come out a rush of air and incoherent sounds.

"Uh huh," she says, swirling her hips and bearing back down on my cock.

Pulling her down, my lips attack hers. She continues to move against me, taking us both towards the edge of release. My heart is wide open and completely hers. This feisty, incredible woman swooped in and stole my heart, ensuring it would never be mine again.

She's everything I never even knew I wanted in my life.

And now we're having a baby.

Together.

It's a damn good life I live, and it's all because of her.

"I can't wait to find out."

Lexi

Four Weeks Later

Do you know what really sucks?

Morning sickness.

Mostly because mine isn't morning sickness at all. Oh, no. I actually get up feeling great. No nausea, no weariness. I feel fine. Not energetic or anything crazy like that, but not any of the typical things associated with pregnancy.

Now seven p.m.?

That's a whole other story.

Like clockwork, my fatigue and nausea kicks in towards the end of my workday, which basically renders me completely useless. I'm suddenly exhausted and cranky and can't keep anything in my belly. I've tried everything from herbal teas to topical oils, but nothing helps alleviate the early evening sickness that sweeps in.

Linkin has been amazing. He's not afraid of a little puke, which is great because there seems to be quite a lot of it lately. He's also turning pro when it comes to shoulder and foot rubs. Seriously, the man is smoking hot, has more muscles than a gym locker room, a dick that would make any man envious, and can practically evoke orgasms when he gives a foot rub.

Yep, I'm one lucky woman.

"How are you feeling today?" Ella asks from her station next to mine.

"Fabulous," I reply, flat-ironing Maggie Drew's long blonde hair until it's silky and smooth.

"Oh, I heard you were pregnant," Maggie says, watching my every move in the mirror. "Your grandma was in the boutique last week and was gushing over some of the new outfits. She's very anxious for the baby."

"It's been a month and she's already bought bags of unisex clothes and wants to go crib shopping. It seems a bit early, considering I've only had one doctor's appointment. Next month, I'm scheduled for an ultrasound since their machine was down at my first one," I say, removing the cape from my client.

"Ultrasounds! What fun. They didn't have those things when I had my Joseph. They just came out a surprise," Maggie adds, carefully standing up from my chair.

"I think I want to be surprised," I say to the room at large. "There are very few real surprises in life, ya know?"

"I agree," Ella says. "Though I'm not sure I could make it nine months without shopping for specifics. I mean, it would be so easy to shop if you knew if you were having a boy or girl."

Very true.

"What does Linkin say?" Barb wonders.

"I'm not really sure," I say somewhat absently. "We haven't really discussed it."

"Oh, there's plenty of time for that, right?" Cecelia adds.

"Right," everyone chimes in.

I send Maggie on her way and glance down at my schedule. I used to be able to work through lunch, but not anymore. Being pregnant has forced a bunch of changes, in addition to the physical ones to my features. The biggest change is my boobs, which Linkin seems to find great joy in. Of course, they're sensitive enough that I find great joy in them too.

My book says I have thirty minutes until my next client, which leaves me just enough time to eat the chicken salad sandwich I brought. The bell on the door rings, announcing a visitor. When I glance up from the desk, I can't stop the smile that spreads across my face.

Linkin.

And he brought Chinese.

The amazing aroma fills the salon and makes my mouth water. Of course, that could be the incredibly sexy man carrying the bag and wearing a smirk. "Hi," I say as he approaches the desk.

"Hi," he answers, stopping in front of me and setting the bag on the counter. "How's my baby mama?"

"Suddenly starving," I answer, grabbing for the bag of food and glancing inside. "Oh my God, you brought kung pao chicken and sautéed vegetables and rice."

"I did," he answers with that smirk and a twinkle in his eyes.

"Your baby mama is hungry. Very, very hungry," I respond, opening up a Styrofoam container and stealing a piece of chicken.

"Take it in the back room before you get sauce on the appointment book," Barb reprimands with a grin.

Gathering up the bags, careful not to spill any of the precious contents, I get up and meet Linkin around the side of the desk. He bends down and places a kiss on my lips, one I'm happy to reciprocate. "Thanks for bringing me chicken."

"It's not for you; it's for the baby." He winks before leading me through the salon and into the back room.

While I pull the containers from the bag, Linkin goes to the fridge. "Got any water in here?"

"Bottom drawer."

He pulls two bottles of water from the fridge and meets me at the table. Like a true gentleman, he doesn't even say anything when he realizes I've already dug in (without silverware). Instead he just smiles down at me and spears a piece of chicken with a plastic fork.

"Can I ask you something?" I ask with a full mouth.

"Anything."

"Do you want to know what we're having?"

He glances up, considering my question. "I guess if you want to know, then I'm cool with it. But it would be pretty awesome to be surprised." His answer makes me smile.

"I kinda want to be surprised."

"Then we'll wait and be surprised." That's it. End of conversation. It makes me incredibly happy that we're on the same page.

When we near the end of lunch, he finally asks, "Have you had any luck with the list?"

"I actually have. I've narrowed it down to three," I say, pulling the sheets of paper from my bag that's next to the table.

Linkin studies the papers carefully, mentally making his own lists of pros and cons. I watch as he keeps going back to the third paper. I hold my breath, anxious to hear what he thinks, especially since that one is my favorite.

"This one," he says, setting the papers down on the table and pointing to the third choice. "Three bedrooms, family room in back, and a fenced in backyard."

"That's my choice too," I beam happily.

"I'll call the number and make an appointment," he says, folding up the paper and sticking it into his pocket.

Linkin and I have shared a bed since we found out we were having a baby. After a few nights of bed-hopping between my place and his, he came to the conclusion that we needed our own place.

While I love staying at the apartment, it has never really felt like my own place. It's Abby's. Almost everything was hers, except for the personal effects I took with me when I left Chris. Linkin says his place has always felt more like a place to sleep and shower. He never really made it a home.

"The boys will love the backyard," I say. Part of what attracted me to the place was the fenced in yard. Not only will that be nice with a small child, but it'll help keep Linkin's crazy brothers from running amuck in the neighborhood.

"Definitely. And three rooms," he points at me. "The Knuckleheads can have a place to stay when they come over."

Karen was able to find a full-time job with more stable hours at Blossoms and Blooms as Payton's full-time employee. Even though she's working day hours now, the boys still look forward to a night a week at our place. Plus, it gives Karen a night to enjoy a little peace and quiet without being slayed by a sword every five minutes.

"Exactly," I reply, smiling.

Linkin comes around the table and kneels in front of me. "How's my baby?" he asks softly, his hand rubbing my still-flat stomach.

"Good, so the little peanut must take after me," I sass.

"Ha! Good isn't one of the terms I would use to describe you," he quips, the dirty smirk cresting his lips. "Unless we're talking about blow jobs. Then, good definitely is on the list."

"Good? That's it?" I ask, fretting outrage.

"Great. Superb. Fucking awesome. The most amazing mouth to ever wrap around my cock," he says, wrapping his hands around my neck.

"Much better," I say before his lips claim mine. The kiss makes my toes curl and my panties damp within the first five seconds.

"How much longer?" he asks, glancing at his watch.

"My next appointment should be here in five minutes," I reply breathlessly.

"Five minutes, huh? That gives me just enough time," he says, that wicked little gleam in his eye that I know and love.

Linkin reaches down and pulls my flats from my feet. He starts with one and rubs the ball, before digging and massaging the arch. "That's what I'm talking about," I groan, my entire body relaxing into the chair. "You're so amazing at this."

"That's what you said last night," he says with a wink.

Yeah, he's right. That's pretty much what I say every night.

Linkin

26

I've developed a foot fetish.

Over these last couple of weeks, I've wanted nothing more than to help alleviate some of the aches that come with carrying a life. It kills me every night when she's throwing up and I can't take that away for her. But she powers through the vomit, even if it pains me to watch, reminding me that it'll all be worth it in the long run.

And hey, morning (or evening) sickness doesn't last forever, right?

But let's get back to her feet. She's on them all damn day, working her ass off and making a living. The least I can do is give them a little rubdown to help ease some of the pain, correct? Plus, it gives me practice for the end of the pregnancy when they're starting to swell and really hurt.

Did you know there are about a million books about babies out there? I know this because I went online and looked, and ordered ten. Each one is different, but the end result is the same. Lexi even reads them with me, even though she had already done a fair amount of research when she was trying to get knocked up the first time around.

Damn, am I glad that douche got his balls snipped. That decision turned out to be the best thing that could have happened to me.

My mom is over the moon and keeps asking when I'm going to pop the question. She's not pushing me by any means, but I can tell she's excited about the baby and the prospect of finally having a daughter (in-law).

She told me a few weeks ago when we were alone that she finally paid off the debt. She was so happy and relieved, and after talking with Lexi, I decided not to tell her what I did. Mom is finally in a good place, even though she's still legally married to the asshole, and I don't want her to feel guilty or feel like she owes me anything. She doesn't. Not one damn dime.

The boys are thrilled, of course. They've already named him Thor because they're both sure he's a boy. They'll teach him to ride his bike and climb trees and use a sword.

I've scaled down my hours at Lucky's, at least for a few more months and then I'll quit altogether. My lease is up this month and I'm gonna move all of my stuff next door temporarily until we get our own place. Every penny I'm making there goes straight into the account Dean helped me set up for the baby. Lexi often comes up on the nights I work, usually sitting at the end of the bar, nursing a Sprite and devouring nachos. Well, until the evening sickness hits and then she's in the bathroom in the back office, praying to the porcelain god and swearing like a sailor.

The wedding is this weekend. Lexi's sister Jaime gets hitched in just a few days. Everyone is getting excited, including me. This family has really welcomed me with open arms, and is treating me like I've been a part of their clan for years. It still makes me wonder how in the fuck Chris could have fucked this all up. How in the hell did he walk away from all of this, making the choices he made?

I don't get it, but I'm damn glad he did.

I check my watch again, anxious to be taking the afternoon off. Ernie was thrilled when I told him about the baby and is letting me flex my time as much as I need to so that I don't miss any of the appointments.

Last month when we were there, the ultrasound machine had an issue. Even though we confirmed the pregnancy with a pee test, we didn't get to take a peek at the baby. We were told that we'd get a look at today's appointment. It's been a constant source of excitement for both of us, especially in the last few days.

At three-fifteen, I head out into the mid-April afternoon and hop in Lexi's car. I dropped her off at work this morning so that we were only dealing with one vehicle. When I pull up in front of the salon, she's already standing by the window, watching and waiting.

She slides into the passenger seat, kisses me on the lips, and buckles up for the short drive to her OB. The Gods of Waiting Rooms is on our side today, too. When we walk in, there's only one other woman there, and she's called back before we even take our seats. Lexi reaches over and links our fingers as I start to tell her about the 454 big block I just started to rebuild. It's going into an old El Camino that's being restored to mint condition. I love the way she lights up when I talk about cars. It's so fucking hot.

The mood is light and playful as we walk down the hallway and she steps on the scale. I turn away, not wanting her to think I care about her weight. I've known enough women in my life to know you never ask questions or act like you care about whatever number is on the scale. It's like sex suicide. You bring that shit up and you're sleeping on the couch for a week, jacking off to old Playboys you found in the basement.

"How have you been feeling this month?" the nurse asks Lexi.

"Not too bad. I'm still getting sick, but not quite every evening."

"That's good to hear," she says, handing her the little cup to pee in. I wait in the hallway while she does her thing, and then we're escorted to our room. "Everything off below the belt. We're gonna get a look at your baby today."

Lexi's smile is infectious as she looks my way. We're about to see our baby for the first time. This moment is making it all seem so surreal. Not that the constant throwing up or the confirmation from our last appointment wasn't an indication enough, but actually getting to see the little bean on the screen is driving it all home.

"Good afternoon," the doc says as he enters the room. He's an older man, probably in his mid to late fifties. I'll be honest, when Lexi told me her doc was a dude, I was a little unsettled. Okay, fine. I wanted to punch him in the face for putting his hands in a place I dubbed *mine* a while ago.

"Hey," Lexi says, lying on the table.

"Well, the machine is all fixed, so we're gonna take a peek at your baby. We'll get a few measurements too to make sure everything is on track for the due date we predicted."

October twenty-third. That date is burned into my memory.

The doc asks a few more questions before firing up the computer-looking thing on the cart beside the table. Lexi reaches for my hand, entwining our fingers together as we wait. We watch as he pulls out this long instrument and grabs a condom.

The hairs on the back of my neck stand up.

"Because you're too early for a typical ultrasound, we're using a transvaginal unit that will be inserted into your vagina. We'll be able to get a good look at the baby this way, as well as measure the heartbeat." He doesn't seem to care at all that he just put a rubber on the probe and is about to stick it inside my woman. In front of me.

What the fuck?

Lexi senses my anxiety (of course she does) and squeezes my hand. "It's okay," she mouths, keeping her eyes locked on mine.

"Might be a little cold," the doc says. I can tell the moment he uses that *thing* on my girl. She tenses a little, which spurs me into action.

I reach up with my other hand and push the hair off her forehead. Then, I place tender kisses along the smooth skin, trying to erase the lines across her face. She starts to relax instantly, which helps my own breathing calm and my erratic heartbeat slow.

"Ahhh, there it is," the doc says, drawing our attention to the screen. There, on the monitor, is this tiny little peanut.

It's absolutely beautiful.

A sniffle pulls my attention from the monitor. Lexi is gazing up at the screen, gentle tears rolling down her face and disappearing into her hair. I quickly wipe them away, letting my hand linger on her face. Unable to stop myself, I bend down and kiss away one of those little drops of moisture. It's salty against my lips, but I don't care.

"Well, hello," the doctor says, a weird hitch in his voice.

Lexi and I both turn back to the monitor. He's marking images on the screen; of what, I'm not sure. I can't really tell what anything is. It all looks a little alien to me.

"Okay, Mom and Dad. Say hello to your babies," he says proudly and turns the monitor to fully face us.

I stare at the image. One bean marked one and a second bean marked two.

"Babies?" Lexi gasps, leaning up onto her elbows to get a closer look.

"Babies," he confirms.

I stare at the man who smiles widely at my girl, not really sure I heard him correctly. When I glance at Lexi, she's staring in shock at the screen, mouth hanging open wide enough to catch flies. Then those emerald eyes turn to me.

"Twins?" she asks like a question, but surely not meaning it as one.

"Wait." I blink at her, the machine, the doctor, and then back to her. "What?"

"Oh my God, we're having twins!" She exclaims, tears rolling down her face.

"You are," the doctor confirms before finishing up whatever he's doing down at the place no man will ever touch again without losing his hand. "I printed off an image for you to take home. Congratulations. Twins runs in the family?"

"It does," she agrees and glances at me. "Actually on both sides."

"Well, they say twins usually skip a generation, but I always say that the human body will do whatever in the world it wants."

"No shit," I say, finally finding my words.

Doc gives me a smile and sets papers down on the counter. "I'll give you both a few minutes to talk. Come out to the desk when you're ready to leave."

Lexi says something to him, but I tune it all out. Twins? Twins?? How in the hell did this happen? Well, I know how it happened. I was there, making the baby… or babies.

"Are you all right?" she asks turning on the table but keeping the paper sheet clutched at her waist.

"Uhhh, I'm not sure how to answer that," I say truthfully, rubbing the back of my neck as I stand up and start to pace.

"I know this is a shock," Lexi starts, her voice getting small as if she's afraid.

Of me? No, not of me, but of my reaction. Holy shit, that can't happen. Kneeling in front of her, I take both of her hands in my own. "It's a shock, yes, but do you know what?" She shakes her head, waiting for me to continue. "We're having twins. Holy shit, I can't believe it," I say, giving her my biggest smile ever. She starts to blur in front of me as realization starts to set in. Two babies. Not just one to read a bedtime story to or teach how to change the oil in the car, but two.

Twins.

"Holy shit," I proclaim, picking her up in my arms and spinning around the little room. The paper sheet falls to the floor, but I don't give a shit.

We're having twins!

"You're really okay with this?" she asks when I set her down on the floor.

"Are you kidding? How can I not be? We're having two babies."

"I know, but things could get a little messy. I mean, it's not like they weren't before, but now this?"

"Seriously? Babe, this is my kinda mess. This is you and me... and our babies."

"It is," she says softly before my lips claim hers. The kiss is tender and passionate and so fucking perfect that I could stay right here, right now, forever.

Except we can't.

It's time to change the game plan. Things are about to get a little chaotic. Life is about to get a little bit crazy.

Or as I like to call it, messy.

The best kinda mess there is.

Lexi

27

I'm standing at the front of the church, waiting for my sister to make her entrance. When she steps around the corner, her arm linked with our father's, I can't stop the tears. Even if it weren't for these crazy pregnancy hormones, I'd be a blubbering mess the moment I look over at the groom. Ryan is fighting his own tears, his eyes glued on the woman he loves and the biggest smile on his face, as she walks towards him in a gorgeous white dress.

It's a picture-perfect moment.

Dad holds up well as he hands Jaime's hand over to Ryan's. He leans forward, grabs Ryan by the back and whispers something in his ear. Whatever Dad says, Ryan agrees as he nods his head decisively, blinks back tears, and gives him a smile. Then Dad takes his seat in the front pew beside Grandma and Grandpa, and my sister and her groom step up to the altar.

My eyes keep glancing to my right where a certain sexy mechanic is seated in the row right behind my family. Linkin is wearing black dress pants with a light blue dress shirt and plaid patterned tie. But it's the way his shirt sleeves are rolled up casually, revealing that incredible ink on his arms that keeps drawing my attention. God, he's so sexy. He's sitting with Levi, whose own eyes are glued to my twin sister's ass. Typical.

The ceremony doesn't last too long, but the pictures are a whole other story. The photographer is a true professional, and ends up taking a billion and a half photos from every angle, in every light, and in every pose. Okay, so maybe not quite that many, but I'm starting to get a little hungry.

Can't a pregnant girl get a little bit of stuffed meatballs and some cheese dip around here?

Finally, we're released to head to the reception. Linkin and I ride with Abby and Levi to one of the hotels along the bay. It's not tourist season, so it's a quick drive and parking is a breeze. I'm seated up front with the rest of the wedding party, while they placed Linkin at the table with my parents, Levi, and Brielle. She looks so stinking cute in her purple dress, her hair full of curls.

The night progresses quickly with dinner, toasts, and the cutting of the cake, all while Ryan keeps close tabs and at least one hand on his bride at all times. When they take to the dance floor, I can't help but smile. They're so in love with each other. It's been evident since they were being arrested for indecent exposure back when they were first dating.

And now here they are.

Married.

Linkin comes up behind me and pulls me into his chest. His muscles flex under my fingers as I wrap my hands around his forearms and revel in his embrace. I can feel his strong heart pounding against my back and his stubble has he drops his chin to nibble on my ear. Whisker burn on my neck is almost as good as whisker burn on the thighs.

His hands automatically go to my abdomen. Ever since he found out I was expecting, he's always touching my stomach. But since we found out it was twins earlier in the week, it's his new obsession. He can't keep his hands off me (and I'm not talking sexually), and at night when we're getting into bed, he actually takes to talking to them.

My heart melts and I fall further every night.

"So, you knocked up my granddaughter, and now she's having twins, eh?" Grandpa asks, coming up to stand beside us.

"That's the rumor," Linkin replies with a smile and wink.

"I'd like to think I had a hand in it," Grandpa says, adjusting his suspenders and wearing a huge grin.

"The only thing you had a hand in is a hard-on that took hours to go down," Linkin retorts, getting a big laugh from my grandpa.

"Yeah, let's talk about those special brownies of yours," Dean says, joining the conversation.

"I was afraid I was going to have to go to the ER. Do you know how embarrassing that would have been if I would have had to go to the place I work and confess that I had an erection that lasted longer than four hours?" Levi adds, stepping up beside me.

"I may have used a few too many. I'm still working on perfecting the recipe," Grandpa says, scratching his head.

"Why do you even need Viagra brownies to begin with?" I ask, flabbergasted.

"Your grandma is an animal, Lexi Lou. I'm man enough to admit that, at times, I require medical intervention to keep up with her appetite."

"Gross," Payton whispers, making a gagging noise.

"Just promise us you won't poison us again with male enhancement drugs," Ryan begs as he escorts his wife off the dance floor and joins us.

"I make no promises," he argues.

"At least have the decency to tell us when we've been drugged. I think we were all a bit nervous as to why four guys were together in the bathroom with boners," Linkin says with a nervous laugh.

"Fine. Anyway, it's been longer than the five minutes Emmie asked me to wait." Then bending forward and dropping his voice, he adds, "She's waiting on me in the coat room just behind the concierge. We're crossing public sex where you could be caught at any moment off the bucket list." With a wide grin, he turns and practically dances out of the ballroom and out of sight.

"You didn't check your coat, right?" Abby asks Levi as all of us watch him disappear.

"Thankfully, no."

Another slow song starts, and I'm pulled onto the dance floor. Payton and Dean, Ryan and Jaime, and Abby and Levi all join us, as well as a few other guests. Linkin wraps his arms around me and pulls me close. My head hits just below his chin, my cheek lining up perfectly with his heart.

"You know, you're lookin' mighty fine in that dress. We could always find our own coat closet and cross something off our bucket list."

"I think you've already managed to cross something off the bucket list," I retort, glancing down at my belly.

"Damn right, I have," he agrees.

"Did you get into the Viagra brownies?" I ask, noting the hardness that's pressed against my stomach.

"Nope, that's just my standard reaction to having the most beautiful woman in the world in my arms."

"A bit cheesy, but I like it."

"Because you like me. I knew it! All those months ago, I knew my charms would win you over."

"It wasn't your charms. It was your mega cock," I answer cheekily. A gasp is heard behind me, followed by the muffled sound of a laugh turned into a cough. When I glance around, I'm startled to see one of my old high school teachers dancing with her husband. She's staring at me with wide-eyes and her mouth gaping open.

"Come on, sweetness. Let's go find a coat closet so I can show you my mega cock."

Linkin

28

I swear I haven't slept a wink since the moment I saw two babies on that monitor.

As the days turn into months and the cravings turn from Mexican food to coffee cake and cottage cheese (and yes, she eats them together), my nervousness grows. The first of July has brought a heat wave like no other in Virginia that even the coastal waters can't seem to cool.

My girl is all baby. Well, babies. At almost six months, she's sporting a bigger beach ball than the one the boys use when we go to the beach to swim. But do you know what? It's sexy as fuck. Like seriously, hard-on inducing sexy every time she walks (albeit a bit of a waddle) into the room, and I can't keep my hands off her. I guess it's a good thing you can't get knocked up further while being knocked up because we'd probably have a dozen babies on the way by now.

Lexi is still working as long as possible, but the belly is already starting to make it difficult. Clients get knocked in the back of the head pretty much daily now, which makes them laugh and Lexi frustrated. She's a worker, and the thought of having to stop working before nine months is stressing her out. Personally, I love it when the ball gets in the way. We've had to be a bit more creative in bed, which my feisty little tiger is all for. She's insatiable, which bodes well for me, since I think she's the most desirable woman on the planet.

I'm on my way home from work after a long, hot day in the shop. Lexi's last client of the day should be wrapping up about now, so she shouldn't be too far behind me. After a quick pit stop, I pull into the driveway. We decided to put my Harley in the second bay of the garage to leave her more room to get in. It's a pretty tight two-car unit with not a lot of wiggle room. I don't mind parking outside so that my girl can get in and out of her car easier.

Inside the house we're renting together along the bay, I preheat the oven before slipping off to the bedroom to shower. The en suite bathroom is a bit on the smaller size with only a shower stall, toilet, and sink. Eventually, we'll find a bigger place, but this place will do just fine for now. At least we're not back at the apartment.

After a quick shower, I'm sporting a clean pair of basketball shorts and a sleeveless shirt in the kitchen when Lexi gets home. With the kitchen just off the garage, I hear her grumble and bitch as she tries to roll out of her car. I snicker to myself, thankful that she's not in the house yet. I'd never laugh in her face; I love my balls too much to be that stupid. Just another reason why we should move up our search for a new car. I think she needs a small SUV so she doesn't have to crawl in and out of a car. Something with a good safety rating.

"Welcome home, mama," I say happily when the back door opens.

"Why are you so happy? It's hotter than the surface of the sun out there," she grumbles as she waddles in the door and sets her bag onto the table. "What's that smell?"

"Soap. I decided to shower today," I retort.

"No, that smells sexy," she says, walking up behind me, wrapping her arms around my waist, and taking a big whiff of my shirt. "I mean what's in the dish? It smells like heaven."

"Homemade mac and cheese with breadcrumbs and grated parmesan cheese," I tell her, mixing it all together and piling the extra cheese on top.

"Oh my God, that sounds amazing. You should hang out with Levi more often," she says, reaching around and taking some of the cheese from the top of the dish.

"It'll be ready in about fifteen minutes." I slide the dish into the oven and turn just in time to catch her staring at my ass. When she glances up, I raise an eyebrow and give her my best smirk. It always makes her horny. "How was work?" I ask, grabbing her a bottle of water from the fridge.

"Fine. Busy. How as your day?" she asks, taking long pulls from the bottle.

"Hot. Jacob finally got himself fired," I tell her as I grab two plates and forks then join her at that table.

"Really? What did the little bag of dicks do this time?"

"Pulled a car into the shop and left it in gear."

She glances up at me, eyes wide. "What happened?"

"It rolled into another car that was there for an oil change."

"Oh, shit. How much damage?"

"Not a lot, fortunately. The car wasn't going that fast. Just a dent in both of them that Ernie is now responsible for fixing."

"Of course. So he was fired?"

"Yep. Ernie blew a gasket, told him that if he couldn't do something as elementary as remembering to put the car in park, then he wasn't needed around there anymore."

A few minutes later, the timer on the oven sounds. The cheese is bubbling on top when I pull it out and set it in the middle of the table. "Drink?" I ask, grabbing a bottle of beer out of the fridge.

"I'd take one of those," she grumbles, which makes me smile.

"Not for another three and a half months, baby," I say gently, reaching in and grabbing the carton of milk. When I hold it up, she grudgingly nods her head. After the glass is poured, I join her at the table and watch her dive into dinner.

"Holy shitballs, this is amazing," she mumbles with a mouth full of food. At least, I think that's what she said.

"Thank you."

"You're really turning into a regular Betty Crocker these days, Stone."

"I am. Turns out, I kinda like to cook. I like to take care of my woman and my babies. It makes me feel like I'm doing something other than just sitting here, waiting for them to be born," I confess, shrugging my shoulders.

"You do so much," she says softly, her green eyes honest and sincere. "You wait on me hand and foot. If you keep this up, I'll want to stay pregnant forever," she quips.

"That can be arranged," I smirk back, wiggling my eyebrows suggestively.

"That *will* be arranged. Later."

"I love later."

"Me too," she says before shoveling another mouthful of food into her face.

After dinner, we stretch out on the couch. Lexi sits at one end while I sit at the other, her feet resting in my lap. With her working on her feet all day, they've started to swell and sometimes, when she finally kicks them up at night, you can barely tell she has ankles.

Like I do most nights, I start to knead and massage her feet. Her head falls back on the couch and a smile plays on her lips. She always says this is her favorite time of night, but the thing is, it's mine too. The part of our evening where we're starting to unwind and just hanging out. Tonight, I stopped off and picked up a total chick flick for her to watch in hopes that she tries to relax. Not only are we dealing with a little swelling, but her blood pressure has been slowly creeping up.

"What's this?" she asks when I press the start button on the remote.

"That new Julia Roberts movie." When she doesn't say anything, I glance over and find her staring at me with tears in her eyes. "What's wrong, baby?" I ask, concerned that I've somehow managed to fuck up our night already.

"You rented me a movie?"

"Don't tell anyone, okay? I have this total bad boy reputation to uphold."

"You're a total badass, babe. I won't tell anyone that you had to help shave my legs last night."

"Pssh! That was total badassery," I defend, pulling her leg a little farther into my lap. "Besides, it was a total badass strategic move to get into your pants."

Her laughter fills the room. "Well, it worked."

"Of course it did. You can't resist me."

"You're so full of it."

"If you're good later, I'll make sure *you're* full of it," I say, waggling my eyebrows and grinning like a loon. "Now, stop talking. The sappy chic flick is starting."

It takes approximately seven and a half minutes before she falls asleep on the couch. Instead of watching the movie, I find myself watching her. She's like a sleeping angel, all relaxed and softly snoring. I also use the opportunity to wiggle in closer to her stomach. It's my favorite time of night where I get to talk to my babies and tell them all about their awesome mom.

"Hey, guys," I say softly to her stomach. "Well, not guys, because you could be girls too. But I'll be honest," I continue, placing my hand under her shirt and resting them on her tight belly, "that thought kinda freaks me out a little. Boys I can handle because I've had my hands full for nine years of your two rowdy uncles. But girls? Your mama's gonna have to help me out with that one. She's got five older sisters so she's a pro at dealing with girls."

My hands are still until I feel that familiar kick that never fails to make me smile. "I feel you in there. Good evening, baby," I say, bending down and kissing where I was just kicked. My other hand wraps around to the other side of the stomach and I wait until I feel movement. It doesn't take long before the entire left side rolls.

"That's the most amazing thing I've ever seen," I whisper aloud, smiling down at the place my babies play. "Now listen, kids, I know you're all wide awake and ready to play, but your mama is feeling a little tired tonight. Her energy is already starting to run out as the days get closer and closer to your arrival. I want you two to take it easy on her, okay?" I ask to the belly. Holding my breath, I wait a few seconds until I feel movement and more kicking. "I don't think you're listening. You're both going to be a bit of a handful, aren't you?"

"They take after their dad," Lexi whispers, a soft smile playing on her lips, but her eyes still closed.

"I'm pretty sure that's a false statement," I defend, content with watching and feeling the babies move around. Lexi's hand joins mine on her abdomen and I link our fingers together.

The clock reads ten when the movie ends and the babies simmer down. Damn I hope Lexi's able to get decent sleep tonight. Gingerly, I slip off the couch, careful not to wake Sleeping Beauty. Once the house is locked up and the lights are off, I bend down and scoop her up in my arms.

"What are you doing? I'll break your back," she asks sleepily.

"I doubt that, and I'm carrying the woman I love to bed."

When we reach the room, I set her on the bed, pulling the blankets up around her.

"I have to brush my teeth," she whispers without moving.

"I think you'll be fine to skip one night."

"I'm still in my tank top and shorts."

"Sleep, baby."

"What about sex?"

"I'll sex you up tomorrow night," I tell her, crawling into bed and waiting until she curls up beside me. Her in my arms is my favorite place to be.

"I'm sorry," she says softly, her eyes still closed.

"Don't be sorry, baby. Sleep." I kiss her on the forehead and turn off the lamp.

"I love you, Linkin."

"And I love you, Lexi. You and the babies."

She falls fast sleep in my arms, for at least a little while. She'll be up at least once or twice to pee, thanks to the added pressure of babies dancing on her bladder. As for me, I'm content with just holding her in my arms and feeling her breathe next to me.

Someday, I'll tell our kids all about how their mom batted her gorgeous green eyes at me and stole my heart. I'm probably gonna leave out the part about stripping, Viagra brownies, and jackass ex-husbands who liked to cause trouble. Instead, I'll tell them that I fell madly in love with her quick wit and her attitude. Her breathtaking smile and her stunning green eyes. I'll tell them that just by being around her, I wanted to be a better man.

Cheesy, but true.

My life began the moment this woman tore me a new asshole in the middle of the hallway of that apartment building. This woman in my arms owns my heart and soul.

Her and our babies.

One big happy family.

Our perfect mess.

Epilogue

Lexi

It's a Summer sister tradition that on the first Saturday of each month, the six of us get together. We take turns picking the location or activity, anything from margaritas and a movie to wine and painting classes at the small gallery uptown. One thing, though, is as certain as the sun rising over the Chesapeake Bay every morning: there will be alcohol involved.

Always.

It was Meghan's turn to pick tonight's activity, which is a Bingo fundraiser at The Beaver. The entire back room is filled with ladies of all ages for this year's Jupiter Bay Fire Department fundraiser. It's not your typical Bingo fundraiser, though. The ladies are here to check out all of the shirtless firemen.

You heard me.

And Meghan picked it! (Which I fully support, by the way.)

All of the guys under thirty gather up prizes from local businesses and call Bingo for the night. There's a twenty-dollar cover at the door, which includes some appetizers and eight games of Bingo, called by our local heroes. Did I mention they're shirtless? And wearing turn-out pants? And boots?

It's a beautiful sight, especially with my raging hormones.

Levi is here, working the board up front. Even though he's on display and all eyes have already undressed him a dozen times tonight, his eyes are only on my sister. He keeps glancing her way and offering her smiles, which she happily returns. It's cute, now that I have my own man warming my bed. But AJ keeps making gagging noises every time Abby fans her flushed face.

Speaking of AJ, she's hitting the booze pretty hard tonight. It's a cash bar, and she's had a drink in her hand ever since we walked in the door (sometimes two). "Looking to get wasted tonight?" I ask AJ.

"Damn right," she says, taking another drink of her beer. "And laid." She glances around at the naked chests and smiles. "Definitely laid."

"Me too," Jaime says, holding up her hand for AJ to slap.

"Me three!" Payton exclaims, glancing over her shoulder into the main bar area where her boyfriend is surely waiting. He'll be there with Ryan and Linkin.

"I guess that makes me four? These hormones are crazy. I dry hump Linkin pretty much twenty-four seven. I should be embarrassed, but the man is giving me O's like a hooker gives BJ's so I'm not complaining," I say, taking a drink of my water.

"Me five!" Abby adds enthusiastically, her eyes devouring her shirtless man up at the front of the room.

"I'm so sad. I'm not having sex," Meghan says, taking another drink of her margarita.

"You could, you know. No one would look down on you in the least," Jaime says softly.

"I know," Meghan replies, shifting a bit in her seat. "I'm just not ready."

"Well, then Meggy Pie, I'll have sex for you tonight!" AJ proclaims, her green eyes already a little glassy.

"Just be careful, AJ. There are a lot of out-of-towners here that you don't know anything about."

"All I need to know is if he has an eight inch dick and knows how to use it. Maybe oral, too. Good oral skills are important," she adds, nodding her head decisively.

"Amen," Payton says, reaching out and slapping AJ's hand. That's when I notice her finger.

"Hey, what's that?" I ask, reaching across the table and grabbing her hand. She tries to pull it away, but my eagle talons are no match for her.

"That's a diamond," Abby says, a shocked look on her face.

Now it's Payton's turn to squirm in her seat. "Look," she starts, but is cut off.

"Oh my God, you're engaged?" Jaime hollers, drawing the attention of those around us.

The five of us bend towards Payton a bit, ignoring the glances from our neighbors. The Bingo is all but forgotten as we stare at our oldest sister and wait for her to elaborate.

"Okay, so you guys aren't going to get mad at me, right?" she asks, clearly nervous about whatever she's about to say.

"Why would we be mad about you getting engaged?" Meghan asks.

"Because we're not engaged." She glances around at each of us before she lowers the boom. "We're married."

"What?!" we all exclaim at the same time.

And that's when we're asked to step out of the room for disrupting Bingo.

When we make our way to the main bar, we all turn our full attention to Payton. The guys notice the commotion and join us.

"Look, we wanted to tell you, but it happened so fast."

"You got married? And didn't tell us?" I ask, unable to stop the tears that are suddenly swimming in my eyes. Stupid hormones!

"Please don't cry, Lexi," Payton says, reaching forward and touching my hand. But I don't want her traitorous wedding ring wearing hand touching me. "Let me explain."

We all stand there and wait. Dean wraps his arm around Payton's shoulder in a sign of support and offers her a smile. It's so sweet and loving and makes me want to cry that much more.

"So we heard from the attorney proceeding over the adoption of Brielle. He said that if Dean and I were already married that the adoption would move quicker. We mentioned it to dad the other night and he made a call. He borrowed the jet from that rich couple he flies for, and flew us to Vegas."

"You got married in Vegas? By Elvis?" Jaime asks.

"Not by Elvis, but at a small chapel on the strip."

"Who else knows?" AJ asks, still drinking her beer.

"Well, Dad knows, of course, and Dean's mom Gretchen was there. And Brielle."

"When did this happen?" I ask, shocked that we didn't know a thing about this.

"Thursday night."

"You flew to Vegas Thursday, got married, and came home?" Jaime asks, the corners of her lips starting to turn up.

"Yeah. We got out there just in time to get the marriage license, bought rings, went to a little place that Gretchen researched on the flight, and flew home." Even though Payton is apprehensive and worried about our reactions, she's radiating with happiness.

Again, we're stunned silent.

Finally, it hits everyone at once. "Oh my God! You're married!" Meghan squeals with excitement before throwing her arms around Dean and Payton.

"Holy shit," I laugh before joining them in the hug. Well, as much as I can, considering my stomach is the size of Rhode Island. The rest of our sisters join in the hug, which leads to more tears. At least they're not all just from me this time.

We opt to grab the big table in the bar and have a little celebration. Of course, I'm not drinking, which really sucks. The guys join us, and as soon as Bingo is finished, Levi comes out to find out what's wrong.

"Nothing, babe," Abby says, a wide smile on her face. "Payton and Dean eloped this week."

"That's awesome," he says, reaching over to shake Dean's hand in congratulations before wrapping my sister in a big hug.

"Thank you," she says, returning the hug before taking her seat beside her husband.

Husband.

That's so strange to say. Even though we've known it was coming, I think we all expected a proposal and wedding, like Jaime and Ryan had back in April. Now here we are: two sisters married and two shacking up with their boyfriends.

It makes me think about my future with Linkin. Even though I'm not sure what it holds, I know that I'm in this for the long haul. This time around, it's not about the perfect car or house or life or husband. It's about finding that one person who completes your soul. Who loves you with every breath of their being, and you love back equally the same.

Linkin.

As if sensing where my mind is, Linkin glances over and gives me that smirk. He moves forward and wraps his strong arms around my neck, pulling me towards him. Our lips meet in the middle in a slow, lazy kiss.

"Get a room," one of my sisters says. I think it was AJ.

"I plan on it," Linkin replies loudly, offering me a wink.

We hang out and visit with my family for another hour, but before long, it's a struggle to keep my eyes open. Exhaustion and fatigue starts to hit in the early evening most nights, and the fact that I've made it until almost ten o'clock is a small miracle.

"Ready to head home?" Linkin asks, rubbing small circles on my lower back. Lord, this man and his magic hands.

"I think so." My words get lost in my yawn.

"I'm taking my girl home," Linkin announces to the table.

"Awww, Lexi, are you feeling all right? You look tired," Abby says with a look of pity.

"Growing babies is hard work," I reply as Linkin helps me out of the chair. I don't really need the help, but he does it anyway. I think he just likes copping a feel.

"You don't have to lie to us, Lex. We know you're leaving so you can give road-head." This from Jaime.

"I wish," I retort. "There's no way I could bend over the console anymore. Not with this basketball attached to my front." I rub a gentle hand across my abdomen, which is quickly joined by Linkin. And then my sisters. It's a good thing I'm not one of those people who minds having others touch their pregnant belly. My sisters have no boundaries.

"Don't worry, Lexi. Since AJ is going to have sex tonight for Meghan, I'll give road-head for you!" Jaime exclaims.

"Uh, babe, that's a little weird," Ryan says, looking strangely at his wife.

"Fine, the road-head is from me," she says, leaning forward and kissing him. "Sorry, Lex." She adds with a casual shrug.

"It's okay," I say as Linkin entwines his fingers with mine. "We're learning to be very creative."

"Damn right," Linkin adds with a wink. "I can't keep her off my body."

I roll my eyes, even though his statement is one hundred percent the truth.

My sisters all give me hugs and rub the belly. "Congratulations," I whisper to Payton before placing a kiss on her cheek. "I'm so happy for you. And I know that the adoption will go through seamlessly now. But just remember, you're already her mom."

My oldest sister blinks back tears and nods her head sharply. "Thank you." The words are so full of emotion that it starts to choke me up. Again.

"Get me out of here before I start bawling over the spilled popcorn by the bar," I instruct to Linkin, who just grins. He's well used to my emotional roller-coaster rides lately.

With one final wave to my family, I turn towards the door. Linkin wraps his arm around my neck, pulling me in close to his body. Neither of us speaks as we step out into the hot night air and to his Blazer. He helps me inside, but my legs are still dangling from the doorway. He steps between my legs, wraps his warm hands around the back of my neck, and kisses me.

His kisses are pure magic.

"I love you," he whispers, his warm breath fanning across my lips.

"And I love you."

The look he gives me reminds me of someone who won a big prize and his smile renders me speechless and powerless. I'm so damn lucky I chewed him out in the hallway of the apartment building all those months ago. Without him, I'd be lonely and probably knocked up with donor number G45629's sperm. And that thought is almost nauseating.

My life might have gotten a little messy, but now it's the only life I'd want to live. With Linkin and our babies.

"Take me home and make love to me," I tell him breathlessly.

"It would be my pleasure."

Another Epilogue

AJ

Tonight, I'm getting hammered.

And laid.

It's a little embarrassing if I were to confess how long it's been since I've had anyone warm my bed. Or his. I'm not picky. Hell, there doesn't even have to be a bed. I'm a fan of shower sex, wall sex, truck sex, elevator sex (happened once during a blackout), and well, any kind of sex that involves me actually getting off.

Anyway, I'm getting off topic. The point is, tonight I'm getting laid. School starts in just over a month and alcohol helps fuel all of my bad decisions, and I'm definitely feeling a doozy coming on.

I'm surrounded by happiness.

Even though we lost Josh last year, our family is growing by leaps and bounds. Jaime and Ryan were married this past April, we found out tonight that Dean and Payton eloped to Vegas, and our baby sister Lexi is about to pop out a litter of babies in just a few shorts months. Okay, so she's only having two, but I wouldn't be surprised if there wasn't one or two more hiding in there somewhere. She's big and glowing and the way Linkin looks at her and constantly touches her belly is almost nauseatingly cute.

Stupid hormones.

I'm not jealous, per se, because I'm definitely happy for my sisters. I'm just lonely, I guess; tired of kissing frogs and them turning out to be just your typical toad.

The Beaver is abuzz with tourists, all here to celebrate the extended July 4th holiday weekend. There's a local guy shooting pool that has possibility; though I'm pretty sure I've already taken a ride on his pogo stick – apparently, it wasn't that memorable. There are a handful of out-of-towners sitting at a table in the back. A few keep glancing over at us, but only one really has potential. And even then, I don't feel like dropping my panties.

I turn back towards my sisters who are all laughing at something Meghan said. I should probably be listening, but I can't seem to concentrate. My mind usually wanders easily, but this is different. It's like some weird electric force is pulling me.

Glancing around, I search for the source of this invisible current. Nothing jumps out at me, yet the hairs on the back of my neck stand up.

That's when my eyes connect with those of a man at the bar.

I tip my beer back, pleasantly passed buzzed and heading straight into hungover territory, and watch. He's sitting at the end of the bar, and even though there's a guy next to him, he appears alone. In the dim light of the bar, I can tell his eyes are the color of the ocean. His dark hair is slightly rumpled; the kind of look you get when you run your fingers through it. Suddenly, my fingers are twitching.

And my lady parts are all but panting.

The man makes no move to hide the fact that he's watching me. In fact, we both just continue to stare, lost in our own little world where no one else exists. For how long? I have no idea; I completely lose track of time. My stomach churns with excitement. The possibility of going home with this man is doing all sorts of crazy things to my brain and my body. I'm drunk on more than just alcohol, but on the prospect of him.

This stranger.

Conversations are had around me. I think I participate, but I have no idea what I say. My eyes keep glancing back at the man at the bar, and every time I look, his eyes are drinking me in.

Finally, he turns without taking his eyes off me and sets his beer bottle down on the bar. He grabs his wallet and throws down some bills onto the bar, never bothering to look at the amount. Then he stands up. Holy shit, he's tall. Like crazy tall. And lean. I'm not talking skinny, okay? He's definitely built under his tight Under Armour t-shirt. Even though it's midsummer, he's wearing jeans that fit his very long legs to perfection.

God, what I wouldn't give to wrap my legs around this man's body right now.

His big feet eat up the floor until he's standing in front of me. I'm faintly aware that my sisters are all staring at us, watching and waiting.

"Hi," the gorgeous stranger says in a deep, masculine voice. Holy shit, his voice! I think I could actually come just from hearing him talk.

"Hi."

"Sawyer," he says, extending his hand down to me.

"AJ."

He smiles, and oh God, that smile. Even through my alcohol-induced fog, I can tell this man is utter perfection. The kinda man who should be pictured on magazine covers or maybe even those dirty romance novels Abby reads. He's also trouble. The kinda man who could definitely do some damage to an unsuspecting heart and thank fuck that isn't me. The stranger looks like the kinda man who wants to have a good time, and hopefully, show me a damn good one at the same time.

No strings. No stupid heart.

Just fun.

He extends his hand down and waits. There's no thinking as I place my own in his. His fingers are calloused and his hands crazy-big as he wraps his around mine and helps me stand. The room slightly moves (okay, it moves a lot), and it makes me wonder how much alcohol I really had tonight.

Enough to follow him out the door.

And that's what I do.

Consequences be damned.

THE END

About the Author

USA Today Bestselling Author Lacey Black is a Midwestern girl with a passion for reading, writing, and shopping. She carries her e-reader with her everywhere she goes so she never misses an opportunity to read a few pages. Always looking for a happily ever after, Lacey is passionate about contemporary romance novels and enjoys it further when you mix in a little suspense. She resides in a small town in Illinois with her husband and two children.

Website: laceyblackbooks.com
Email: laceyblackwrites@gmail.com

Sign up for my newsletter so you don't miss a single sale, reveal or release!
www.laceyblackbooks.com/newsletter